Timm felt her breath
warm on his neck

Angel's soft hair brushed his chin, tantalizing him, reminding him of his adolescent hopes and dreams, always of her. He experienced a moment of disbelief that the one he'd wanted was here, now…with him.

She gripped his biceps, her hands warm through his cotton shirt, her fingers tight. Her nails bit into his skin, bringing him firmly back into the moment.

He pressed closer. Her hip, firm beneath his other hand, burned his palm. With his eyes closed, he feathered the skin above her jeans, and it was softer than anything he'd ever felt.

He was drowning in her scent and her heat. He had to touch her more.

Dear Reader,

Most people wander this earth wearing hard outer shells to protect their vulnerable cores. But those exteriors don't reflect who they really are. The problem is that the world assumes what they see on the surface is all there is. What a shame. I wanted to explore this idea and look at what kinds of problems it can cause.

Angel Donovan has been forced into a certain role by fate and, no matter how hard she tries, can't get her hometown to see her differently, to recognize that she is not the same person on the inside as the beautiful face and killer body lead people to believe. I liked the idea of a woman breaking free of preconceived perceptions to show the world that she has depth, that the person on the inside is every bit as beautiful as the one on the outside.

Timm Franck has the opposite problem. He is a decent, smart, nerdy guy who was burned and still carries the scars. He has no problem showing people who he really is on the inside. He just doesn't want to show them his chest full of scars.

I know of too many people who worry about their outer shell not being beautiful enough and fail to show that what they have in their cores is much more worthy than surface beauty. Revealing ourselves to others can turn out to be the best thing we've ever done! May you find the courage to do it.

Happy reading,

Mary Sullivan

P.S. I do love to hear from readers! Please contact me through my website at www.marysullivanbooks.com.

Beyond Ordinary
Mary Sullivan

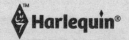

TORONTO NEW YORK LONDON
AMSTERDAM PARIS SYDNEY HAMBURG
STOCKHOLM ATHENS TOKYO MILAN MADRID
PRAGUE WARSAW BUDAPEST AUCKLAND

Recycling programs
for this product may
not exist in your area.

ISBN-13: 978-0-373-71717-0

BEYOND ORDINARY

ABOUT THE AUTHOR

Mary likes to break through the shells of new people she meets, discovering the pearls of their personalities. We all seem to have so much to give to each other. She has enjoyed meeting so many great people through her writing career, especially readers. This is her fourth Harlequin Superromance novel. Mary loves being part of the Harlequin family!

Books by Mary Sullivan

HARLEQUIN SUPERROMANCE

1570—NO ORDINARY COWBOY
1631—A COWBOY'S PLAN
1653—THIS COWBOY'S SON

Don't miss any of our special offers. Write to us at the following address for information on our newest releases.

Harlequin Reader Service
U.S.: 3010 Walden Ave., P.O. Box 1325, Buffalo, NY 14269
Canadian: P.O. Box 609, Fort Erie, Ont. L2A 5X3

To my mum,
who enjoyed reading her daughter's books.

Love always.

CHAPTER ONE

ANGEL DONOVAN LIMPED home to Ordinary, Montana, on her wounded Honda Gold Wing, pulling to a stop on the shoulder of the highway a couple of miles shy of town.

Out of gas.

She'd been gliding on fumes for the past quarter hour.

She tugged off her helmet and brushed sweat-dampened hair from her forehead, then dismounted.

The hot breeze outrunning nightfall across the prairie feathered her hair around her arms and her back, in the space between her vest and the waistband of her jeans. She should cut off every last black inch of it.

With one strong swing of her arm, she heaved the helmet into the closest field where it rolled across dry soil beneath yellow wheat, its red gloss disappearing under the dirt it picked up.

She unhooked her saddlebags and laid them down a few feet away, took out the can of lighter fluid she'd bought in Bozeman and sprinkled it over the bike.

It glowed golden in the horizontal rays of the setting sun, its chemical scent a counterpoint to the dry, earthy aroma of the fields.

When a pickup truck flew past, its rush of air pushed her toward the bike. Farther down the road, it slowed.

Whoever you are, keep moving. I don't need you meddling.

Striking a wooden match on the tight denim across her thigh, she threw it onto the bike and the lighter fluid ignited with a satisfying *whoosh*.

It crackled and whispered, spoke of things best laid to rest, smoked like a demon and obliterated the scratches and dents on the nearly new bike.

Neil, baby, this is for you.

The heat rising off the burning bike distorted the horizon in shimmering waves.

The pickup reversed down the road and came to a stop ten feet away. A man exited the vehicle with a fire extinguisher in his hand.

"No," Angel screamed, and tried to head him off, but he scooted around her.

He sprayed the bike and the fire sputtered, the flames hissed then died. Acrid smoke swirled into the air, choking her.

"Stop." She threw herself at the man and sent him staggering. His finger slid off the trigger, but not before he sprayed both of them.

Angel coughed. Her eyes watered.

"You *want* this to burn?" he asked. She didn't recognize him, or care who he was.

"Go away," she cried. "Mind your own business."

"I can't."

"Leave," she ordered. "I *have* to do this."

"The county's under a fire ban." He pressed the trigger to spray the bike and Angel launched herself at him again. She scratched his neck above the collar of his shirt and slapped his face.

He pushed her away, but she attacked again. His arms

busy with her, he dropped the extinguisher and it rolled into the ditch.

It could rot there.

"What the hell? Back off, woman."

"You back off," she cried. "You're ruining everything."

"You haven't changed a bit, have you? Still as self-centered as ever."

He knew her?

He grabbed her arms, wrapped them across her body and hauled her back against his chest. Her struggles were useless. The guy was stronger than he looked.

"Listen to me," he said close to her ear. "We're in the middle of a heat wave."

He thought she didn't know that, with sweat dripping down her back?

"I don't care why you need to burn a perfectly good bike," he said, "but we're under a fire ban. You think the ranchers want you starting a wildfire, burning up their crops and their homes?"

He was right, damn him. She'd come close to screwing up again.

She'd failed.

Timm Franck had always dreamed of holding Angel Donovan, but not like this. Not with anger and frustration. Not as though they were wrestling.

She breathed hard.

The full breasts that probably half the men in town had had wet dreams about at one time or another rested on his forearm where he'd wrapped it across her ribs to hold her still. The other hand cupped her stomach and held her steady against him. On her abdomen, above her jeans, his thumb touched a strip of bare skin that felt like velvet.

She squirmed. Air hissed between his teeth. "Stop it."

An erection threatened. Thirty-one-year-old men weren't supposed to behave like randy teenagers. He wasn't a trigger-happy guy. But then, this was Angel.

When enough of the fight left her that he thought he could let her go, he eased his grip and stepped away. There was only so much he could take.

"Come on," he said. "I'll take you home. I assume you're heading to your mother's?"

She nodded, her attention on the foam-covered bike.

For a minute, Timm could only stare.

Disheveled dark hair fell to her waist. Red spots rode on her cheeks. One pale blue vein at her temple beat beneath her translucent skin. The deep V of her black leather top showcased a mile-long neck and the sweetest cleavage this side of the Rockies.

She had always been too pretty for her own good, or for the good of his peace of mind. Damn, she'd been away for four years and he still had it bad.

He reached a hand to her face and she pulled back. "Hold still." He wiped a spot of foam from the corner of her lip. Her peach-soft skin burned beneath his thumb.

There wasn't a square inch of her body he hadn't fantasized about touching over the years. She was even softer than he'd imagined and an urge rose in him—to stake his claim on the playground of her body like the worst neighborhood bully.

He shook his head, snapping out of the daze Angel

always inspired, disappointed that his reaction to her hadn't changed.

He was supposed to be a smart man. He owned and edited the largest newspaper for miles around. But it seemed that when it came to Angel Donovan, he was as brain-dead as every other man in Ordinary.

Assuming she would want the saddlebags lying on the side of the road, he picked them up and led her to his truck with a hand under her elbow.

"Neil," she whispered. "I'm so sorry." He glanced at her to make sure she hadn't mistaken him for someone else, but she was talking to herself. What was driving her to burn what looked to be a fairly new bike? Any bike, for that matter?

As they approached the truck, she stiffened and resisted his hold.

"Who are you?"

Not one trace of recognition shone in those brilliant eyes. He might as well have been a stranger.

It shouldn't bother him.

It did.

He'd always suspected he was invisible to Angel. He'd been invisible to everyone in his teens. Since then, he'd become a force to be reckoned with in town, but Angel hadn't been in Ordinary to witness it.

"I'm not getting into a truck with a stranger," she said with a pugnacious jutting of her jaw.

Tough and unafraid, the Angel he'd known could slice the balls off a man with the sharp edge of her tongue. Looked like she hadn't changed.

"I'm not a stranger," he answered. "I grew up in Ordinary."

"Never seen you before in my life."

Like he said, it shouldn't hurt, but it did.

"Get in the truck, Angel. I'm driving you into town."

"I'd rather walk."

"There's a bad element hanging around these days." Beneath his fingers, her pulse thrummed and that heart-beat warmed her perfume—patchouli—and it swirled around him, heating his blood. Angel would have made a great hippy—free love and all that.

"I'm not letting you walk two miles into town," he said. "It will be dark by the time you get there."

She stared at him with her full lips pinched into a flat line. "Who are you?"

"Timm Franck," he said, hoping like crazy his name would spark a hint of recognition. It didn't.

"How do I know you?" Her gaze strayed to the top of his shirt, to the collar buttoned to his throat, and her eyes widened. "You're the guy who—"

"Yeah," he muttered, resigned to the fact that she remembered him for the wrong reason. "I'm the guy who—"

He released her.

"Get in and close the door," he said, quietly.

She blushed and slid into the truck with her eyes averted. Timm wished he didn't have this big sign stuck around his neck that pretty much said, This Guy Isn't Normal. When You Look At Him, Be Embarrassed. Be Very Embarrassed.

He hadn't been treated as *normal* in nearly twenty years.

He tossed her bags at her feet, left her to close the door and then walked around the front of the truck, in and out of beams of the headlights.

When he climbed into the driver's seat and slammed

his door, her face came alive. Her blue eyes widened. Her mouth dropped open.

"Wait a minute," she said, and Timm saw the moment full recognition of exactly who he was hit her.

"You." She lunged out of the truck.

Timm prevented her escape with a hand on her arm.

So she finally remembered what he had written about her mother. It had been more than a dozen years ago, but she'd reacted badly then and she was reacting badly now.

"Stay in the truck, Angel," he said. "I'm driving you into town."

"Over my dead body."

"If I have to."

"I'd rather walk."

"Look, there's a new bar that's attracting bikers. They're tough and itching for trouble."

Her expression was mutinous, but she remained where she was. "Why did you interfere?" she asked, crossing her arms. "What I was doing was none of your business."

"If the gas in that bike's tank had ignited…" Imagining the destruction to the land around them, he shook his head.

Why hadn't life beaten even a modicum of common sense into the brain lurking behind that perfect face, or a soul into that stunning body?

Once a shallow beauty queen, always shallow.

"I ran out of gas," she mumbled, staring out of the open window as they drove past fields fading in the dying light.

That stopped him for a minute. "Why were you burning the bike?"

"Never mind. If I told you, you'd tell your father and he'd publish it in tomorrow's paper."

She *did* remember him, and his family.

"My father died last year," he said.

"Oh. I'm sorry," she said, her tone laced with sadness uncharacteristic of the Angel he knew. "I hadn't heard."

He nodded, but didn't respond.

"How did he die?" she asked.

Timm faltered—he still couldn't talk about Papa. Finally, he responded to her accusation of a few minutes ago. "I don't publish the *Ordinary Citizen* on Tuesdays."

"Don't be a smart-ass." In a split second, she reverted to sharp-tongued Angel. "Your paper is a rag full of nothing but gossip and innuendo." Yeah, she remembered him, and *definitely* for more of the wrong reasons.

"That's not true and you know it," Timm said. "I'm not apologizing for that story I wrote when I was a teenager. If you didn't like it, tough, but it was neither libel nor gossip."

At the time, he couldn't write about Angel without the whole town figuring out he had a crush on her a mile wide, so he'd written about her mother. And what was the difference? They were two peas in a pod.

He watched her stare out the window. One strand of hair had snagged on a silver hoop earring and he wanted to tuck it behind her ear, so he gripped the steering wheel.

"It was a *story,*" he pressed. "Fiction."

In his irritation, his foot came down heavily on the accelerator and he picked up speed. He forced himself to relax. It was weird to have Angel in his truck, sexy and smelling of retro perfume.

"Everyone in town knew the story was about Mama."

That's because it was. "I never called her by name."

"You didn't have to. Everyone knew it was Missy Donovan." Her laugh sounded brittle. "You all but called my mother a slut and you were right."

A slut? He shot her a glance. "I did not."

"Yeah? What exactly did 'she can take a man anywhere she wants him to go' mean?"

He smiled. "You can quote my story?"

She paused a moment before saying, "I only ever saw the one written about Mama."

"I meant that she was sexy and knew how to use it to her advantage, that she knew how to get whatever she wanted from men."

She drummed the fingers of one hand on her thigh. Timm wondered how it felt to be the daughter of the town's…for lack of a better word, slut. "Missy brags about how you've changed your life. Your mom is proud of you."

So was he. During his adolescent years, while everyone else had been out doing things, he'd been at home sick, sitting at his bedroom window, watching people, studying human nature, wanting to believe the best of people. They didn't always measure up.

Angel had fascinated him. Most of the time she'd risen only as far as her trailer-trash background would allow, but he'd thought there might be more to her than she let people see.

Then, four years ago, at twenty-four, she'd left for college and Timm had thought, *Yes! Surprise us all!*

If she had indeed turned her life around, why was

she here pulling a stunt like burning a bike on the side of the road?

In the barely visible light, her lips twisted. "Mama needs to get a hobby and stop talking about me."

"In high school, you were voted Most Likely to Succeed."

"I remember," she answered, her tone a trace bitter. "As an exotic dancer."

"No one ever expected you to end up at college, studying math of all things."

She didn't say anything. If silence could be qualified, this one was heavy with significance.

Had he gotten it wrong? He usually had a sharp memory. "You did study math, right?"

She nodded.

What was up? Why wouldn't she look at him or answer his questions?

He flipped on the interior light. She faced him with a stunned expression then, just as quickly, turned away. He noticed a mottled blush on her neck. She was hiding something.

What had happened to her at college?

A sharp flash of disappointment flooded him. He'd thought that, given half a chance, Angel would have used college to break out of the mold fate had pressed her into. Too bad he'd thought too highly of her.

He shut off the light. "You didn't do well at college, did you?"

"I excelled," she snapped.

In some weird way, he thought he knew Angel too well. "You didn't finish, did you?"

With her thumbnail, she worried a hangnail on her index finger. "No," she mumbled almost too low to hear.

The intensity of his reaction took him by surprise.

He'd made the ultimate sacrifice after Papa's death, had left college early to come home and take over the family business, to think more of others than of himself.

"So you threw away the education Missy paid for."

"I didn't throw it away."

"Then what?"

She shrugged. "None of your business."

Angel hadn't changed one iota.

"Figures," he said under his breath. "You really didn't change one bit while you were gone."

She jabbed a finger against her chest. "I'm not as stupid as you think I am."

Stupid? "I've never thought that, Angel. Not with the way you had the boys dancing to your tune in high school."

She turned to look at him. In the dim illumination cast by the dashboard, he could barely make out her expression, but it might have been self-mocking. Or was she mocking him?

She'd never invited him to any of her metaphorical dances.

Unblemished beauties like Angel had no use for scarred beasts like Timm. They preferred the athletes of the world, the movers and shakers, the doers, not quiet, thoughtful boys who were forced to watch life pass them by. Who figured out the problems of the world and some of the solutions and wrote about them.

Who had learned, by watching, exactly how imperfect his fellow man was.

He'd changed since then, had become successful, was well respected in town. His scars were a fact of life that he didn't think about most days.

He no longer considered himself a beast. Angel, on the other hand, was still an unblemished beauty.

How lowering to find himself, all these years later, still mooning over a shallow beauty queen.

He wanted her.

ANGEL DIDN'T WANT TO be here with brainy Timm Franck. She hadn't recognized him at first, but she remembered him now. She had almost blurted, "The guy who'd been burned." So stupid.

Timm would never have left college before finishing his degree. He would never torch a bike on the side of the road during a burn ban. He would never screw up as badly as she had.

Too smart to be human, to indulge in human mistakes, Timm was a robot, with a mind and no feelings.

She studied him. He'd grown into his height. His shoulders looked broader, his biceps bigger. His cheekbones stood out more than they used to now that his face had become lean and strong. He'd grown up well. So well.

Yeah, she remembered him now.

At a guess, she'd put him just over thirty years old. He'd been three grades ahead of her in high school. When he came. When he wasn't having an operation, or recovering from one. In the later grades, he'd been around more often, because the doctors had done all they could for him by then. That's what she guessed, at any rate.

Wire-rimmed glasses rested on his straight nose. With his quiet, thoughtful gaze, he looked like he chewed encyclopedias for snacks.

How could a girl like her compete with a mind like his?

He'd perfected that brainy look to a fine art. For the first time, she found it attractive.

Damn, that bothered her.

She reached down to pull the lever that pushed her seat all the way back. Then she slipped off her red cowboy boots and leaned her feet on the dashboard, the vinyl warm under her soles, and wrapped her arms around her knees.

She caught Timm staring at the red polish dotting her toenails. Let him look. No way would he ever get to touch.

She used to like the jocks—big dumb boys who wanted nothing more from her than hot sessions in the back of their trucks. That was no longer true. She'd known some great guys at college attending on athletic scholarships—ambitious and self-disciplined guys, smart men who didn't try to grab her in dark corners.

But then, Bozeman hadn't been Ordinary. No one there had known her as Missy Donovan's daughter.

"When you wrote that story," she said, "you pretty much said Mama was too stupid to get a man without using sex."

"We're still on that subject?" He sighed. "Listen, I like Missy. She's sweet and generous."

"Did I hear a *but* at the end of that sentence?"

"Yeah. She isn't too bright. Men have taken advantage of her over the years."

Angel knew how…simple…Mama was, knew that she only wanted a man to take care of her and love her. Too bad so many of them had wanted only sex.

Then Timm said, "She took advantage of them, too."

"And why not?" Angel went on the offensive. "She had no skills. She was poor. She had to survive." So why did the way she chose to survive embarrass Angel so much?

"The town decided the second I was born to Missy that I was as cheap and easy as she was. Boys started sniffing around me before they were able to tie their shoelaces."

What would sanctimonious Timm Franck know about growing up in poverty? About growing up in a town that saw only what it wanted to see about a girl? His family had been respected pillars of the community.

What if she gave in to the urge to grab his glasses from his face and crumple them in her fist? Man, she felt wound up, all of her emotions strung too tightly.

"Illegitimate, trashy Angel Donovan. That's all the town ever thought of me." She didn't want a brainiac like Timm telling her there was no escape for a girl born into poverty to a woman who knew how to live off men, but not much else.

Angel needed to escape.

She'd tried to change while at college, in a new place where no one knew her, or her mother, or her mother's reputation. Where there were no preconceived notions about her.

Neil had treated her like gold. He'd seen who she wanted to be, not who she was expected to be.

That hadn't lasted, had it? She'd tried to be a better person. She'd failed. When you try so hard to change and it doesn't take, it hurts so damn much. After Neil died, she'd felt vulnerable and uncertain. But here in Ordinary, she knew *exactly* who she was, who she was expected to be and how to act to get through every day.

In Ordinary, she was confident and tough.

She would deal just fine here until she could get grounded, get clear about who she wanted to be. Then she'd head out of town and reinvent herself again.

She wasn't ready to quit. She'd come out of her mother's womb a fighter. This was a temporary setback. *Ordinary, Montana, the second I have enough money to leave, you can kiss my butt goodbye.*

She felt Timm's gaze on her as palpably as a touch.

"Why were you burning that bike?"

"Never mind." She couldn't talk about it. The words were too big, too enormous in their dark intensity, and clogged her throat.

She wanted to yell, to act out, to smash something.

That's why she liked cool, logical math so much. It didn't have miles of shit-kicking emotion attached to it the way everything else in her life did.

They traveled the length of Main Street, then turned and stopped in front of her mother's house. What should she say? *Thanks for stopping the only thing that could have eased my pain?*

She slipped her feet into her cowboy boots. Offering him a terse "Thanks" she stepped out of the truck, dragging her saddlebags with her.

Behind her, Timm sped away.

She trudged toward the bungalow. The rosebushes that lined the walkway were well cared for, the green cushion on the wicker chair on the veranda well used.

Mama had done well for herself in the past five years. She'd nursed her former boyfriend until his death. Hal had left everything to her—the house and enough money to leave Missy secure for years. The first thing she'd done was pay for Angel to attend college.

Mama no longer *had* to depend on men—she had security. Yet she was on the verge of throwing it all away on another man. Somehow Phil Butler—a slimy example of the worst of his gender—had convinced Missy to marry him.

"Angel," Mama had said in yesterday's phone message, *"Phil and me are getting married."*

Maybe that's all Donovan women were good at—squandering their advantages when so close to success.

But Angel couldn't figure out why Missy was so dependant on Phil. Why did she defer to him in her own house?

Angel knocked so she wouldn't scare Mama, then used her key to enter.

"Is that you, Phil?" Mama called, her voice huskier with age.

"No. It's me." So Phil wasn't home? Perfect time to confront Mama about him.

"Angel?" Mama rushed from the living room with a broad smile creasing her face. "Oh, honey, I wondered when you'd get here. You didn't call." She pulled Angel into a hug.

Angel filled her lungs with Mama's scent—Avon's Sweet Honesty and cigarettes. She'd missed this. She liked the perfume Mama had used all her life, but wished she would give up the smokes.

Oh, it felt good to be cradled in Mama's arms. Mama might be the town tramp, but she'd always been a good mother.

Missy pulled away to look at her. "I missed you."

"I missed you, too, Mama." She fingered a lock of Mama's hair. "Why did you go back to the blond?"

Missy had stopped dyeing her hair after Hal died. Now she was using again.

"Phil likes it this way. He says it makes me look younger."

Phil was an ass. He was a big part of the reason Angel had come home instead of heading off to a big city, any city where people didn't know her. The moment she'd heard her mother's message, she'd packed her saddlebags and set out for Ordinary.

Mama would marry Phil over Angel's dead body.

Of course, that was only part of the reason she'd run home. To be honest, she was also here for Mama's TLC. Mama always knew how to make her feel better about things. At the moment, Angel needed a double dose of her mother's care.

Angel tried to turn away before her mother could read her expression. But Mama held her still and saw everything Angel tried to hide.

Mama's happiness turned to concern. "What's wrong, honey? What happened?"

Giving in to the impulse to lean on someone else for a minute, to let someone take on her battles, Angel hid her face against her mother's shoulder and sighed.

"Oh, Mama, I screwed up so badly."

CHAPTER TWO

"YOU QUIT COLLEGE?" Mama asked.

Angel nodded.

"But—" Mama sighed. "I wanted you to do good. What happened?"

Angel shook her head, mute in the face of Mama's disappointment in her. Resentment burbled beneath the surface, though, that Missy had never tried to change, to become someone better than the town tramp, but she had expected Angel to fight the good fight, to put the effort into overcoming her roots.

Angel had at least tried.

They sat in darkness, on Mama's rose-patterned sofa, illuminated only by the streetlight filtered through the trees and sheers on the window.

Angel couldn't tell Mama about Neil. Not yet. How could she tell her that she'd crumpled like a day-old balloon when Neil died? How could she explain how hopeless and hard trying to change was? Or how difficult it was to outrun a reputation? How could she say any of it without hurting Mama's feelings? After all, it had been *Mama's* reputation she'd been running from.

She'd wanted to settle *anywhere* but here.

Then Mama had called and Angel had come running to Ordinary to save Missy from herself.

Mama must have seen the turmoil on her face, because she rubbed Angel's knuckles and said, "Never mind for now. Let's find you something to eat." Before Angel could start in on what she thought about Missy's fiancé, the front door opened and she tensed.

Phil. Her skin crawled before she even saw him.

He stepped into the living room. "Why is it so dark in here?" he asked, his tone brusque.

Mama flicked on the lamp. "Look who's come home, Phil," she said, her voice soft, tremulous.

Angel bit her tongue so she wouldn't say what she thought. *For God's sake, Mama, stand up for yourself.*

In the split second before Phil realized Mama wasn't alone, he looked severe. That changed when he saw Angel.

His manner became snaky. Oh, Lord, he could be the villain in a silent movie, scrubbing his hands in glee over the heroine tied to the train tracks. The word *unctuous* came to mind. Yuck.

That image was only her imagination, though. Phil was an ordinary man, not a cardboard villain in a movie. Still, Angel had trouble liking him.

Was hating a person as much as she loathed Phil illegal?

His crafty gaze took in the tension between Angel and Missy. Phil never missed a thing. Chances were he would somehow use this to his own advantage.

"Angel," he said. "How's my favorite daughter?"
Daughter? Gag me.

Just because Mama had agreed to marry him, Angel was suddenly his daughter? No freaking way. Never. That was too creepy.

When he approached the sofa, Angel remained seated and held her breath while he embraced her, endured it because Mama watched her with such hope, as if to say, *Please, Angel, like him, for me.*

Oh, Mama, you're all I've got. I would die for you, but put up with Phil? No way.

Angel smelled beer on Phil's breath.

She pulled away. "You've been drinking. Where?"

Mama gasped. "Angel, that's rude."

Phil watched Angel with a smug grin. She could see the hamster maniacally spinning the wheel of Phil's mind, calculating how much he could get away with because he knew she didn't want to hurt Mama more than she had to. He knew she would do whatever she could to ruin his chances with Mama. He also knew that Mama's happiness mattered more to her than anything.

Phil made her think of rodents. Too bad for the rodents.

"At the new place," Phil replied. "Chester's Roadhouse."

"Why did you go alone?" Angel asked. Mama placed a soft warning hand on Angel's shoulder that she ignored. "Why did you go without Mama?"

"Your Mama doesn't like it there. Right, Missy?" Phil looked at Mama. She nodded.

"Do you remember Chester Ames?" Mama asked.

Angel remembered Chester. He used to treat Mama and her like gold.

"He opened a bar on Main Street," Missy said.

Okay, that answered her question why Phil hadn't taken Mama with him. Chester had a giant crush on Mama that time had never dimmed. Mama had always had a soft spot for him, too. Angel used to fantasize about how good life would be if Chester were her father. Chester had been married, though, and faithful to his wife.

Clearly Phil had picked up on that mutual attraction.

"Good for Chester. He's a *great* guy," Angel said, her emphasis implying that he was a better man than Phil.

"I can take you there tomorrow night," Phil said.

Not on your life. "No, thanks. Mama, I'm heading to bed. We can talk more in the morning."

Angel passed Phil without a backward glance. For the sake of Mama's happiness, Angel would consider that he might be good for Mama in some way that Angel hadn't yet determined. She would try as hard as possible in the next few days to see him from Mama's point of view. But no way was she ignoring her instincts. While checking for the good, she would also watch for the ways in which Phil was trouble.

MISSY FELT PHIL STIR beside her and roll out of bed. Sitting on the side of the mattress, he pulled on his underwear then left the room.

Her breasts hurt, ached, and a weird sort of…stopped-up feeling…throbbed in her lower belly. Sex with Phil never satisfied her.

He wasn't big enough—in his size or in his attention to *her* needs. Sex was about him and what he wanted. She was dumb enough to always give in.

Lord knew she had needs. Always had.

Face it, Missy, you're forty-five years old. Phil is thirty-five. You'll do anything to keep him.

You would think a man Phil's age would have more energy, more to give a woman.

She listened to him shuffle down the hall, noted that he slowed in front of Angel's room. She bit her lip.

A grown woman shouldn't be jealous of her own daughter, but Missy was feeling her age.

Angel was young and beautiful. Men fell all over her. They used to do that with Missy.

What if Phil left? Where would that leave her?

With no one.

The darkness pressed in on her. She remembered those days after her own mother had left.

"You're sixteen now, kid. Take care of yourself."

"Mama, not yet. I can't. I'm not smart like you."

"With a body and face like yours, you'll do fine."

"Please don't go." Missy had pleaded more.

Mama had left anyway.

In the trailer alone, with no way to support herself, to finish high school, with no skills, Missy had turned to men. They liked her body. She had learned early to lean on them.

What if Phil left and no other man ever found her attractive again?

She was so pathetic, clinging to Phil as though he was the last man on earth. What if this was the rest of her life? What if she never enjoyed sex again? What if she kept on being jealous of her own daughter?

Missy heard Phil exit the washroom and walk toward their bedroom.

He stopped in front of Angel's door.

Angel's doorknob rattled, ever so slightly, but Missy heard it.

She held her breath. *Don't go in there.*

He continued toward Missy's room and the breath she'd been holding flew out of her. She rolled away so Phil would think she was sleeping.

He hadn't gone into Angel's room tonight, but he'd thought about it.

AFTER MIDNIGHT, ANGEL lay on her bed, watching the headlights of a car sweep across her ceiling.

She couldn't sleep, not with her mind traveling a mile a minute with memories of Neil. She picked up a stone from the bedside table. Neil had given it to her because somehow time and the elements had shaped it into a heart.

He'd said it reminded him of her, of how time and life had shaped her into a truly good person.

Horse poop. It had done no such thing. As she rolled over, though, she clutched the stone.

The night lay still around her. She couldn't breathe.

Someone stirred in Mama's room. She knew what was coming. Or who.

Here we go again.

Phil's footsteps whispered along the bare floor in the hallway.

He stopped at her door.

She flipped a sheet over herself and gripped it.

Come on in, Phil. I'd love to clock someone right now. Come in, buddy. Give me a reason to hit you.

He moved on, his footsteps entering the bathroom. She heard the door close.

When she'd come home on Christmas break, he'd played the same game every night.

A couple of minutes later, he retraced his steps, stopping outside Angel's door long enough to turn the doorknob.

The door wasn't locked. He could enter if he wanted to, and Angel would fight him tooth and nail.

After rotating a few degrees, the knob returned to its normal position and she heard Phil move on.

He was teasing her, letting her know that while

he was in this house, he was the boss. He controlled everything.

Only because Mama let him. *She* owned it.

Angel uncurled her fingers, releasing the bedsheet she'd been gripping.

If Mama wasn't bright enough to protect herself, Angel would have to do it for her.

At 1:00 a.m., she gave up trying to sleep. She sat on the bed and hung her head, tired of trying so hard to forget.

She dressed in the outfit she'd arrived in. Tomorrow, she'd unpack the saddlebags she'd left in the hallway.

Quietly, she stepped out of the house. These nights Angel haunted hallways and streets. After Neil's death, she'd walked the many paths and trails of the campus every night, because to stay in bed with no distractions from thoughts of Neil and her own guilt in his death was murder.

In a strange way, it soothed her that Ordinary, Montana, never seemed to change. The street Missy had lived on for the past several years, in Harold's house, was more upscale than what Angel had grown up in.

She rushed through the poorer part of town, where their old trailer still sat, and headed toward Main Street to see what the brouhaha about Chester's was all about.

TIMM STOOD AT THE FRONT window of his apartment above the newspaper office trying to catch any hint of breeze to cool off.

He had a gift for insomnia. Probably did it better than anyone else he knew.

Glancing toward the end of Main Street, he watched

several of Chester's bikers drift out to their bikes, some of them none too steady on their feet.

The sheriff should be sitting out there every night, arresting them. But really, what could he do when he worked a twelve-hour shift every day and had only one deputy to take over for the night?

That issue needed to be addressed in Timm's bid for mayor.

A movement from the other end of Main caught his eye. Angel Donovan. What the hell? He'd warned her that the town wasn't the same one she'd grown up in now that Chester's drew the worst clientele from the next county.

She always had been stubborn, though.

She was out there, in the dark, alone and he didn't like it one bit.

She just had to pull old tricks and court trouble. She had a real talent for it.

He pulled on a shirt and jogged downstairs. He let himself out of the office, locking the door behind him.

From the recess of his door, he watched her. No need to tell her he was there. With a little luck, nothing would happen and she would wander home.

As Angel passed on the opposite side of the street, the bar's door opened and a bunch of bikers stepped out.

Timm watched and waited for her to move on, but she didn't. She'd always had too much curiosity for her own good.

A couple of the bikers mounted their hogs parked out front. Another one noticed Angel and wandered over. She stood her ground.

For God's sake, Angel, do you have to stand up for every fight? Walk away. Run.

She didn't.

He'd watched her fight since she was old enough to understand the names kids called her mother.

"Haven't seen you here before," the biker said, his voice tobacco-roughened, his posture aggressive he-man. "Who are you?"

His gaze traveled her body, slowly, as if he already owned it. The hair on Timm's arms rose. He shifted his stance, ready to defend Angel.

"No one," she answered, obviously not impressed by the bruiser. He had a layer of fat padding his belly, but enough muscle on his bare arms to bully.

"Let's party. Come on." He turned but when she didn't follow, he looked back at her. "I wasn't *asking.*"

Timm straightened away from the wall. Bastard was going to cause trouble, all right.

"No, thanks," Angel said. "Not if you were the last Neanderthal on earth."

For God's sake, Angel, don't be stupid. Grit and balls are admirable in life, but with a guy like this?

The biker didn't take her comments well. He grabbed her arm, and Timm shot out of the doorway.

As a teenager, he'd been helpless because of his injuries and had watched her fight her battles alone. He wasn't helpless now.

"Get your hands off her," he ordered.

At the same moment, Angel kicked the biker's shin and he slapped her.

Timm was on the guy in an instant. Not a fair fight. A hundred and eighty pounds of intellectual versus a two-hundred-and-thirty-pound wrestler look-alike.

Timm smashed the heel of his hand against the bruiser's nose.

"Angel, run!" he shouted.

The biker slammed his fist into Timm's jaw and he saw stars and staggered, but caught himself before he hit the ground.

Angel jumped her attacker and grabbed a fistful of hair.

"Move on." A voice called out from across the street. Brawny Chester Ames, with a good set of biceps, a tough attitude and a baseball bat in one hand, ran toward them and shoved the bat into the guy's ribs.

With a roar, the biker pushed Angel away from him and spun around.

Chester held the bat raised and ready to do serious harm if the guy didn't leave.

"You want to drink in my bar again, you go on home and stop bothering her." Chester ground out the words. "Now."

The biker hesitated. Chester waited. Timm bounced on the balls of his feet, ready to try to take the guy down if he dared to touch Angel again.

When the guy finally walked to his bike without a word, the breath whooshed out of Timm. Then he cursed his lack of control. He'd been too angry—he knew better than to be so emotional—and because of that emotion, he'd lost the fight. Sensei Chong had taught him how to fight smart, how to remain calm and rational.

He looked at Angel. What was it about her that called up so many feelings? That cost him his precious self-control? He only knew that he'd gone into a rage when the biker had hurt her.

Chester approached Angel. "Why are you out here this late at night?"

"Hey, Chester," she said, her tone soft and affectionate, raising Timm's hackles. Had she been with him at some point? But he was old enough to be her father.

"You shouldn't be here alone," Chester scolded, his tone stern like a father's, easing Timm's tension. A bit.

"I'm not alone." She gestured toward Timm.

Chester eyed him dubiously, and not as a friend. He returned his attention to Angel. "D'you want a drive home? I can be ready in ten minutes."

Before she could answer, a flash of possession roared through Timm, and he interjected, "I'm taking her home." He wasn't much better than the Neanderthal Chester had chased away.

Chester gave him a cold look, nodded, then crossed the road to go back inside.

Angel confronted Timm with her fists on her hips. "What are you doing here?"

"Watching out for you." He stepped closer to her. "Making sure you don't get hurt. I saw you from my window."

Before she could respond, he said, "The next time I tell you to run, do it."

"Don't tell me what to do. I don't run away from battles. I'm not a damsel in distress who needs a man to rescue her."

"And yet, you just needed two of us."

Framed as she was by the streetlight, Timm saw her cheeks fill with color.

"That guy was typical of Chester's clientele."

"I can take care of myself."

His jaw ached where he swore he could feel bruises forming already. "I don't doubt it, Angel, but why would you put yourself in a situation in which you would have to?"

"That's my business." She strode away and turned down a side street.

She got under his skin, made him angry, but he trailed her home. He hadn't liked seeing her hurt. No woman deserved that.

She spun to face him. "Why are you following me?"

"Seeing that you get home safely."

"I told you, I can take care of myself. Stop following me."

"No."

"I don't want you to."

"Tough. That biker could circle back, looking for you."

He trailed her to her old neighborhood. The landscape changed from well-to-do to not on the flip of a dime. Heads, you're rich. Tails, you're poor. Heads, you live on pretty, tree-lined streets. Tails, you live behind the ugly, industrial feed store.

She stopped at the trailer she'd grown up in. After Missy and Angel had moved to Harold's house, no one else had taken up residence. It stood lonesome, threadbare, neglected. Even so, it didn't look much worse than the other trailers on the dead-end street.

What are you thinking, Angel?

He'd had so much room in the four-bedroom brick house where he'd been raised, yet it hadn't been enough to separate him from his father on the nights he drank. On those occasions, the house had been claustrophobic. So, how had Angel felt in this little tin can while her mother's boyfriends cycled through Missy's revolving door?

Had those men ever bothered Angel once she became a teenager? God, he hoped not.

"How did it feel to grow up in there?"

She stared at him for a protracted minute. Then

swearing, she picked up a stone and tossed it at the trailer, where it pinged off the metal loudly enough to awaken a nearby dog.

After a couple of barks, someone yelled and the barking stopped. The night turned quiet again, still and hot.

Breathless and waiting.

In front of the trailer at the end of the short street, Timm spotted the red tip of a burning cigarette. Was that a man? Was he watching Angel?

Timm's muscles bunched and tightened, waiting for trouble.

He stepped closer to protect Angel if he had to, but at that moment she moved on, cutting through the trees and someone's backyard to access the next street.

He followed her until she reached the short sidewalk to her mother's house.

"Good night, Angel," he called softly.

Nothing but the gentle click of her front door closing behind her answered him.

ON TUESDAY MORNING, Timm finished proofreading a hard copy of the Wednesday issue of the paper, then sat at his desk in the storefront to input the changes he'd made.

Megan and Mason, a pair of his reporters, had written excellent articles. He had to remember to tell them so.

As soon as he finished, he sent the file off to the printer in Billings.

They would print twelve thousand copies overnight and deliver them to Ordinary and other small towns throughout the county early tomorrow morning.

On page one was the announcement for the meeting he planned to hold on Thursday night. The town had a problem with Chester's bar and it was time they organized and did something about it.

As important as the issue was, Timm's mind had only been half on the job. The other half had been thinking about Angel.

He was a fool. He didn't rate even a second thought from her, while he fell right back into his old crush the second she came to town.

As if his mind had conjured her, Angel walked into the newspaper office wearing dark jeans and a white T-shirt, the sun behind her skimming her body with loving hands. On anyone else the clothes would look normal, but on Angel? Well…wow.

"What can I do for you?" With her in his space, Timm was surprised that his brain functioned well enough to string together a whole sentence.

"Hey," she said, her eyes hard, as though she thought he'd kick her out or something. "Do you have any copies of the latest issue?"

"Sure," he answered. "That would be last Saturday's. Here."

He pulled one from a pile under the counter.

"Or you can wait for tomorrow for the next edition."

"This will do." Angel reached into her pocket. "How much?"

"Nothing. The next issue comes out tomorrow, so this one's dated."

Slow to pull out her hand, she stared at him as though he were a liar.

"Honest," he said. "Anyone who walks in here on a Tuesday gets Saturday's paper free." Not that anyone ever did come in on Tuesday for last week's paper, but Angel didn't need to know that.

"Thanks," she said. "Do you have a piece of paper and a pen?"

He handed her both. Without a word, she approached the small tables he provided for people to use when filling out ads or obits.

When she sat, her low-riding jeans gaped away from her back, just far enough to bare a tiny fraction of skin. Timm's hands recalled the feel of holding her last night when he stopped her from burning her bike.

He tried not to pay attention to Angel, but couldn't stop himself from counting the pages she turned too quickly before finally stopping.

Reaching under the counter, he unfolded the paper and thumbed through the same number of pages. She'd stopped at the want ads.

Angel needed a job.

If she'd bothered to finish her degree, she could do a hell of a lot better than anything available in the want ads in Ordinary. A fresh spurt of disappointment ran through him. The woman had wasted a great opportunity. Probably spent too much time partying with men the way she had as a teen.

He'd seen it all from his bedroom window as he'd watched the world go by. When boredom nearly killed him, Papa would move him for a few days to the apartment above the newspaper offices, where he could watch the happenings on Main Street.

All the while, he kept a journal, chronicling his feelings of isolation and the yearning to be normal and his observations of his fellow man's behavior, as seen from a bird's-eye view. That journal, about to be published, was paying off for him now.

When he'd turned twenty, he'd moved to the apartment for good.

He read the list of job openings: Bernice's Beauty Salon, the New American diner and Chester's Roadhouse. Even a wild girl like Angel wouldn't work at the Roadhouse.

Angel put the notes she'd taken in her pocket. She folded the newspaper neatly and handed it to Timm along with the pen.

By way of thanks, she nodded then walked out of the office and turned left toward the beauty salon and the diner. Appeared as though she was being smart, keeping away from Chester's at the other end of Main.

Good.

At that moment, Sheriff Kavenagh entered the office.

"Cash," Timm said. "How's the law-enforcement business today?"

Cash barely noticed Timm. He was watching Angel walk down the street.

"Angel's back," he said, a big grin flashing. The sheriff was a good-looking guy. He and Angel had made a handsome couple for a while before Angel headed off to college.

Timm wondered if they'd ever—

Probably.

His inner bully resurfaced. He didn't want Cash sliding around on the playground of Angel's body. Or any other man. It seemed that where Angel was concerned, Timm was one big lusting, *jealous* male hormone. And that bothered him.

Get a grip.

Cash finally turned to Timm and said, "You hear things around town. You know anything about a bike that's stranded on the side of the road out past Sadie Armstrong's place?"

"Angel rode in on it last night."

"Why did she leave it on the road?"

For some reason he didn't look at too closely, Timm didn't want to tell the sheriff about Angel trying to set fire to that bike. "She ran out of gas."

"Yeah? She should have gotten Alvin to tow it."

"I picked her up when I saw her stranded," Timm said. "It was already dark. She'll probably take care of it today."

"Someone tried to burn it." Cash didn't look happy. "Idiot could have started a fire. I need to find out who did it and put the fear of God into him. Give him a ticket. He could have burned up a fair portion of the countryside."

Now was the time for Timm to admit that Angel was the culprit. He was normally an honest man. Why protect Angel? She was a big girl and plenty capable of taking care of herself. As far as Timm could tell, Angel's attitude hadn't changed one bit while away. So why was she worthy of his protection?

He held his tongue.

"So Angel's back," Cash mused, with a smile playing at the corners of his mouth. "She'll perk up the town."

Timm stepped around the counter, edgy today, but he couldn't pinpoint why. "The town's already *perked up* enough with the bar full of bikers every night."

Cash grew serious and nodded. "I know. Williams had to break up another fight there last night. His report said it happened about ten. He'll be on shift again at eight tonight if you want to talk to him."

"Thanks," Timm answered, walking beside Cash to the open doorway. "I'll interview him for Saturday's paper."

Sweat beaded on Timm's forehead and he fingered

the button at his throat, tempted to open it. He might have come to terms with his scars, but he doubted that anyone in town wanted to see them.

"I'm organizing a town meeting for Thursday night at the Legion Hall," he said. "We need to get Chester's closed down."

"Good luck with that. He's not breaking any laws."

"I know." Timm had looked at the problem from every angle. "All I can do is gather the citizens and mount a protest."

Cash pointed a finger at Timm. "You be careful. Those bikers aren't going to be happy about this. Watch your back."

Timm nodded. He wasn't worried for himself, but what if they bothered Ma, or his sister, Sara, now that she was home from school?

"You'll get a lot of support," Cash said, stepping onto the sidewalk. "The townspeople respect you, Timm. As future mayor, you know they'll listen."

Timm smiled. "I'm not mayor yet."

"Don't worry. You will be."

"We'll see." The election was in two more weeks and Max Golden, his only competition, was a popular guy. "I don't like to make assumptions."

Cash was right, though. As publisher of the most well-read small-town newspaper in the state, he held a good position. People respected a man when he was good at his job. Timm had been born to use his brain and, with the paper, he got to use it all—creativity and research and reporting the facts. Yeah, he did his job well.

He'd see if that parlayed into votes.

"Will you come to the meeting?" Timm asked. "It would look good if you showed up. Seven o'clock."

"I'll still be on duty, but if nothing's going on in town, I'll be there." Cash walked away.

Timm focused on the building at the end of the street. Six months ago, Chester had rented the last two storefronts on Main and had turned them into one large space.

Any new business in Ordinary should have been a relief to the town. In the summer, they usually appreciated tourist dollars, but that source of income had dried up this year a few months after Chester's grand opening, when the bikers had appropriated the bar as their own.

Main Street pretty well became theirs after eight every night.

Timm's concern had nothing to do with money or tourists, though.

For him, this fight was personal.

CHAPTER THREE

ANGEL ENTERED BERNICE'S Beauty Salon.

Bernice was a good person—she'd never looked down on Angel.

"Hey, honey," Bernice said with a smile, stopping the sweeping she'd been doing and resting one hand on her ample hip. "Haven't seen you in a while, Angel. How's school?"

It had been good, but had ended badly. Angel's smile felt sickly, but she hoped it looked normal. "Good. I'm home for the summer and then heading to the city for a job."

Angel looked around. The shop hadn't changed one bit in the time she'd been gone. Red geraniums dotted the windowsill and a monster jade plant stood in one corner.

"You getting your hair cut?" Bernice asked.

Angel shook her head.

"Good. Don't think Missy or the men in town would like that much." She laughed.

"Bernice, I'm here about the job you have open."

Bernice's smile fell. "Honey, I hired a girl yesterday."

From the back of the room, a teenager Angel recognized, but whose name she couldn't remember, stepped out with another woman and walked her to a salon chair.

When the woman unwrapped the towel from her wet hair, she looked at Angel. Her mouth fell open, then quickly closed.

"Well, well, well. Look what the cat dragged in. Angel Donovan. What are you doing in town?"

Elsa. Scotty's daughter. Scotty owned the hardware store. The town liked him, but disliked his daughter.

Elsa had hated Angel in high school, even though Angel had been a few years behind her. Didn't matter. Boys and men of any age were attracted to Angel.

Angel tipped her head and smiled. If it felt a little mean, so be it. This was Elsa, after all, herself the meanest woman in town.

"My mama lives here, in case you've forgotten." Angel turned toward the front door.

Before she could open it, Elsa said, "William married me, you know."

Angel turned back. "That's nice."

"We have three beautiful children and a perfect life."

"Fine, Elsa. Let's get it all out now, 'cause I'll be in town for the summer and I'm not taking crap from you for the next three months." She stood, arms akimbo. "To confirm what you've always suspected, Bill and I made out one night after a football game."

Elsa's face contorted into a mask of rage. "Proving you're no better than your mother."

"Who were you? Snow White? You'd been dating Bill for two years—you were still dating him—when you got busy with Matt Long and wound up pregnant. Behind Bill's back. After that, he wanted revenge. You're a hypocrite, Elsa, no better than any other woman in town, including me and Missy."

Angel stomped out of the shop. She was so tired

of the fight. It would never end as long as she lived in Ordinary. She stood on the sidewalk to get her rowdy anger under control, then crossed the street toward the diner.

When she stepped inside, the old familiar scents assailed her—bacon and eggs, grilled-cheese sandwiches, burgers.

Within seconds, all conversation seemed to stop.

Someone yelled, "Hey, Angel, when did you get back?"

Sam Miller sat in a booth across from the counter.

Angel walked over and leaned her hip against his table.

"Hey, Sam, how've you been?" Angel smiled at the three men with him even though she didn't know them. By the glances skimming her body, they liked her. Men always did.

Except for Timm Franck.

So what? You don't want him attracted to you anyway.

She'd been celibate since Neil and planned to keep it that way here in Ordinary. No men. No hanky-panky.

She wrapped up the pleasantries, then made her way to the cash register. George, cook and owner of the diner, asked her what she wanted to order.

There was a time when George had been one of Missy's boyfriends, but that had changed once Angel had become a teenager and George had wanted to switch daughter for mother.

Both Missy and Angel had booted him out of the trailer and had told him to never come back.

He still gave her the creeps.

The words *I'm here about the job* stuck in her throat.

Could she work here every day with George watching her the way he was looking at her now—with greed?

She almost decided to take the job so she could put him down the first time he tried to touch her, by "accident," in passing, the way he used to before Angel learned how to fight back.

Man, she would enjoy giving him a piece of her mind.

She wasn't in town to fight old fights, though, despite what had happened with Elsa. She was here for Mama, and she needed money to leave the second she got Phil out of her mother's life.

"I changed my mind. I don't want anything," she muttered, then left the diner.

Fuming, she strode down the sidewalk to Chester's Roadhouse, betting that he'd still have enough affection for her and her mom to give her a job.

She'd come home broke. She'd wasted her money on that bike, thinking that she would have her degree in a couple of months and would get a full-time job.

Then Neil…then Neil had—

Chester needed a bartender. Angel hadn't gotten her degree, couldn't do much else, but bartending was something she did really well. She made people happy.

A niggling feeling caught her unawares. Someone was watching her. She stopped before entering the bar and glanced around.

Timm crossed the street toward the diner, looking at her. When they made eye contact, he changed direction and approached her.

What could he possibly have to say to her that they couldn't have said fifteen minutes ago in his office?

Sunlight did good things for Timm. It warmed his

light brown hair to honey and highlighted that face that had matured into strong planes and angles.

He was taller than she'd remembered, and lean. For a nerd, he walked with a surprising athletic grace.

When he got close enough for her to see his eyes behind the wire-rimmed glasses, she realized they were chocolate-brown. He wasn't fast enough in masking his look of admiration of her.

It warmed her. It shouldn't have.

Timm fit into this town too well.

She didn't.

"Hi," she said. Brilliant. Wow, it wasn't like her to be tongue-tied. But she didn't want to say anything that would make her look stupid in front of this guy. He was too smart.

"Sheriff Kavenagh saw your bike out on the highway," he said.

Angel swallowed. Shit. All she needed was to be fined or arrested for starting a fire during a drought.

"So you told him I tried to burn it?" She couldn't help the aggression in her tone.

"No," he said. He shifted his gaze away from her, studied the shops across the street, wouldn't look her in the eye.

"You didn't? Why not?"

He shrugged. "I was there to stop the fire, so no problem."

"Thanks," she mumbled. There was a whole lot more she should say, but the words wouldn't come out. "Well. I gotta go." She stepped toward the Roadhouse door.

"The bar's not open for another hour." Something in his voice—disapproval, maybe—set her hackles on edge.

"I'm heading in for a job."

"You don't want to do that." The helpful man of a minute ago was gone, replaced by a hard-edged judgmental prude.

"How is it any of your business?"

"I plan to close this place down."

"Why would you close Chester's?"

"You saw the bikers last night. They're ruining the town. Decent people stay away."

The implication being that she wasn't decent. Surprise, surprise. The town's attitude hadn't changed about her. Why should it have?

Timm had always seemed different, though—smarter—and she was disappointed to find he was no better than the rest of Ordinary's residents.

Obviously, attending college made no difference in how the townspeople viewed her. They still had her pegged as the trailer-trash girl with the slutty mother.

"Great talking to you," she said, her sarcasm tainting the sunny day.

Without a word, his expression flattened, and he turned and walked away.

Angel opened the door of Chester's Roadhouse, irritated by Timm's assessment of her. Seemed that, in his eyes, the bar was exactly where she belonged.

Stepping into the dark interior, Angel shook off her funk. She gave her eyes a moment to adjust to the dimness. It was at least ten degrees cooler in here than outside, thank goodness. Must cost Chester a fortune to air-condition, though.

The place smelled like beer.

Chester had spent his money freely decorating the huge room. Red leather and oak booths lined two walls. The center of the room housed chairs padded with the same upholstery surrounding large round tables.

Angel approached the bar.

Chester was doing well for himself. The bar must bring in good money.

"Hey, Freddy," she said to the bartender, recognizing him from school. "Haven't seen you in a while. How have you been?"

"Hi, Angel." Freddy was a good guy, not too handsome, but not ugly, either. He leaned on the bar and assessed her. "You're looking well. College treated you okay?"

Angel ignored her spurt of guilt for not finishing and smiled. "I did all right there."

"What can I get you? Bar isn't open yet, but I can pour you a soft drink."

"Thanks, but nothing. I'm here to see Chester."

Freddy indicated a nearby archway. "Down the hall, last door on your left. Should be open."

Angel made her way to Chester's office, where she found him sitting in a leather office chair behind a huge desk covered with piles of papers.

She rapped on his open door. "Hey, Chester."

He looked up, startled, and smiled. "Angel. I didn't have a chance to talk to you. When did you blow back into town?"

Angel smiled. "Last night. I'm here for the bartending job in the paper."

Chester leaned back in the chair and wrapped his fingers behind his head. It made his biceps look huge. Angel totally understood Mama's crush on him.

"How's Missy?" he asked quietly. He always asked about Mama.

"As good as can be, considering who's living with her right now."

"Yeah, I hear you." He frowned. "Hey, I thought you

finished college. Is the economy so bad you can't get a job even with a degree?"

Angel sat in the chair in front of the desk. "I'm hanging around for the summer. To help Mama with the wedding and to take care of her place while she and Phil take a honeymoon." The lies rolled off her tongue easily. If she felt any guilt about lying to a good friend like Chester, she ignored it.

Chester shuffled papers on his desk. He blushed the way he always did when Missy was around.

"So, I see you've got Freddy working behind the bar. What hours do you need me for?"

"Freddy's going to night school."

"No kidding? What's he studying?"

"He wants to be an accountant."

"Cool. I can mix drinks. I worked as a bartender in Bozeman when I was at school. Do you need a reference?"

"Nah. I trust you, Angel." He leaned forward and rested his elbows on the desk. "I need a bartender for the evenings—from six until one-thirty. There's usually a bit of cleanup after the bar closes, but you'd be out by two, latest. I'm usually here until three, going through the receipts and counting the cash, so you'll never be alone."

He stood to walk her out. "You'll be a great asset here, Angel. With your looks..." Chester grinned. "You're a hell of a lot prettier than Freddy is."

Angel laughed. "Yeah, I'm pretty good at having fun, too." She knew her place. Knew exactly her value. Here in Ordinary, she was a party girl, through and through.

She left the bar after agreeing to start work that evening and walked down the street to the candy store,

Sweet Talk. While she was home, she would reconnect with the only other family she had.

Two years ago, she'd found out that she had a half brother—Matthew Long. Matt's dad and Missy had had a relationship for years when Matt was young and Angel had been the result of that affair. Mama had never told her who her father was.

Not kosher of Mama to sleep with another woman's man, but so like Missy.

Fortunately, them both being only children meant that Angel and Matt had latched onto each other. From the very beginning, he'd insisted that he was her full brother—there was nothing *half* about their relationship, he was her brother in every way that counted. She couldn't imagine being closer to him than she was now. And she adored his wife and children.

In fact, she needed to pick up candy for her nephew and niece, thus the visit to Sweet Talk. For six-year-old Jesse, she chose a chocolate rabbit that wore a housecoat and carried a candle and a book, all decorated with icing sugar dyed in pastels. For two-year-old Rose, she bought a small chocolate rabbit with pink lips and a pink icing dress. Adding to her purchase, she selected a bag of humbugs for Jenny and salted Dutch licorice for Matt.

She tipped her head through the doorway to the candy-making room and waved to the owner, Janey Wilson. Looked as though Janey was about to pop out another kid. How many were Janey and C.J. up to now? Four? Five?

Angel returned home to ask Mama if she could borrow her car to drive out to Matt's ranch.

Angel stepped into the quiet house. She'd noticed that the garage door was open and the car gone. Nuts.

When she walked into the kitchen, she found that she wasn't alone.

Phil sat at the table, drinking coffee.

He glanced up when she entered, his eyes skimming her body before settling on her face.

His demeanor always surprised her—so mild-looking, yet there was something behind his pale eyes that sat wrong with Angel. Something like…a banked hunger, as if he could never get enough to satisfy his cravings.

Not a tall man, why did he *seem* so much bigger than he actually was? Wiry strength threaded his forearms, though, and crafty knowledge gleamed in his eye. Angel would be a fool to underestimate him.

"Where's Mama?"

"Grocery shopping."

Phil had a mass of grocery-store coupons spread neatly across the table. Angel felt vaguely nauseous. Mama was still hoarding those stupid things?

"Don't tell me you collect coupons, too?" Angel asked, her tone derisive.

"Why not? If you work at it hard enough, you can save a lot of money."

Angel turned and poured herself a cup of coffee. Mama had pinched every penny until it squeaked and her obsession with discounts and coupons had sparked a loathing for them in Angel.

"What's so wrong with using coupons?" Phil asked.

She wasn't about to tell him that they reeked of poverty, and reminded her too much of growing up in that crummy old trailer.

Phil stacked the detergent coupons on top of each other and fastened them with a paper clip. Then he picked up assorted coupons and fastened those together.

Control freak.

"Why did you clip those?" Angel asked, despite not wanting to care. "They're different products."

"They're only good until the end of the month, so your mother and I will watch for specials and use them before the expiry date."

Cheapskate.

Almost as if he'd read her mind, he peered at her sharply. "No one handed me an education. I get by in this life however I can."

They both heard the car rumble down the driveway along the side of the house.

A minute later, Mama walked in the door. Still a beautiful woman, voluptuous and sensuous in the way she moved, she looked tired this morning.

Angel knew she'd put those dark circles under Mama's eyes with her attitude toward Phil. Despite knowing it was the right thing to do, Angel felt a worm of disgust at her own behavior crawling under her flesh.

She looked out the window. The barely driven Grand Am Mama had inherited from Hal sat inside the garage.

"Phil, can you close the garage door?" Missy's arms were full of groceries. "It's sticking again."

Phil stood and took the two full grocery bags from her and placed them on the counter.

"Any more bags in the car?"

"One more."

"I'll get it." He left the kitchen.

Okay, so he was more a gentleman than Angel had given him credit for.

Missy hugged Angel. "Can I get you some lunch?"

"I can make my own."

"I know, but you're home and I want to do it."

Angel stopped her with a hand on her arm. "Mama, can we talk?"

A flash of fear flittered across Missy's face. "About what?"

"Phil," Angel rushed on, determined to say something before Phil returned.

The garage door screeched.

"No," Missy breathed.

"Mama, please," Angel said, but heard Phil on the stairs. A second later, Phil entered with the last bag. It joined the others on the counter.

Angel's frustration mounted.

"How much did we save?" Phil asked Missy.

"Four-thirty-five." Missy smiled at him, obviously absurdly relieved that Angel hadn't been able to vocalize her thoughts about Phil.

"Good girl." Phil caressed her hip and she preened under his attention. Phil sat at the table again.

Angel turned away.

Missy pulled a frying pan out of a cupboard.

"What are you doing?" Phil asked.

"I'm making an early lunch for Angel."

"So this is what you're planning to do here?" He directed the question toward Angel. "Have your mother cook for you?"

"I didn't ask her to cook," Angel said, hating the way Phil questioned everything Missy did.

"I want to make her lunch, Phil." Missy's placating tone grated.

Phil stared at Angel with a thunderous frown and asked, "Are you planning to freeload off your mother?"

"What about you?" she snapped. "Are you working?"

"No."

"Then *you're* freeloading," she shouted.

"Angel, he can't work," Missy explained. "He has a disability."

"Yeah? I didn't know they considered being brain-dead a disability."

Phil surged out of his chair.

Missy slapped a restraining hand on his chest and held him back. "Angel!" Distress rode high in her voice.

Phil breathed loudly and stared at Angel with something close to hatred in his eyes.

The plastic clock on the wall ticked a loud cadence in counterpoint to Angel's hard-driving pulse.

"Go ahead," Angel said. "Take a swing at me, big man. Prove to Mama who you really are."

Too clever to show his hand, Phil retreated, his thin smile bordering on insolence.

"While you live in my house, Angel," Missy said, "treat Phil with respect."

Angel reeled from the disappointment on Mama's face. What? Had that really happened? Had Mama taken a *man's* side against Angel? Mama and she were a team. The Donovan girls against the world.

What were they now? A crowd of three, with Angel the odd person out? Shocked, she left the kitchen, shaken by Mama's need to defend Phil over her.

She sat on the bed in her room and hung her head, so scared. What if she lost Mama?

Phil was too clever. Angel led with her emotions, going off like lightning, while Phil calculated every angle, every advantage.

A short time later, she heard Phil leave. Wherever he was going, it was without the car.

She rushed to the kitchen.

Mama sat at the table with her cheek resting on one hand, looking so despondent that Angel put her arms around her from behind and whispered in her ear, "I'm sorry, Mama."

She couldn't bring up the issue of Phil again today. She'd handled it all wrong. Time to regroup and figure out how to do it better.

Missy patted her arm and said, "I know, honey." There was a subtle but tangible distance in her.

Abruptly, she stood and said, too brightly, "Let's have lunch."

Throughout the meal, Missy maintained that distance. For the first time in their lives, the chatter between them was uncomfortable, made more so with her forced gaiety and Angel's equally forced responses.

God, how was Angel going to get rid of Phil? For the first time, it occurred to her that if it came to a showdown, Mama might choose Phil over her. The prospect seemed impossible, but Angel could never have predicted her mother's earlier behavior.

Oh, Mama, I don't want to lose you.

Angel swallowed the last mouthful of her sandwich, and it felt like sawdust clogging her throat.

Refusing to believe that anything would come between her and Missy, she forced the dire thoughts from her mind.

They'd be okay. They always had and always would be.

Deciding to stick with her original plan to visit Matt—and to put some space between Mama and her—Angel asked to borrow the car. Before leaving, she kissed Mama's forehead. Her responding smile was so vague it chilled Angel.

What was going on in Missy's mind these days? Was it only the outburst between them and Phil that had her distracted? Or was something else bothering her?

Angel worried that question all the way to her brother's place with no resolution.

Matt's ranch was large and prosperous. Matt and his wife, Jenny, worked hard for what they had.

As she drove up the lane, Jesse ran out of the stable.

"Auntie Angel," he screamed when he realized who was in the car. A second later, Matt stepped out into the sunlight with a big grin splitting his face.

She stepped out and Jesse threw himself against her legs, wrapping his arms around her. He was getting so big. She adored this little guy.

Her blue funk fell away.

Here, with these people, she found a peace foreign in every other area of her life.

This was a good family that Matt had made work by overcoming all of the pain and sorrow of his past. Angel wondered whether someday she would be able to do the same for herself. She planned to. Somehow.

"Where are Jenny and Rose?" she asked, her voice muffled by Matt's chest because he'd wrapped his arms around her tightly.

Angel loved having an older brother. Maybe if she'd known about him in high school, she could have gone to him for advice when boys started to sniff around her once she'd started to develop this double-edged sword of a killer body. Maybe things could have gone differently for her....

"I can't breathe," Jesse wailed against her thighs, and Matt pulled away, laughing.

"How long are you staying this time?" Matt asked.

"I'm staying in Ordinary only a few weeks." She refused to call it home. As soon as she figured out how to deep-six Phil and Missy's marriage, she was getting out of here and staying away. She'd warned Matt enough times that she wouldn't end up in Ordinary permanently. At some point, he would have to believe her.

They all entered a house that smelled like bananas.

They found Jenny and Rose in the kitchen. Half a pot of chicken-noodle soup sat on the stove and a loaf of banana bread cooled on the counter.

Angel spotted the mix box in the recycling bin in the corner of the kitchen. Jenny was a terrible cook. She did *nothing* from scratch.

She rushed to give Angel a big hug, but not before Angel noticed her belly and hooted.

"Another baby?"

"Yes," Jenny said, beaming.

Women everywhere were having babies, while Angel...well, none of her encounters with men seemed to last long enough to reach the let's-commit-and-make-babies stage. She swallowed her sorrow.

Enjoy your niece and nephew.

She walked to the table and kissed the little blond-haired, blue-eyed doll sitting in the high chair.

Rose giggled and kicked her feet. "Up, Auntie Angel."

Angel lifted the tray away from the chair. It looked as though more noodles had ended up on it than inside her niece.

Rose kicked her feet and said, "Angel. Up. *Peese.*"

Angel laughed and blew her a raspberry. "Hold your horses, squirt."

Rose blew a raspberry back at Angel, sending spittle

flying. Angel made a show of jumping out of the way, and Rose giggled.

Angel unbuckled Rose's belt and lifted her into her arms, sniffing her kid scent of powder and baby shampoo and chicken-noodle soup.

She kissed Rose's nose. "What are you up to today?"

"I played dollies and bocks and pee-peed in my potty."

"You did?" Angel exclaimed.

Rose nodded emphatically. "Big girl now."

"You certainly are."

Rose picked up a strand of Angel's long hair. "I grow up pitty like you."

No, don't. It's too much. It's a burden. I want to be loved for myself, not for my face and my body.

She wanted the same for Rose, to be loved for the beautiful person she was inside.

"Auntie Angel?"

"Yes, Rose?"

Rose spread her hands, as if puzzled. "What you bring me?"

Everyone laughed and Angel sent Matt and Jenny a wry smile.

"This habit of bringing gifts every time you show up is going to have to stop," Matt said.

"Sure," Angel said. "Next time. Come on. There's something for each of you in the car."

Matt wrapped his arm around her as they walked outside.

Here is where I feel at home, where I'm accepted and loved, completely and utterly. On Matt and Jenny's ranch, she wasn't trashy Angel Donovan. Here, she wasn't Missy's daughter. In this house, she was a good sister-in-law, a loving sister and a world-class aunt.

WHEN PHIL RETURNED TO the house, Missy still sat at the kitchen table, exactly where she'd been when Angel had left, with her head in her hands, trying to figure out what to do.

"Hey, babe." Phil said. "Come on." He walked down the hall to their bedroom.

Missy followed him, less and less happy about their afternoon "dates," as Phil called them. Why couldn't Phil ever get enough no matter how often she satisfied him— every night, most mornings and every afternoon?

Her frustration grew. Maybe today she could change that. How? For a woman who knew as much about sex as anyone could, she was drawing a blank.

She *had* to make this work with the man she was about to marry.

When she entered the room, Phil was naked from the waist up and unbuckling his belt.

His pants dropped to the floor. Skinny legs. Small chest. It was hard for Missy to whip up enthusiasm day after day.

Phil's face turned hard. "Where's the car?"

Warily, Missy said, "Angel took it to visit Matt."

She pulled off her blouse and Phil stared at her breasts. She swore he liked them better than her face.

"You shouldn't have let her take it." His lips pulled back into a snarl. Phil was angry. Could she use it to charge up the sex?

She dropped her pants and the tiny scrap of red lace of her thong. She turned her back to him and climbed onto the bed, hoping that the sight of her would excite him to new heights.

"Hurry up," he said. "Get under the blankets."

She didn't want to hurry, was sick of hurrying, of giving and not getting. She turned onto her back but didn't climb under the covers. Instead, she bent her knees and spread her legs. *Go down on me, Phil.* He never had before. She wasn't sure what he would do if she asked. She needed satisfaction today.

"Please," she whispered. *Phil, honey, give an inch.*

He shook his head, pulled off his boxers and lay on top of her, entering her without foreplay.

He worked on top of her while Missy pictured massive biceps, big penises, large hands rough on her skin, anything to excite herself.

"Do that thing," Phil ordered.

"What thing?" she asked, trying to spike his anger, trying to spark an unpredictable reaction, hoping he would get a little rough with her.

"Move your muscles inside."

She did and he shook. His arms trembled and he dropped onto his elbows.

He was done.

"Thanks, babe." He breathed heavily in her ear.

For a second, she held him close to bind him to her, afraid to let go. *Phil, I need you. Angel will be gone soon. Then all I'll have is you.*

In only one more week, they were getting married. Then everything would be fine. It had to be. She had no one else.

Phil rolled off her. "Move, babe." She did and he slid under the covers.

Missy opened the drawer of the bedside table and handed him a big cotton hankie. "Here," she said. "Don't mess my sheets."

He took it, cleaned himself, handed it back to her and said, "Wake me at four."

As if she could forget. He did the same thing every day. Such an overgrown boy. A child in a man's body. What had happened to him when he was a kid?

Missy had asked, but Phil wouldn't talk about it.

She showered, dressed, then returned to the kitchen, where she stood in front of the window, frozen by her own unanswered needs.

The grass needed mowing.

TIMM SAT IN FRONT OF his computer. There was something he needed to know, not quite sure why he felt guilty delving into Angel's business.

He was a reporter. Reporters were naturally curious people.

He looked up the bike's license plate. It had been a Montana plate. His memory was one asset that worked in his favor as a journalist.

Angel owned the bike. Even more curious, he typed her name into an internet search engine and found an article dated nearly three months ago.

Young Man Dead—DUI

Both Neil Anderson's motorcycle and his girl-friend, Angel Donovan, came away from a single-vehicle accident with minor scratches.

Neil, a promising young student at Bozeman University, wasn't so lucky. He died on impact when he was thrown and his head hit a tree.

At the autopsy, he was determined to have had a blood alcohol level higher than .08.

Close friends and family of the victim ex-pressed shock, since Anderson never drank and didn't frequent bars.

The officer who investigated the crash stated that Montana has the highest incident rate of alcohol-related car accidents in the country.

Timm jumped up from his desk to pace. Angel hadn't changed. He'd watched the impetuous fool try to burn a bike—scratched and dented, maybe, but nearly new. He remembered the party girl she used to be. Clearly she'd gotten the Anderson kid started on drinking. Timm was a fool to like her, to defend her, to lie to Cash through omission.

So, she was burning the bike…because? Probably because it had killed her friend.

Angel was wrong, though. The bike hadn't killed her friend. *She* had.

CHAPTER FOUR

ANGEL, MATT, JENNY and the children sat amid the detritus of cannibalized chocolate animals. They'd fought the good fight, but hungry mouths had prevailed.

Jenny stood to take the kids to the washroom to clean up, leaving Angel and Matt alone.

"Matt, I need to talk to you."

At her serious tone, he nodded. "Let's step outside."

They wandered to the corral, where Masterpiece joined them at the fence. Angel scratched the horse's jaw, while Matt took a caramel from his shirt pocket, unwrapped it then offered it to Master.

"What's the problem, sis?"

"I need to ask your advice. About Phil. And I hate to ask because I know you probably don't like Missy."

"I never had anything against Missy. Your mom doesn't have a bad bone in her body. She just lacks good judgment." He leaned back against the white fence and crossed his arms. "Besides, that relationship gave me you. You're my only blood relative on this earth, except for my children."

The sun glinted from hair a dozen different shades of brown and blond. He studied her and she felt his affection like a gentle stroke.

"Shoot, Angel. What's bothering you?"

"Mama's going to marry Phil at the end of next week. It's why I came back."

Master nudged her shoulder and she scratched his forehead. He closed his eyes and pushed against her palm. "I have to stop it, Matt. Phil doesn't love Mama."

"I don't get a great feeling from the guy, but if Missy wants to marry him, that's her decision. How do you think you can stop her?"

"I don't know." Frustration ate a hole in her gut. "Any ideas?"

"Have you told Missy about your concerns?"

"She knows how much I dislike Phil. You know me. I'm mouthy and come out swinging. I haven't had a chance to tell her about the way he stops by my bedroom in the middle of the night and rattles my doorknob, but I don't want to hurt her."

Matt straightened away from the fence. "He does what?" His voice had gone flat with a dangerous depth.

"He doesn't come into my room. He just pretends that he will."

"Come on. I'll drive into town and have a talk with him." When he said *talk,* Angel had no doubt that Matt had no intention of simply talking.

On impulse, she threw her arms around him. "I love you, Matt. You're the best big brother."

His arms snapped around her. "I love you, too, girl. I'm not going to let Phil get away with that shit."

Angel pulled back. "It's okay. Don't get into a fight over it. I just need to convince Mama to not marry him."

Matt shook his head. "I don't know what to say other than to be honest and tell her what's happening."

"Yeah, you're right. I'll try it again—she didn't take it well earlier when I said how I felt. Mama's being pretty stubborn right now."

As Matt walked Angel to her car, he said, "You call anytime day or night if Phil threatens you. Got it?"

"I can handle Phil." She climbed into the car.

"Uh-uh. I think there's a hell of a lot more to that guy than meets the eye. Don't trust him, Angel. Don't turn your back."

"You really think he'd hurt me?"

Matt leaned on the open window. "Don't know, but my gut tells me he can't be trusted. Be careful."

Angel kissed his cheek and nodded. "Say goodbye to Jenny and the kids for me, okay, big bro?"

"Will do."

Angel drove away, feeling worse. His assessment of Phil was much the same as hers, but Matt's interpretation went a step further. So, if Phil could be a danger to her, could he also be one to Mama?

AT A QUARTER TO SIX that evening, Angel headed to work at Chester's Roadhouse.

Since returning from Matt's, Angel hadn't had the chance to talk to Mama, because Phil was hanging around. She wanted to confront Mama alone, so she and Phil wouldn't have a chance to form a united front against Angel.

Cash Kavenagh pulled up in his cop car and grinned at her through his open window. "Hey, Angel." He pulled off his aviators and his hazel-eyed glance skimmed her body. "You're looking as good as ever."

She grinned right back. She liked Cash. She remembered one heavy petting session she'd had with him before she left for college.

His smile told her that he was remembering that particular evening, too. Cash was handsome and a couple of years older than she and he'd sure known his way around a kiss and a woman's body, but Angel was glad they hadn't taken it all the way. She'd already started to want more for herself, to shake off Ordinary's expectations of her.

She wandered closer to his cruiser. "Hey, Cash. How's it going?"

"Timm told me that bike out on the highway is yours. Said you ran out of gas. Listen, sorry to be the one to break it to you, but someone tried to set it on fire."

She widened her eyes and tried to look surprised.

Apparently it worked. She had no idea why Timm had covered for her, but she appreciated it.

"Maybe it was one of the bikers who hang out here these days. They drive in from Harris County."

Angel nodded, but didn't say anything.

"Alvin will pick it up free of charge if he can use the bike for parts."

"I'll talk to him tomorrow."

"Want me to go ask him now?"

"That would be great, Cash. If you don't mind."

Cash jerked his thumb in the direction of the bar. "You're not heading in there, are you?"

"Chester gave me a job as a bartender. Evenings until closing."

Cash frowned. "You're going to work there? What about college? Your degree? You can do better than this."

Why didn't people shut up about her degree? It wasn't a crime to leave college without getting it. Even so, pride wouldn't let her tell people she'd quit a month shy of finishing.

"This is just for the summer, Cash." She repeated her lie about taking care of the house while Missy and Phil went on their honeymoon.

"How late are you working tonight?"

"Chester says I'll be out by two at the latest."

"Is he going to see you home?"

"No, after hours he counts the cash and cleans up."

"I don't like it, Angel. You didn't drive over?"

She shook her head. Phil wouldn't let her take the car, controlling a-hole. She'd been able to borrow it earlier because he hadn't been home. He'd gone ape-shit about it when she'd returned from Matt's ranch.

"You're going to *walk* home?" It was obvious what Cash thought of that idea.

"Cash, I grew up here. Ordinary's safe. I'm used to walking these streets day or night. I can take care of myself."

"I know, Angel, but the crowd that rides in every night is real bad. Ordinary just isn't the same as it used to be. You take care, y'hear me?"

"Thanks, Cash. I will."

She stepped back and he drove away.

Feeling herself being watched, she glanced down the street. Timm stood in the open doorway of the newspaper office. Details about him were slowly coming back to her. She remembered Timm used to be in the background a lot, used to do a lot of watching, used to sit in his bedroom window while the kids walked home from school. She wasn't sure why there had never been a creep factor attached to it. With a lot of other people there would have been. Maybe it felt okay because the whole town knew about the operations he'd had in those years. The guy had no doubt been bored to tears not being able to go to school. She would have been.

She couldn't believe she hadn't recognized him at first. She'd probably hurt his feelings. Then again, why would that hurt his feelings? He probably didn't give a fig about her.

He was frowning while he watched her.

He gestured to Cash to pull up, then approached to lean on the patrol car's door. They talked for a minute before Timm straightened and Cash drove on. Timm stood in the middle of the street, turned his head her way and stared at her.

They'd been talking about her. What had they said? Something bad?

The slowly dissipating heat of a scorching day shimmered between her and Timm. Even from this distance, his gaze felt hot on her.

What was he thinking? What went on in Timm Franck's head when he watched the folks of Ordinary so steadfastly and quietly?

He nodded and returned to the newspaper office.

Angel shook herself out of her daze and entered the bar at six on the dot. Half a dozen people sat scattered throughout the tavern.

Freddy stood behind the bar, drying glasses. He waved a greeting.

"Hey, Freddy." Angel joined him. "Tell me what I need to know."

Freddy glanced above her face. "I like your hat." She'd worn her favorite red cowboy hat.

"Thanks. It puts me in a party mood."

Freddy grinned and put a clean glass on the shelf below the bar. "I thought you were *always* in party mode."

That was the problem. She'd always played that part too well, and she was sick of it, but…

"I'm hoping to make a lot of good tips here."

He looked at her strangely. "Hoping to? Of course you'll make good tips. These guys aren't coming in here to look at my ugly mug. You're a good change." He dried another glass and put it on the shelf.

"Thanks, Freddy." She'd been feeling too low for her first day at work and had spruced herself up with the hat and her reddest of red lipsticks. She planned to make good money in the next month or so, to purchase a one-way bus ticket out of town to…wherever. Las Vegas. L.A. Maybe New York City.

Freddy showed her the cash drawer and covered the prices. "Do you know how to mix drinks?"

"I bartended in Bozeman." So she wouldn't feel like a complete loser sponging off Mama for four years.

She'd tended bar in a lounge, and the worst trouble she'd ever gotten into was when a guy tried to short-change her. She'd called the manager to deal with him.

Thinking of the bikers, she knew this place would be different. So what? She knew how to handle men.

She recognized only a couple of the patrons as locals, and they weren't exactly the cream of Ordinary's crop.

Kurt Glass sat in a booth against the wall. He raised his empty mug and motioned to Freddy that he wanted another beer.

"I'll get it," Angel said, and pulled a draft. For sure, Kurt wasn't drinking any of the premium ales listed on the chalkboard beer menu behind the bar.

She sauntered over and smiled. Harmless and sweet, Kurt had been homeless for as far back as Angel's memory ran. His ripe aroma greeted her a good ten feet from his booth.

He nodded to her. "Angel. Thank you."

He pulled a buck out of his pocket and fumbled with change. He didn't have close to enough for the beer.

Angel laid her hand over his. "I got it. My homecoming treat."

Kurt smiled. "Thanks, Angel. You're a good girl." He sipped from the glass.

"You're probably the only man in town who thinks so, but thanks, Kurt. I appreciate it."

In his simple-minded way, he had always been able to glimpse past the outer shell to her core.

At college, she had started to think she was a good person inside, but that was before killing Neil.

The clientele built steadily over the next couple of hours. Angel touched base with a few people she hadn't seen in four years.

Most customers, though, were bikers. Seemed the good people of Ordinary didn't want to rub shoulders with them. Despite that, most of the bikers acted fine. Some others, though...

Angel took orders, delivered beers and spent a lot of time telling off guys who tried to pat her tush.

After one pimply faced biker put his hand on her ass, she turned to give him a piece of her mind, only to have a woman sitting at the table glare at her.

"You keep your hands off my man," she ordered, her voice whiskey-slurred.

She had to be kidding. "I'm not touching him. *He's* touching me."

"I saw the way you were looking at him. You were egging him on."

"I was not."

The woman stood, tossing her chair to the ground, and suddenly everyone's eyes were on Angel.

Angel didn't care whether this woman's anger was alcohol-fueled or whether she was simply mean on principle, because there was no way Angel would back down. If the woman wanted a fight, Angel would give it to her.

The woman reached for Angel's hair and Angel reared back, but stayed posed to tangle.

"Back off," she yelled. "I don't *want* your man."

"What's wrong with him?"

"What? Nothing. He's not my type."

"You're too good for him?"

Okay, this was deteriorating into the surreal.

She wanted to tell the woman she'd get no competition from her. Not one of these Neanderthals turned her on. To say that out loud, though, would probably bring both the bikers and their chicks down on her. She knew how to defend herself, came out swinging when she had to.

Protecting herself was a skill Angel had learned well at an early age. If these people thought they could push her around, they had a rude awakening in store.

One thing, though. These guys tipped well. She needed those tips.

Deciding this was a fight she wasn't going to win no matter what she said, she walked away.

"Hey," the woman yelled. "Get back here."

"If you want your drinks," Angel yelled to the bar at large, "get that woman off my back."

A couple of bikers managed to get her to sit and shut up, but only after a lot of grumbling from her.

Her man, in the meantime, wore a drunken grin, proud to be the cause of a fight between women.

Disgusted, Angel grabbed a towel and slapped it onto the bar to wipe up a spill. As she served the patrons, she took note that too many of the bikers—men and women—made too many trips to the washrooms. She didn't know what drugs they were doing, or what they were smoking, but she figured the smart thing to do was to turn a blind eye.

Chester kept the lighting dim for a reason. Even so, she'd seen the exchange of small packets of powder and money under tables.

She passed a table and a guy with huge fists wrapped one around her upper arm, stopping her from taking a tray of empty beer mugs to the bar.

"Hey, what time do you finish?" he asked. Menace rolled from him in waves. This guy liked to bully. No way did she put up with men like him.

"Late." She tried to pull away from him, but his fingers dug into her arm. "Back off, buddy."

"I said—" his mouth formed an ugly slash across his face "—what time do you finish?" The blue of his eyes pierced her. If he weren't so mean-spirited, he'd be a good-looking man, despite the ratty Fu Manchu.

"I'm staying late to help Chester go through the receipts. Then he's driving me home." Not true, but no way did she want this guy waiting for her.

This time, he let her go.

Putting these guys off was tiring. As her tips accumulated, though, she stuck to it. *Think of where you can go with the money. Think of L.A. Think of New York.*

As she approached a table with another order, Kenny Blake rested his palm on her behind. "Kenny," she said, "if you want to keep that hand, get it off my ass."

Kenny laughed and removed his hand. She'd known him in high school. Looked as though he was still a bit of a loner with a drinking habit, if his bloodshot eyes were any indication.

The night wore on, her feet ached and she was less and less in the mood to put up with much from a bunch of drunken fools. She counted to ten, so she wouldn't blast Kenny from here to kingdom come when he tried to touch her again. Ten minutes ago, he'd given her a five-buck tip for a draft.

Chester walked over and said, "Kenny, behave."

Kenny grimaced, but didn't argue.

Chester followed Angel to the bar. "No one wants to get kicked out. This is the only place around."

"You're raking in the cash, Chester. Even on a Tuesday night."

"Yeah, and the place isn't even half-full. It needs to pay, 'cause I sank a fortune into the renovations before I opened. I got debts."

When Angel sighed as she set her loaded tray of empties on the counter, he said, "Friday and Saturday, you'll have a couple of local girls waiting on tables, so you can stay behind the bar."

"Sounds good, Chester. I'm pooped."

The door opened and Phil walked in. He didn't sit in a booth or at a table. No, he sat on a stool and made no secret of watching her.

Great. Just great. Angel raised her chin. Let him look. *Think of how great you'll feel when you finally get him out of Mama's life.*

"What'll you have, Phil?" Chester asked.

"Corona."

Angel served it, squeezing the juice from a wedge of lime into the open bottle, then dropping it into the beer.

Phil pulled a ten out of his pocket and said, "Keep the change." Angel felt dirty taking money from him, but she did nonetheless.

Think about New York.

The way Phil watched her with a sly grin told her he knew she resented taking his money and that he enjoyed it.

Think of Neil.
Think of Matt.
Think of Chester.
All good men.

TIMM PUT LEFTOVERS FROM the dinner his mother had cooked into the fridge and the dirty dishes in the dishwasher.

Sara washed the last of the pots.

Ma sat at the kitchen table, letting the two of them clean up while she spent time with her grandson.

Sara and Finn had arrived home yesterday to stay for a couple of weeks before she headed back to work for the summer, to earn her tuition for the fall.

Sara was studying to become a nurse.

The simple chores reminded Timm of their teenage years. The only things missing were Papa and Davey, both dead now.

Timm had always felt bad for Sara. He wasn't the only one who had lost his adolescence. Even though she was younger than he, she'd had to take on some of the responsibility to help care for Timm.

His care and recovery had consumed so much of the family's time that there was nothing left for Sara. Timm had watched her fade into the background—while he remained powerless and without resources to help her. The pain and discomfort of his poor health, brought on by being burned, distracted him from anything that resembled a normal life for a long time.

Then Davey had been killed by a bull in the rodeo,

and both Timm and Sara had disappeared from their parents' radar. Mama had rallied eventually. But Papa? He'd been lost to them.

No wonder some stranger had been able to take advantage of Sara one night. Nine months later, Finn had been born.

Finn begged his grandmother to play cards, drawing Timm out of his memories.

"Go and get them," Mama said, and he ran to the living room.

"Ten years old already. Can you believe it?" he asked his sister.

Sara didn't respond. She'd been distracted all evening. He nudged her shoulder. "It feels like you gave birth to him yesterday."

"What? Oh. I know," she finally answered. "Yes, he's getting big."

Finn ran into the kitchen and Ma dealt the cards for a game of Polish poker.

"Are you sure you don't want to leave him here for the summer while you work?" Timm kept his voice low so neither Ma nor Finn could hear him. "Mama would love to have him."

Sara stayed quiet for a minute before looking at Timm. What he saw on her face sobered him—sadness and need.

"I can't, Timm. I miss him so much when he's not with me. Come here."

He followed her into the hallway.

"I don't know what to do." Sara, his überpractical, eminently capable sister, actually wrung her hands.

Timm took them in his. "Take a breath. What is it?"

"Finn has been asking who his father is."

"Then tell him."

"How can I? His father was a one-night stand. He's too young to know that. What would he think of me?"

There was no right answer to that. "You knew that this would come at some point. Why weren't you prepared?"

"I thought he would be older."

"Sara, that's unreasonable."

"I know," she snapped. "I *hoped* he would be older. Okay?"

"Did he never ask about his dad on Father's Day?"

"Yes. I told him he was dead. It was better than telling him the truth. But now he wants to know *who* he was and he asks for photographs."

"And you don't have any."

Sara crossed her arms over her chest as though she had Finn in an embrace and was trying to keep him safe form the world. "And I don't have any."

REMINGTON CALDWELL WALKED up the Franck walkway to the front door with a determined stride.

Tonight was the night. *The* night.

Timm answered the doorbell. "Hey, Rem. My gym bag's in the truck. We can leave in a minute."

Rem raised a staying hand. "I'm not going to aikido tonight."

"You drove all the way into town to tell me that? You could have phoned."

"I, um, I…heard Sara was back." He glanced at her standing behind Timm, wearing a worried frown. Had he interrupted something?

As usual, her clothes were nondescript. He swore he put more effort into looking good than she did, and that was only a few minutes a day. Did a less vain woman exist?

"Do you want to go for a drive?" he asked.

Timm glanced at Sara, then at Rem. "Are you asking me or Sara?"

"Sara." Rem saw fear, uncertainty on her face. He felt the same way. This was uncharted territory for him.

"Please," he said.

Timm watched their interaction, seeming on the verge of asking for the lowdown.

Don't ask, Timm.

"Well?" Rem asked her. "Do you want to?"

Sara nodded. "I'll go say good-night to Mama and Finn."

As soon as she left, Timm asked, "What's going on, Rem?"

Rem shrugged. "Later." He didn't like keeping stuff from his best friend, but he didn't want to jinx anything that might happen tonight by talking about it.

Sara returned from the kitchen and stepped outside.

Rem felt Timm's eyes on them as they walked to the car, Sara stiff and he with his hands shoved into his pockets so he wouldn't take her into his arms and blurt out the reason for this outing.

He opened Sara's door and closed it after she settled in. She inspired that kind of formality in a man.

As they drove out of town, the silence in the car unnerved him. He never knew what to say to her.

Correction. He did know what he *wanted* to say, but she never accepted it. Tonight would be different.

He turned onto the long driveway to his ranch—his, now that his father was dead. Rem couldn't believe his dad had been gone for six years already. Rem had grown up in that time, had gone to college and veterinary school, had started to make something of himself. Had been preparing for tonight for all six of those years.

"This is all mine now," he said.

"Yes."

That was it. One word. Nothing more.

C'mon, Sara, meet me halfway.

In the yard, he parked. "Do you want to go inside for a minute to visit Ma?" He knew they liked each other. Always had. "Afterward, meet me at the corral. Okay?"

"Sure," Sara said, her soft voice always at odds with her no-nonsense exterior. Tonight she seemed different, though. He glimpsed that vulnerability again—or something close to it that he couldn't put his finger on.

She entered the house, while his nerves danced all over the place.

Crap. Was his timing wrong for some reason? Seemed it was always bad with Sara.

Not this time, though. He'd worked hard to fix his life. He'd succeeded. She would see that.

He wandered to the stable to check everything for the night. One skittish mare, Rosie, was in the corral, but his own horse was in his stall for the night. Ordinarily, Rusty would be out in the corral for a couple of hours, but no way would Rem let Rusty anywhere near a client's horse, especially one as high strung as Rosie.

He straightened an already tidy stable, his fingers itching to do something, *anything,* to relieve the terrible antsyness he felt with Sara.

The stakes were higher than usual and his nerves skittered and sparked off each other. He needed to get this over with.

Rosie whickered, and he left the building and walked

to the fence. She approached, but not close enough for him to touch.

Rem grinned. "Still shy, darlin'? That'll change."

"It always does with you and females, doesn't it, Rem?"

Rem spun around. Much like the gun-shy mare, Sara kept her distance.

"You know how to charm the ladies." She stood with her arms crossed, as though to protect herself from him.

Ah, Sara, I don't have a mean bone in my body. You're the last person I would hurt.

"I would never charm you," he said, and meant it. She was immune, but aside from that, he didn't *want* to use charm on her. With Sara, he wanted to be his honest self. Just him. He wanted her to come to him willingly.

Here goes nothing.

"I'm a vet now, Sara. I graduated a month ago."

"I heard. Congratulations, Rem." She showed no emotion.

"I'm moving into Russell Carter's office, which he runs out of his house. He'll continue to handle domestic animals, while I do the large ones."

Sara nodded.

"Aren't you happy for me?"

"Yes." Not even a smile. "Did you do well?"

"I excelled."

"You always were smart, even when you were letting your life fall apart."

"See, Sara, that's what I want to change here to-night. Your perception of me. That was the old me. I'm a changed man. I want you to see the new me."

"You've said that before. How long will it last this

time, Rem? When will the drinking and recklessness and women start again?"

"It's been six years, Sara. Give me credit. Even with the crazy college crowd, I never drank."

Looking oddly hesitant for Sara, she said, "That is a long time. I really am proud of you, but—"

"But you're afraid I'll slip back."

"You've done it before."

"I've never lasted this long before—years instead of months."

She didn't respond.

"Damn it, Sara, why are you so stubborn?" He pressed his lips together. Yelling at her and questioning her character would get him nowhere.

He could charm any woman on earth, but how was he supposed to get romantic with Sara when she wouldn't bend? There was only one thing to do.

Stepping away from the fence, without giving her time to move, he wrapped his fingers around the back of her neck, registered a moment of shock in her eyes before he hauled her against him and put his mouth on hers.

She wouldn't open for him, but he knew how to be persuasive. He'd practiced on too many women.

Her lips gave way and he entered with the tip of his tongue and she tasted sweet. So sweet. This pliable Sara got to his heart, stole his breath. *Aw, Sara, honey, open more.* He pressed lightly and she did.

He felt her fingers in his hair and her breasts touch his chest and he wrapped his arms around the tight little body that had always called to him. Home.

Sara felt like home.

Rem pulled away slowly, watching her face as

he did. With her eyelids closed, she looked young, impressionable. He couldn't let go of her yet.

She opened her eyes slowly and their gray depths weren't as cool as they had been. Instead, they were seething with love and resistance and doubt.

He wanted to erase that doubt.

"What are you feeling, Sara?" He needed to know, but asking had broken the spell and, true to form, Sara came out swinging.

She pushed out of his arms. "Why did you do that?"

"Because I needed to soften you up."

Warily, she watched him while she wiped her lips with the back of her hand. "Soften me up for what?"

"To ask you to marry me." He hadn't meant to blurt the question, but Sara wouldn't let him be romantic.

He took her hands in his and squeezed her small fingers. "I love you, Sara. I always have. You know that."

Her eyes widened before she shuttered them quickly enough to cause a draft.

"I want you here with me," he continued. "While I run this ranch and my veterinarian business. Finn, too."

"Rem, no." She shook her head. "Don't do this. Everything is fine the way it is."

Desperation took hold. "I'm sober. I've got a good job. I've got a place to live. I love you. I want to get to know Finn. What more could you want?"

She retreated. "You're ruining everything. My life works. I don't need you in it."

That hurt.

"Is it because of Timm?"

She responded with one terse nod and Rem lost it.

"I was only eleven," he yelled. "Burning him was an accident."

He knew that was true, had told himself that so many times over the years. Still, all of these years later, he blamed himself.

"Six years, Sara," he whispered. "Why isn't that enough?"

"Because it won't last."

Sara confirmed what he knew about himself. That she would never forgive him.

"Take me home," she murmured.

Rem nodded and led her to the car. He drove her into Ordinary, watched her enter her mother's house, all without a single word. No regret. No apology. No goodbye.

And his heart broke.

CHAPTER FIVE

AFTER WATCHING REM and Sara leave, Timm returned to the kitchen.

"Sara's gone out for a little while with Rem. Okay?" He kissed his mother on the cheek. "Thank you for dinner. It was good. I'm heading out now."

Ma's smile was radiant. Her daughter was home and her grandson was with her. She was happy.

Finn jumped out of his seat and hugged his uncle. God, Timm loved this kid. He wanted kids of his own. It was almost time to start dating. No one in Ordinary stirred his blood, but that wasn't necessary. Respect was enough to make any marriage work.

He climbed into his truck. The fliers he'd printed earlier waited on the passenger seat. Time to brave the lion's den on his way out of town.

A block away from Chester's, he parked, picked up his fliers and got out. Save for a huddle of bikers smoking outside Chester's, the street was empty.

He passed through the smokers and the scent of marijuana surrounded him.

He opened the door of Chester's Roadhouse and nearly stepped back out. The noise and the stink of beer slapped him across the face.

The beer nauseated him, making him think of his father. After Timm had been burned, he'd smelled alcohol on his father at times. Years later, after Davey's death, though, Timm had been forced to grow up too quickly, had taken more responsibility with the newspaper. Dad had begun to drink heavily, every night, and Timm had carried him to bed too many times, nearly choking on the reek of the tavern on his clothes.

Eventually and against all expectation, he'd seemed to get better, so Timm had left to study journalism. He had been ridiculously glad to leave Papa's troubles behind to attend college in New York City.

Without Timm knowing, Papa turned bad again. This time, without Timm around to cover for Papa's poor performance at the paper, the circulation had fallen to a new low. Ma had kept the truth of the situation from Timm and she had been alone in trying to deal with his father.

And in that fact lay the source of Timm's guilt, and a sense of responsibility for Ma's happiness. How hard it must have been for her to watch the man she loved deteriorate so badly, while Timm was away reveling in his newfound freedom.

One evening while working on his master's degree, Ma had called him at school. Papa hadn't come home the night before. He'd driven head-on into a tree and had died. Timm still wondered whether it was an accident or deliberate.

Timm had come home, his master's in journalism unfinished and no longer as important as picking up where Papa had left off before Timm's accident. The Francks used to be a prominent family in town and he was determined to restore their good standing. Slowly, he was accomplishing that. Despite the internet, under his leadership the *Ordinary Citizen* was more popular than it had ever been.

Small towns were the backbone of America. He'd

realized that when he'd lived in New York, attending Columbia. Most universities themselves were small towns. New York, though, had been insane.

So many people. So little caring about fellow man. New York was a huge machine that ate up people and spit them out tired. As much as he had loved the city's energy, had thrived there, he'd been very aware of not being one of its victims. Those years had taught him that a person needed community, needed to be surrounded by people who cared—which he had in his hometown.

So Timm did his best to preserve Ordinary and keep it alive.

Someone yelled, snapping Timm from his memories.

Time to get down to business. He was here for a reason.

He placed a couple of fliers onto each table, then approached the bar. Angel watched him silently.

He placed a flier in front of her, wondering if she drank on the job, or only later, at home. For all intents and purposes, this woman had killed a man.

She turned the flier around, read it, then leaned close. "Are you nuts, handing these things out in here?"

He shrugged.

One of the bikers glared at Timm and crumpled the flier in this fist. He stood and stalked to the bar.

"You need to leave," Angel said. "Now. This guy's mean. Go!"

If he didn't know better, he'd think she was concerned about him. When a couple of more bikers rose from their chairs and stalked to the bar, Angel ran to the hallway and hollered, "Chester, get out here!"

She *was* worried about him. Imagine that. Him, the man she'd remembered only as the guy who—

A big bruiser grabbed Timm by one arm and spun him around.

Chester ran in, grabbed his baseball bat and ordered, "Eddy, sit down. I'll take care of Timm."

"You need to take a look at the shit he's handing out in your bar, man." Eddy strode to his table, followed by his cohorts.

Chester read the notice then looked at Timm. "You got a lotta nerve coming in here with this. Get out."

"Just giving you fair warning about Thursday night's meeting."

"Don't worry," Chester said, his jaw tight. "I'll be there."

Timm nodded. He glanced at Angel then left.

His nerve endings hummed along his skin. He'd never been a violent man, but that big biker had tempted him. Maybe it was thinking of Papa's useless death, or Ma's grief that wouldn't quit, her loneliness when Sara and Finn were away from home, or Angel getting a young kid hooked on alcohol—and who knew what else—then getting him killed. Or maybe it was simply his need to close this damn place for good, but Timm was itching for a fight.

He threw the papers onto the passenger seat. He'd plastered the town with them earlier. Chester's Roadhouse was a hot topic in Ordinary these days and he planned to end it. Soon.

He revved his truck, half hoping someone would come out of Chester's to give him that fight he craved, then he peeled out of Ordinary.

On the way to Haven, Timm calmed himself. He'd spent too many years learning to control his impulses for him to lose it so easily now.

There had been too many things during his teenage

years that he hadn't been able to control—his scars, his confinement, his physiotherapy, the operations, his father's drinking—so he'd worked at controlling his reactions to those things, and had achieved a certain acceptance and peace.

These days, he never lost his temper. Until tonight.

Aikido would help to bring his unruly emotions under control.

Half an hour later, Timm grabbed his gym bag and headed into Silver Dragon Martial Arts Academy. He changed in the dressing room and emerged only a minute before Sensei Chong started the class.

As if sensing his turmoil, Sensei Chong demonstrated a move for the newer students with Timm as his partner. Still jittery, Timm used the sensei's momentum too harshly and sent him sprawling.

"*Osu!*" Sensei Chong shouted!

Timm stepped off the mat. Yes, be patient, indeed. He knew what he needed to do. He sat on a mat in the corner and meditated, zoned out of the world around him and concentrated on breathing and being.

Aikido was described as the way of harmonious spirit. Timm got that. Totally.

When he felt centered, as though he'd left the world outside these four walls far behind, he rejoined the class.

Timm lost himself in the rhythms and soothing ebbs and flows of the stretches. The tightness of the skin on his chest eased gradually, and he could breathe deeply again.

He paired up with another student and commenced training, honing the techniques he'd learned over the past five years. They took turns acting as *uke* and *shite*.

First the student acted as the attacker and Timm

easily used the force of his opponent's own movements to send him off balance.

Timm loved the sense of letting go, of setting aggression aside, of fighting without resistance.

Then Timm attacked and the student redirected the force until Timm was off balance and fell. He attacked again, and his partner used Timm's own momentum against him. Timm ended up on his back on the floor, contemplating the ceiling.

The perfect simplicity and logic behind using the attacker's force in defense resonated in Timm.

Two hours later, he showered then left the studio, bowing to Sensei Chong on his way out—more cool, more calm, human again and ready to deal with problems rationally.

Another two hours later, Timm approached Chester's. *Why are you standing here, waiting to walk Angel home, to make sure she gets there safely? Why do you care?*

She probably doesn't give you a second thought.

Probably not.

So why do you care?

Damned if I know.

So why are you here?

I promised Cash I'd get her home safely.

As one-thirty approached, Timm watched bikers leave the bar, mount their bikes and peel out of town with as much noise as their machines could muster.

Deputy Williams sat in the cop car across the street, waiting for trouble, no doubt. Why wasn't he ticketing all of these drivers? Their blood-alcohol levels had to be sky-high. They were going to kill somebody.

Earlier, Timm had interviewed Williams about last night's fight and had written up the article.

Timm wiped sweat from his forehead. Another hot night. His shirt stuck to his back.

He waited and watched. He was good at that. He'd had years of practice.

Finally, Angel stepped out of the bar, but even from this distance, he could tell she wasn't happy.

When Phil emerged behind her and put his hand on her waist, Timm understood why. Missy's latest lover was a creep. Even Angel didn't deserve to be bothered by a sleazeball like Phil.

Angel knocked his hand away from her and Phil scowled.

Time to make good on his promise to Cash, then get himself home, away from this hellhole and Angel.

"Angel," he called as he jogged across the street, his body limber and free-moving after tonight's workout. She brightened, and his steps faltered. She was glad to see him?

"What are doing here?" Phil asked, his tone hostile.

"I told you I didn't need you to walk me home," Angel told Phil. "Timm's doing it."

"We can all walk home together," Phil said.

Angel slipped her arm through one of Timm's as though they were on a date and said, "We're taking the long way home." She cuddled against his side and Timm died and went to heaven on the spot. He might dislike Angel's character, but he didn't have issues with her body.

Angel pulled him down the sidewalk, then looked over her shoulder and told Phil to go home.

When they were out of earshot, she said, "What are you doing out so late?"

"Waiting for you."

In the glow of the last streetlight on Main Street, her face showed surprise. "Why?" She dropped Timm's arm as though it were a hot potato and put distance between them once they had cleared Phil's sight line.

"I'm making sure you get home safely."

"You're the one who needs protection these days. Handing out those fliers in the bar wasn't real smart."

"Says you."

"Yeah, says me." He heard a smile in her voice. They walked in silence for a beat. "Why is closing the bar down so important to you?"

"Isn't it obvious? Those bikers are bad for the town."

"Yeah, but it seems like more than that with you. What is it?"

Angel's intuition prickled his skin and made him defensive. Evidently, she was smarter than he thought.

Still, he couldn't tell her.

Timm took her elbow and steered her around the spray from a lawn sprinkler. "Just a second," he said, and ran to the side of Mrs. Allen's house, where he turned off the water.

Mrs. Allen poked her head out of her front door and called, "Is that you, Timm?"

"Yes. The water's off. You can go to bed."

"Thank you. Who's that with you?"

"Angel Donovan."

"Oh." Mrs. Allen sounded uncertain. Maybe she didn't remember who Angel was. "I see."

They walked on, and Angel said, "Do you do that all the time?"

"Often. She turns it on earlier in the evening and then forgets about it. If I see it on, I turn it off."

"Every night?"

"Most nights, if someone else doesn't come along first and do it."

They turned down Missy's street.

"I think her hips pain her so much that once she settles in front of her TV for the night, she doesn't want to come back out again."

They stopped in front of Missy's house.

"I'd better go in," Angel said, and stepped away from him. She spun back halfway down the sidewalk.

"Why did you wait to walk me home tonight?"

"I promised Cash I'd make sure you got home safely."

"Oh." In the soft shine cast by Missy's porch light, she looked disappointed, the expression come and gone quickly.

He hadn't imagined it, though, and didn't like that she looked hurt.

ON WEDNESDAY MORNING, Missy left Bernice's Salon with a new hairdo. Before she'd taken three steps she ran into a wall of solid muscle.

A pair of strong hands gripped her upper arms and steadied her.

She looked up. Way up.

Chester.

Oh. He looked so good.

Adrenaline shot like liquid fire through her veins to settle low in her belly.

While she stared, his hands still gripped her arms. Such a hard touch—firm, decisive, hot. She wanted those big hands on her everywhere.

Phil's touch is too soft. The second she thought that, Missy felt bad. She shouldn't betray Phil, even if only in her thoughts. She was marrying the man next week, for Pete's sake.

Besides, Chester was married and off-limits.

"Missy." Her name on Chester's breath washing her face with warmth doubled the heat in her lower belly and she knew she would make a fool of herself if she didn't escape—right this minute.

"I—" She searched for something to say.

"Are you two going to stand there gawking all day?" Angel's voice came from behind them.

Chester dropped his hold on her and Missy spun around. Her daughter, eating an apple, had a big smile on her face, so pretty it almost hurt to look at her.

"Where are you off to?" Angel asked.

Missy wondered how long Angel had been witness to her and Chester staring at each other like a pair of deer stunned by headlights. She couldn't stand here another minute feeling brain-dead and struggling to find something to say.

"I have to go," she whispered.

"Yeah, sure." Chester stepped around them. With one big finger, he pointed vaguely in her direction and said, his face tinged with pink, "You look good."

He strode to Scotty's Hardware and entered the shop while the heat in Missy's belly traveled to her heart. Chester thought she looked good.

Angel accompanied Missy down Main Street.

Had Chester been talking to Angel instead of her? In the sun, Angel's hair shone like a blue-black waterfall down her back. Her cheeks had a healthy pink glow. Her skin was flawless. Straight white teeth bit into the apple.

Missy and Keith had made a beautiful girl. Stunning, really.

But Missy was pretty sure Chester had pointed at her. Hadn't he?

A woman shouldn't be jealous of her own daughter. It wasn't right. Especially not when they'd always been a team, the two of them protecting each other against the world. She'd made sure to be in Angel's life for as long as she needed her. She'd never abandoned her.

Missy didn't like the look on Angel's face. She was about to get serious and Missy knew it probably had something to do with Phil.

"Honey, did you like college?" Not the most original topic, given that she'd spoken with Angel several times a week the entire time she was at school.

Angel looked at her askance. "Yeah, a lot, Mama. Why?"

"I want what's best for you, Angel. You know that, right?"

Missy had certainly wanted more for Angel than she'd had for herself. That's why, using Hal's money, she'd sent her to college, even though the thought of Angel leaving her alone had terrified her. She'd had a tough couple of years before Phil came along—a new man in town, who was interested in her.

Missy had never been so glad to feel a man's attraction to her, before she went completely over the hill.

And now? Missy knew Angel wasn't home for good, wouldn't hang around forever. With Phil stopping outside Angel's door every night, maybe that was a good thing. But when Angel was gone, Missy would need Phil even more.

She felt the beginning of a headache form behind her right eye.

Angel tossed her apple core to a small border collie

sitting in the back of a pickup. He caught it and ate it in a couple of bites.

Missy forced herself to set aside her jealousy of her daughter.

Angel took a breath to speak and Missy cut her off again, desperate to stay off the topic of her future husband. "How was work last night?"

"Good," Angel said, "except for the guys who got drunk and wouldn't stop touching my behind."

They used to do that to Missy. "Did things get out of hand? Were you okay?"

Angel wrapped her arm around Missy's shoulders. "Don't worry about me, Mama. You taught me to take care of myself."

Missy had done her best, but she knew men, knew what they could do even when a girl didn't want it.

Angel still looked as though she was chewing on a problem.

"Angel—"

"Mama, stop. I want to say something. You need to ditch Phil. There are still men around who find you attractive. You can get another man and ditch that loser. Look at Chester. He's still crazy about you." The words rushed out of Angel, as though she didn't dare take a breath in case Missy interrupted.

"Have you forgotten that he's married?" Missy deliberately avoided talking about Phil.

"That never bothered you in the past," Angel said. "You made me with Matt's dad."

"I shouldn't have. And I don't do that anymore. I haven't been with a married man since Keith died." And with good reason. Keith's wife had discovered Missy and him together in a motel room. She shot Keith dead and then took her own life. The trauma of that experience had been enough to make Missy avoid any man who was even casually involved with another woman.

"I'm real glad, Mama. It was never good for you to come in second in a man's affection."

"Honey, with Keith, affection had nothing to do with it."

"And with Phil?"

Heaving an exasperated sigh, Missy stopped walking. "Phil loves me. He told me so."

"Then why does he—"

"Stop! I don't want to hear it."

"How do you know what I'm going to say?"

"Angel, don't. Phil is the only man who ever asked me to marry him."

"But—"

"Out of all of those men, those *dozens* of them, he's the only one who asked." Missy pointed a shaky finger at her own chest. "He asked me to spend the rest of my life with him. No one else ever wanted to."

Angel tried to say more, but Missy wouldn't let her, desperate to abandon this whole conversation. "At your age, you can't understand, Angel, but try to see it my way. At forty-five, I can't attract many more men."

Angel obviously didn't have anything to say to that.

"I'm walking home now," Missy said. "Alone."

She rushed away. Angel called her name, but Missy ignored her. She'd heard enough.

As she came level with Chester's Roadhouse, Lisa Ames pulled up in a Town Car, parked and ran into the bar, looking like a million bucks. Lisa always looked good. No wonder Chester had married her.

It seemed that all Missy did these days was envy

other women—her daughter, her youth and Lisa, the most decent man Missy had ever known.

She practically ran the rest of the way home.

AT LUNCHTIME, TIMM stepped into his mother's house, hoping he'd catch Sara at home.

He found the family in the kitchen.

"Timm," Ma said, jumping up from her chair. "I didn't know you were coming. Sit down. I'll make you something."

"Ma, don't worry about me. I'll get a burger in town. I just want to talk to Sara for a minute."

"Nonsense. You will sit and you will eat here."

Timm sat beside Sara and leaned close. "How are you today?"

"I'm fine. And you?" She didn't look fine. She looked as though she hadn't slept a wink last night.

"What happened last night?"

"Nothing."

"I'm worried about you."

"Don't be. I'm fine."

"But—"

"Let it go, Timm." She shook her head sharply.

Finn captured his attention and Timm knew he wouldn't get anything else out of her. So what had happened last night between Sara and Rem that had put the dark circles under his sister's eyes?

As far as Timm knew, Rem and Sara had had very little to do with each other. For the life of him, he couldn't come up with a plausible reason why Rem would want to speak with her alone. And by the closed expression on her face, she wasn't going to share.

Stubborn woman.

THE SECOND REM GULPED down the last bite of his mother's stew, he stood, rinsed his plate and cutlery and put them into the dishwasher.

He kissed his mother on the cheek, said, "I'm going out for a while," then quickly left the house.

On the drive into Ordinary, last night's conversation with Sara went around and around in his head. He couldn't turn it off any more now than he'd been able to all day.

He'd put too much hope in the outcome. He'd spent six years anticipating Sara saying yes. He'd been a fool.

In his despair, his old urges sank deep claws into him.

He parked in front of Chester's, his dashed hopes eating away at his guts like acid. He needed to be numb, to not feel one goddammed thing.

He went in and sat on an empty stool at the bar. "Angel, hit me with a shot of whiskey," he said without preamble.

What the hell was the point of trying to straighten out a life when it got you nothing?

Angel set the drink in front of him. "You okay, Rem?"

"Don't you worry about me, Angel. I'm fine. Just F-I-N-E." Throwing a handful of cash onto the counter, he said, "You keep these coming all night, y'hear? The second I finish one, you bring me another, starting right now."

He picked up the glass, gulped its contents, then slammed the glass onto the bar.

"Rem…maybe this isn't a good idea. Do you want to talk?"

"Talk? God, no. I'm here to drink. Hit me, Angel."

She didn't look happy, but she poured him another.

He stood, grabbed her face and planted a big kiss on her lips. "You're a good woman, Angel. I shoulda stuck with you in high school." They'd dated for a year. They'd been good together—the sex had been fantastic.

But sometime toward the end of that year, Rem had realized that his best buddy, Timm, had a crush on Angel a mile wide. He'd dropped her right away.

It had taken a long time for them to be friends again after the incident when Rem had burned Timm by mistake. Rem would never do anything to compromise their relationship again. So when he noticed that dating Angel was causing Timm to drift away, he stopped seeing her. She'd been philosophical. After all, they hadn't loved each other.

To this day, Timm had yet to figure out that Rem had guessed about the crush.

A couple of hours, although to Rem's inebriated state it could have been only twenty minutes—or a lot of drinks—later Timm walked in.

"Timm, buddy, sit." He patted the stool beside him. "Right here, man. What can I buy for you?"

"Rem, what the hell are you doing? You haven't had a drink in years." Timm didn't look happy.

"Wanna know somethin'? They still taste good." He had to concentrate to get the words out through lips that would not cooperate.

"What happened last night?"

Rem barked a bitter laugh. He couldn't help himself. "Funny. I asked a girl to marry me. She said no."

"You asked Sara to marry you? Why?"

To Rem's regret, he sobered instantly. "I love her." He wanted out of this chat. "She hates me." He wanted that smooth, easy, happy place back.

"You love Sara? Since when?"

Rem shrugged. "Since forever."

"Why didn't you ever tell me?"

"Because I knew she was mad at me about you." Rem pointed in the direction of Timm's chest. "I thought I didn't stand a chance. But I've been trying to change."

Timm nodded. "I know. You've been doing well, but honest to God, Rem, you're breaking my heart tonight."

"My heart's broken, too." He could feel it breaking now. Too hard. Too sober. "Angel, another drink. Hurry."

"For God's sake, Rem, buck up," Timm snapped. "You can't do this again. Don't screw up after six years."

Rem spread his hands. "It didn't mean nothing, good buddy. She still didn't want me anyway."

"No wonder she doesn't want you if you fall into drinking so easily."

"Not easy. Pain. Hurts." He drank so he wouldn't blubber like a baby. *Blubber.* Weird word. *Blub-ber.* Great word.

"One setback and that's it?"

"'Fraid so." Rem laughed again. When he stopped, Timm was gone. Good. He didn't need talking to sober him up. What he needed was another drink. Yeah. Another drink would hit the spot.

He raised his arm to signal Angel.

THE WORKING HOURS were dragging on too long for Angel. In addition to the usual dodging of roving hands, she was witness to Rem soaking his liver in whiskey. Tragic.

When she finally left the bar at the end of the night,

she spotted Timm leaning against a lamppost across the street. Why was he waiting for her? Had Cash asked him to meet her again?

Eddy came out of the bar behind her. Where had he come from? The bar closed down twenty minutes ago and all the patrons had—apparently—cleared out.

Oh, good lord, the guy was a pain. Why could some men not take no for an answer?

He took her arm in one of his big fists. "Hey," he said, but before he could follow up that brilliant remark with anything coherent, Timm stepped away from the post and crossed the street in long strides.

"Let her go," he said quietly. How on earth did a guy as tall and thin as Timm think he could face down a gorilla like Eddy?

The door of the bar opened behind them and Angel turned. Chester, armed with his baseball bat, stood behind Eddy.

"Was that you I heard coming out of the washroom a minute ago, Eddy? Were you hiding in there?" He pointed the bat at the biker. "The next time I hear you in my bar after hours, I'll break your skull open. Got it?"

"Yeah, I got it."

"Next time, leave with your buddies. Let go of Angel and get out of here."

Eddy released her slowly. He climbed on his bike, the engine roared to life and he peeled out of town. But not before giving Chester, Angel and Timm the once-over.

"Are you walking Angel home?" Chester asked Timm.

He nodded.

Chester returned to the bar. The lock clicked into place behind him.

"Come on," Timm said.

Rattled by Eddy, Angel couldn't refuse. In fact, she couldn't think of much to say about anything. A rarity for her, especially with a guy.

But Timm confused her, unsettled her, and she didn't know why.

CHAPTER SIX

THE NIGHT SPOKE around them while Timm and Angel walked side by side, with her setting the pace. Crickets called to each other. The barest hint of a breeze whispered through the leaves of a maple above. Something quick and agile scurried under a hedge.

"Do you know why Chester closed down his bar in Monroe?" Angel asked.

"Same thing as here. The town didn't like the rough crowd. They booted him out. He should have gone somewhere other than Ordinary after he closed."

Angel opened her mouth to say something, but stopped at the sound of a motorcycle starting down the side street they'd turned onto, the rumble an ominous menace on the sleepy street.

Timm felt Angel's tension and understood it. There was no reason for a biker heading out of town to take this residential route. Eddy looking for Angel, maybe?

Timm thrust her behind a big oak tree. He stood in front of Angel in the shadows where no light penetrated. Mrs. Johnson's porch light across the street didn't reach this far.

When the biker passed in front of them, slowly, as though he were peering into shadows, Angel gripped Timm's biceps, her hands warm through his cotton shirt, her fingers tight. Her nails bit into his skin.

She trembled. Had the biker spooked her? He wanted

to ask. Knowing Angel, she'd tear a strip off his hide for insinuating she was anything less than tough. Stubborn woman always came out swinging.

The bike stopped in the distance, toward the end of the lane. Neither of them moved. In the next second, the bike turned the corner, its engine revving loudly.

With the danger gone, Timm's senses became deluged by all that was Angel. Her warm body heated her patchouli scent and it clouded his reason. He pressed closer, his knee fitting into the perfect space between her legs.

Angel breathed hard. Her chest rose and fell against his. Cursing the scars on his torso that were too thick for sensation, he closed his eyes and willed the rest of his body to feel.

He felt her breath warm on his neck, and her soft hair brushing his chin, tantalizing him, reminding him of his adolescent hopes and his horny dreams. Always of Angel.

He'd spent too many years watching life go on around him. Hell, as a teenager, he'd dreamed so often of doing…*something*…with Angel, anything. Of leaving the window from which he watched life and the world go by, and of stepping out of his parents' house to run to her. To pretend to be normal. To walk up to her and ask her out. To hold her exactly as he was doing at this moment.

He wanted to start doing something, here, on this hot summer night, with Angel real and in his arms.

Impatience ate at him.

He wanted.

Go on, then. Do something.

The bark of the tree abraded his fingertips. Angel's hip burned his palm. With his eyes closed, he feathered the skin between her top and her jeans, and it was softer than anything he'd ever felt.

He was drowning in her scent and her heat.

He had to touch her more.

The silent street held its breath, waited for Timm to make his move, so he did.

He slid his hand up her side, his thumb skimming her ribs, and he sighed. He'd never felt anything so beautiful in his life.

Doing was a *hell* of a lot better than watching. Angel was…was… Where were his words, his eloquence that he used every week in his paper?

Angel felt divine. It was that simple and that schmaltzy.

His thumb glided across her ribs again and he felt her stomach quiver. He grazed the underside of her breast.

She inhaled sharply and pushed him.

"Get away from me," she ordered, but her voice lacked its usual bite, as though she was as rattled as he was. "You're as bad as all the other men in town, feeling me up in the dark because you think I'm easy."

Probably. Yeah. Wasn't she? Not that he liked being grouped with the kind of men who took advantage of women and grabbed at them given half a chance.

"Or did you think I'd be grateful to you for trying to protect me? Don't go thinking I owe you anything. I didn't ask you to interfere." She tugged her vest down and stepped away. "Leave me alone."

Timm watched her walk away. His body hummed, every part of him vibrating. Every part but his chest— the only area that hadn't been able to experience the exquisite pain of Angel's body against his.

She had a lot of nerve getting mad at him for trying

what most men in Ordinary had tried—and a good many had been successful doing.

So, she'll put out for any guy but the scarred nerd. He laughed roughly. At least she wasn't willing to screw him out of pity.

He followed her home, because even in his bitterness he knew it was the right thing to do, even if she had rejected him.

ON THURSDAY MORNING, Angel woke up out of sorts.

She cast about to find out what was wrong with her, then remembered Timm touching her in the dark.

She'd thought he was better than most men. Had wanted to believe he was different, that given half a chance he could respect her.

To find out he was like all the others…well, she couldn't quite explain the disappointment.

No amount of physical attraction would tempt her to do anything with Timm or any other Ordinary man.

Enjoying a man's touch so soon after Neil's death felt like disloyalty to Neil. And Timm Franck had no business tempting her when she had a mission here in Ordinary and would soon be gone.

She showered, dressed and entered the kitchen, ready to go another round with Mama about Phil. She had to get her point across.

The two of them sat at the table. So…no discussion right now. The man was around most of the time, severely limiting her time alone with her mother. That's why Angel had been so happy to see Mama on Main Street yesterday.

That hadn't gone well, though. She understood all of Mama's arguments, but Phil was the wrong man for her. Even if she was afraid that he would be the last one to ever find her attractive, he wasn't worth tying herself to for a lifetime. Besides, Missy had no idea how pretty she still was.

Angel caught the smug smile Phil directed at her. Yeah, he thought he had it all figured out. But she had no intentions of backing away from this fight. She'd catch Mama alone later and set her straight about a few things. Then Mama would boot Phil out. And then Angel would wear her own smug smile.

In the meantime, Angel needed to be anywhere but here. She'd head over to the newspaper office to give Timm a piece of her mind. He had no right touching her without her permission.

And she'd tell him so in no uncertain terms.

TIMM SAT AT HIS DESK, poring over the many emails he'd received in the past week about Chester's Roadhouse, trying to pick the one that articulated the problems and concerns best.

The editor hat was one of many a small-town newspaper publisher was called on to wear. Timm also wrote articles, reported on sporting events, drummed up advertising sales, monitored circulation and distribution... and took out the garbage when necessary. In effect, he did almost everything, including writing more than half of the content of the two issues published weekly.

Each issue of the paper carried a column he called The Sound of One Voice, in which he printed an anonymous editorial from anyone in town who wanted to speak about any issue.

Today, though, how could he choose only one letter about Chester's when so many spoke passionately about the establishment and not, to Timm's surprise, all on the side of closing it?

For the first time in the paper's history, Timm would be publishing a total of six different letters in the article rather than only one. Chester's was, indeed, a hot topic.

Timm's problem was keeping his objectivity when his emotions, despite his best efforts, threatened to become engaged. Knowing his potential prejudice, he selected the half dozen he'd publish, being ruthlessly fair to the opposing side.

Sometimes newspaper publishing was thankless, when he had to keep the town's best interests at heart despite what he felt personally about a particular topic.

The sound of a throat being cleared startled Timm. He hadn't heard anyone enter.

Angel stood at the counter, wearing a thunderous frown. "Stop waiting for me after work. I can get myself home safely."

Timm rose slowly, forming his words carefully. Angel's tone could castrate a bull.

Warily, he approached and put his hands in his pockets, staying calm.

"What would you have done last night when Eddy came looking for you?"

"Hidden behind a tree. Only, I wouldn't have had someone pawing me in the dark."

That's what she thought of his touch? It hadn't felt as though he was *pawing* her. Had he been clumsy? It hadn't felt that way.

But if that was how she saw things, fine. He'd never try another thing with her. "My apologies," he said. "You were right. I shouldn't have done that."

He hadn't slept last night. His fingers had remembered too much about Angel's body. And all the while, his mind had spun in disbelief that he'd had the nerve to go as far as he had, out of his dreams and straight into reality.

"What about when someone in the bar tries to do something you don't like?" he asked. "What will you do if Eddy waits for you outside again?"

"I can handle Eddy. I can kick and scream and bite. I've found a knee to the groin pretty effective." Her mean little smile was full of sarcasm.

"Angel, get real. There's no way you can fight him and win."

"So, you could?" She glanced down his body, no doubt checking his size against Eddy's.

"Believe it or not," he said, "yeah, I could."

She seemed to be on the verge of questioning him. That bugged him, wounded his ego.

"Come back here," he said. He gestured for her to move to his side of the counter.

She did, and followed him into the back room.

"What?" she asked, belligerent and doubting.

"For the sake of demonstration, pretend I'm Eddy."

"*O-kay.*"

She had no idea what he was capable of doing to her. Without warning, he executed an aggressive move and Angel ended up with her back flush against his chest and his arm across her neck. The other arm, like a steel band, held her close.

"What will you do now?" he said in her ear. His breath feathered her gorgeous dark hair across her cheek.

"Can you bite me?" he asked.

"No." She sounded reluctant to admit to her own defenselessness.

"Can you kick me in the groin?"

"No." It sounded as though it killed her to admit that.

He put his hand over her mouth, firmly so she couldn't move her head. "Can you scream?" He uncovered her mouth to allow her to answer.

"No."

"I know you think I'm a lot weaker than Eddy. So imagine he's holding you hostage."

He felt her swallow.

"What would you be able to do now?"

"Nothing."

He released her and she stepped away from him with surprising speed. She obviously truly couldn't stand his touch.

Nevertheless...the woman needed protection.

"I can teach you moves that work. I mean, really work, even on people like Eddy, even though you're smaller than him."

"I don't want you to teach me anything." Hostility poured from her in waves and Timm wondered what her problem was.

"Don't meet me after work," she said. "Is that clear? Or do I have to tell Cash you're stalking me?"

He couldn't believe she would say something like that about him.

"No," he said. "No need to tell Cash. I won't be coming around anymore."

She left and Timm almost choked on his indignation. Some thanks that was.

ANGEL STALKED HOME, so freaking disappointed in herself and her reaction to Timm holding her.

She liked it too much. She barely knew the guy, for

Pete's sake, and yet her body wanted him. Every time he put his long-fingered hands on her, she wanted them everywhere. She'd gone to his office to give him a piece of her mind and to get her frustration and anger with him getting under her skin off her chest.

Instead, he'd touched her and she'd wanted to melt in his arms.

Anger didn't begin to cover what she felt toward her own foolish, foolish body and toward Timm for growing up so damn fine.

Too bad. She really *did* want him to teach her how to defend herself against idiots like Eddy, but that wasn't going to happen.

She wouldn't let it.

ON THURSDAY EVENING, Timm entered his mother's house to find her in the kitchen. Sara had called to tell him that she was taking Finn out for fast food in Haven.

He knew how Ma would feel being alone tonight. He dined with her often because he knew she got lonely.

"Why didn't Sara take you with them?"

"I didn't want to go. I don't eat that fast-food junk."

"Do you want to go to the diner?"

"No, I'll make sandwiches."

"Stay seated. I'll make them."

"What's going on, Timm? What did Rem want?"

"Ma, he asked her to marry him."

"What? Why?"

"He loves her."

"Ah."

"Ah?"

"Yes. Don't you remember how he used to take

care of her when she was little? He did better than you did."

Timm bristled.

"Oh, relax," she said. "You were her brother and she was a pesky little sister."

Timm grinned. "Yeah, sometimes I wanted to get rid of her, but you always made me let her play with us."

"I know. And Rem watched out for her. Nobody dared to hurt her when he was around." She smiled. "So, he loves her."

"Yes."

"Poor boy."

"No fooling. She'll never forgive him."

"I don't know why she is so stubborn."

Timm went to the fridge and took out sliced turkey and Swiss cheese. He found a loaf of rye in the cupboard. When he finished making the sandwiches, he put one in front of her.

"Eat," he ordered softly.

She nibbled on hers, while he dug into his. "I don't want to leave you alone tonight, but I have this meeting I organized. I have to go."

"I will be fine."

"Ma, you don't get out of the house enough. I worry about you. Doesn't the church have a social function on Thursday nights?"

"Yes, but I don't want to go."

He crouched on the floor in front of her and took one of her hands in his. "Ma, Papa died two years ago. No one in town would hold his problems against you. You know that."

She brushed a lock of hair from his forehead. "I know. I am still embarrassed, though."

"Ma, he was a good man for so many years—the

best father, the best husband. Can't you remember those times—before I was burned? Before Davey died?"

"I do, Timm. I remember it all."

Papa had been a pillar of the community and Ma had enjoyed their status. So had Timm, but hadn't realized how much until Papa's drinking had threatened their good reputation.

Since he'd returned from college, Timm had succeeded in rebuilding that reputation. And he was taking it one step further in his bid for mayor.

"I've grown up fine," Timm said. "You've adjusted since Papa's death. Why not go out more?"

"The town might have forgotten what he became after...your accident and then David's, but I—I can't."

"Why did he take so much responsibility when I got burned? Rem was only eleven. It was a kid's accident. Papa couldn't have prevented it."

Emotions flitted across Mama's face faster than Timm could identify. Her gaze shifted away from him and, in that moment, he knew she was hiding something.

"What is it? What haven't you told me about Papa?"

"Remember the fire when he was young? At home in Germany?"

"Of course, Uncle Derick still has the scars. They lost their family. I know the whole story already."

Ma shook her head and looked at him with such sorrow that he filled with dread.

"Not the complete story," she said.

"What?" He wanted to be out the door and ten miles away from here.

"Papa started the fire that killed his family."

"*What?* Impossible. Derick never told me that."

"Karl never told your uncle. He was a child, playing

with matches. The fire started at the back of the house. He got scared and ran to his bedroom and hid under the bed. The next thing, he is choking on smoke and Derick is pulling him out and carrying him outside and the rest of the family is dead." Mama's lips quivered.

"Oh, my God." This explained so much about his father that Timm hadn't understood before. The poor man. Talk about a child's innocent mistake causing tragedy.

"He was such a good man, but that mistake—" She took a breath. "It never left him. It made his whole life a trial."

"You knew this before you married him?"

Ma nodded.

"Yet you married him anyway? You must have loved him very much."

"Yes." She stared out the kitchen window, lost in a world of her own. "Your father was a good, good man. He worked hard for a successful life here. He had a good reputation."

Timm finally understood why Papa had been so driven, had fought so hard for respect, had succeeded so well here in Ordinary, in the town he loved.

Fate hadn't let him continue forward, though. One son had been burned and the other killed.

Sometimes, life was too tough.

"Mama—" He wanted to ask whether she thought Papa had fallen asleep at the wheel the night he'd died, or whether he'd committed suicide, but how could he possibly ask her to speculate?

Timm sighed and stood. He wasn't going to convince her to go out tonight.

"Can I do anything for you?" Timm picked up his keys from the table. "Get you anything?"

"No. You go have a good night. I am fine."

Timm pretended to take her at her word, but he knew the truth. Papa's death had changed her, yes, but not as much as what had come before he'd died.

She wasn't getting any younger, but she was still too young to live the rest of her life alone. He glanced at where she sat, backlit by the evening sun streaming through the window. He knew a couple of the older men in town found her attractive. Why couldn't she give one of them a chance?

Timm felt the responsibility of her happiness hang around his neck like a burden, and felt guilty about that. He should enjoy making his mother happy, but these days found it an impossible task.

He strode toward the Legion Hall.

The janitor had already set up rows of wooden chairs facing the stage on which bands played for Ordinary's summer dances. On the stage sat a table with a few chairs behind it facing the audience.

That's where Timm would sit. If Cash showed up, he would join him. Timm's uncle Derick, who was the incumbent mayor, would also have a seat there.

As if on cue, Derick entered the hall, stopping to talk to citizens as he made his way to the front.

"Timm," he said when he got close enough, "looks like a good turnout." He shook Timm's hand, his own crippled into claws from contracture scars he'd suffered rescuing his little brother from the fire. The fire that same little brother had started. The tragedy struck Timm anew and he vowed never to reveal the truth to Derick. At this late date, what would be the point?

"Let's see what we can do about getting rid of that junk heap at the edge of town," Derick said.

"It isn't a junk heap, Uncle," Timm responded.

"Chester did a good job of turning those two empty stores into one. He decorated it decently."

"Yeah," Derick replied. "It's just too bad that, when he closed down his roadhouse in Monroe, Harris County's biker population decided to follow him here."

Timm nodded, stepped onto the stage and looked out at the audience of fifty or sixty people. Most of the citizens had shown up, including those from the ranches and farms stretching across the prairie surrounding Ordinary.

Cash entered, in uniform. Timm motioned for him to join him on stage.

When they all settled in their seats, Timm called the meeting to order.

The crowd quieted and Timm leaned toward the one microphone in the center of the table. "Thanks for coming out tonight."

There was a time when it would have bothered him to speak in front of so many, to be the object of curious stares. He'd grown up since the days of being whispered about behind his back. He enjoyed the respect of his townspeople. He would love to be their mayor, to carry on the family tradition now that his uncle had decided not to seek reelection.

Tonight, he wasn't acting as a reporter or publisher. He was here as a citizen. And as such, he intended to articulate his own feelings, to be subjective, unfettered by the objectivity of his role as publisher.

"You all know why we're here. Chester's Roadhouse has caused a disruption in our lives."

The crowd murmured their agreement.

"With all of the bikers hanging around, the town doesn't feel safe after seven or eight at night. Except for the activity around the roadhouse, Ordinary becomes a ghost town after sundown."

"Used to be that people strolled the streets on nice summer evenings," Angus Kinsey called out. "Now they're afraid to." He sat in the front row with his arm across the back of his wife's chair.

"Yes." Timm emphasized his agreement with a sharp nod.

"Aw, come on, Timm." Chester spoke from the rear of the room. "Don't you think you're making this bigger than it really is?" He stood inside the door with his arms crossed over his chest, exaggerating the biceps below his short sleeves. "No one is in danger. There haven't been men killed or women raped."

The uproar from the crowd drowned out whatever else Chester had to say.

Good, Timm thought, *keep up that kind of talk, Chester, and you'll help my cause more than your own.*

"Are you blind, Chester?" Matt Long shouted. "You've lived outside Ordinary for a few years. You don't value it the way we do."

"That's not true," Chester responded. "I'm bringing much-needed money to this place."

"How do you figure that?" Matt stood to make his point. "All of that money's going into your pockets and no one else's."

George stood. "That's not true. A lot of those bikers come into the diner to get a bite to eat before heading to the bar."

Max Golden, Timm's competition for mayor, stood next. "Chester paid a lot of men and women to renovate those two vacant storefronts. He employs locals as wait-staff and bartenders."

"And Kurt earns a few extra bucks sweeping up

every morning," Chester said. He pointed to Scotty, who owned the hardware store, and his brother, who owned the grocery store. "I buy as many supplies as I can locally. I pay taxes at the business rate. Any of you running businesses know that's a lot higher than Ordinary's residential rates. I live here and shop here."

Hank Shelter stood and approached the stage. "May I?" He waited for Timm's nod of approval, then turned to address his fellow citizens.

"Chester, everyone here believes that a man has a right to make a living however he can." Hank's gravel-rough voice carried to the back of the room without a microphone. "The problem is that your living is causing people a lot of grief."

"Why do you care, Hank?" Chester stalked up the aisle, obviously not going down without a fight. "You don't even live in town."

"Ordinary has been home to Shelters going back four generations. Whether we—" he gestured with his head toward the crowd "—live *in* town or *on the outskirts*, this issue affects us all."

"What about the businesses?" A petite, dark-haired woman in the middle of the room stood. Janey Wilson pointed a finger directly at Chester. "Back to the issue of who's making a living these days in Ordinary. *You're* costing *me* money."

Janey had come to Ordinary a grieving mother after losing her child and was now a married woman and a respected business owner in town.

"What about Sweet Talk?" she asked. "It's right in the middle of town. I used to stay open late to accommodate tourists. Those tour buses have stopped coming because of the reputation your bar has given the town. I'm losing money."

Chester frowned. "I'm sorry about that, Janey, but what am I supposed to do? Turn away good business at the door? I—"

Whatever else he'd been about to say was lost in shouts from outside the Legion Hall. Kurt Glass ran into the assembly, and Chester had to reach an arm in front of Kurt to bar him from crashing into the last row of chairs.

"There's a big fight!" Kurt yelled, his face white.

Cash ran down the side stairs from the stage and into the centre aisle. "Where?"

"At the bar. Those biker guys is giving Angel a hard time." Kurt pressed one hand against his chest and panted. "You gotta help her. They're hurting her."

Timm's breath caught in his throat. Forgoing the stairs, he jumped from the stage. Pushing through the crowd to get out the door, he caught up with Cash on the sidewalk, and ran beside him.

If she'd been hurt badly, someone was going to pay.

Cash had a walkie-talkie to his mouth. "Erma, call Williams and get him in early. Tell him to pack his gun and to stop for a couple of stun guns on his way over to Chester's."

The fight at Chester's had spilled into the street. Where was Angel?

Darting between the milling groups, Timm searched for her. "Angel," he yelled.

No sign of her. His pulse pounded and he forced himself to calm. He needed his wits about him.

While Cash dealt with the bikers outside, Timm squeezed by and made it into the bar.

Outside a gun report sounded. Timm didn't care if all the bikers died. Where was Angel?

A bruiser of a man stepped in front of Timm. "You're the guy trying to close our bar."

He made a grab for the front of Timm's shirt, but Timm stepped to the side and pulled the guy's arm forward until he was off balance and landed on his face on the floor, hard. Timm felt the vibrations through the soles of his shoes.

Before the biker could stand, Timm lifted his arm high behind his back and pressed his knee against it, the entire time scanning the bar.

She had to be here.

"Where's Angel?" he shouted, but the guy only whimpered.

Timm's breath stopped again. What if one of these idiots had already taken her away?

His grip on the biker must have tensed. "Hey, man, that hurts," the guy wheezed.

"Shut up. It's supposed to." Frantically, Timm scanned for Angel.

A scream from the hallway curdled the blood in his veins. He dropped the biker's arm and ran in that direction.

Timm entered the hallway in time to see a big guy carrying Angel to the back door. She was putting up a good fight, but didn't stand a chance against the guy's size. When she bit the man's shoulder, he slugged her. Timm roared his fury.

Angel went limp, and the blood in Timm's veins turned to ice. As he reached the biker and caught his ponytail in his fist, Angel rallied. Timm yanked hard and the guy dropped her. She landed on her butt and hissed, but jumped up. While Timm held the man's head immobile by the hair, she kneed him in the groin.

Timm caught Angel's eye and grinned.

When he let go, the biker dropped to the floor, curled up like a fetus and, moaning, cradled his balls.

Angel leaned over and got into the biker's face. "I told you, Eddy. I don't want anything to do with you. Leave. Me. Alone."

Eddy lurched to his feet and raised his hand, but before he could connect with her face, Timm grabbed his wrist and swung him into the wall, where his head hit with a loud crack. He went down and stayed down.

Angel's stare shifted between the unconscious biker and Timm. Her jaw dropped. He could see the wheels turning. *Timm Franck took down a biker?* He might have been an observer for most of his life, but he knew how to defend himself and a woman in distress.

Before giving Eddy a chance to gain consciousness, Timm grabbed Angel's hand and led her out the back door.

"The bar— I can't leave—"

"After what just happened, yeah, you can."

"Cash will want to talk to me."

"He can do that later. Right now, I'm getting you home safe."

Once in the alley, he headed away from the bar, prepared to avoid the mayhem by taking the long way.

"I don't care if you want to tell Cash that I'm stalking you. I'm walking you home tonight."

"I won't tell him you're stalking me."

"Good."

He hadn't let go of her hand yet. Was afraid to. He'd just had the proverbial wind knocked out of him with the horrible visions of Angel's rape that had flashed through his mind.

Angel stopped so quickly that Timm was pulled up

short. She looked at him strangely and said, "You're squeezing too tight."

He released his grip. "God, Angel. I'm sorry."

"Are you okay?"

"Am *I* okay? *You're* the one who nearly got ra—" He couldn't say that hideous word out loud.

She nodded. "I know." They'd exited the alley at the far end of Main Street. The sun hadn't yet set and Angel looked ghostly pale, but her mouth was firm, her expression determined. "I've never been so mad."

"You fought like a hellion."

"Thanks." Her eyes widened. "So did you. Eddy went down like a stone."

Timm hadn't done enough to Eddy. "He should be tarred and feathered."

Angel snorted a laugh. "Yeah." She glanced away and when she met his gaze again, he could see her resolution. "That's it. I'm sick of these fights. I'm sick of being rescued. Something has to change."

He asked the question that had been bothering him since they'd left the bar. "Why doesn't Chester have bouncers?"

She touched the bruise forming on her chin. For the first time, he noticed that her lip was split. She'd been hit more than once. Timm didn't know how long he'd be able to control this surge of violence he felt seeing that damage. For Eddy's safety, Timm hoped he never met the man again.

"Chester's the bouncer," Angel said.

"He should have been there instead of leaving you alone."

"If your meeting hadn't been on, he would have been in the bar."

"It's not my fault he doesn't have enough staff. He should have left someone there to protect you."

"I can protect myself."

"I know you've been doing it all your life," he said, "but you were no match for Eddy."

"I know. I need to fix that." She put her hands on her hips and cocked her head. "Where did you learn to do those moves? That some kind of self-defense trick?"

"It's aikido. There's a martial-arts center in Haven."

"I need to know how to do that. Can you teach me?"

He stilled. Touching her to prove her own helplessness in the newspaper office had almost killed him. Too much temptation for his own good. In order to teach her, he would have to have physical contact with her. Sure, the touching would be innocuous. But the entire time he'd be thinking about putting his hands all over her, everywhere, in every sweet nook and sexy cranny. And all of those places were forbidden to him. She'd made that perfectly clear.

"Sensei Chong teaches classes every day," he said.

"I don't have enough time to start at the beginning. I want a few key moves so I can defend myself."

When he didn't respond right away, she said, "I'll pay you."

Great idea. I'll take it in trade. Let's trade spit. Let's trade body fluids. Let's trade who we are. Let's trade… confidences.

Those thoughts were exactly why he should avoid having anything to do with Angel.

"I'm going to keep working there, you know," Angel said. "I need the money."

She was the very last person he should be spending

time with, but she was also a woman he never wanted to see hurt again.

"You don't have to pay me," he said quietly. "I'll teach you."

Her answering grin was brilliant, blinding, and he wondered if he'd made a big mistake.

No. He could control himself. He was a master.

"I'm busy today and tomorrow," he said, "and you work nights."

"How about Sunday?"

"I take my mother to church and then in the afternoon I have my book launch."

"What book launch?"

"My book. I've advertised in the paper for the past month."

"You have a book out? What's it about?"

"Stuff I wrote after I was burned, parts of the journal I kept during my convalescence."

"What kind of stuff?"

Timm grinned. "You'll have to buy a copy of the book to find out."

She smiled. "Okay. I will."

"How about you come to my apartment Sunday evening? I can teach you some of those moves we were talking about."

She nodded, her expression pensive. They stopped in front of her house.

"How will you stay safe Friday and Saturday nights?" Timm asked.

"Chester will be there."

"How about on the walk home?"

She shrugged. "I can ask Chester to walk me home for two nights. I'm pretty sure he won't mind."

Timm nodded, but found that he didn't like that solution one bit. He wasn't sure why.

CHAPTER SEVEN

THE FOLLOWING MORNING, Timm entered Cash's office. He wanted to gather all the necessary facts for the paper. And…yes, he'd make sure Cash knew the full extent of Eddy's crimes.

"Hey," Cash said, looking up from a pile of papers on his desk.

"Is that everything involving last night's arrests?" Timm asked.

Cash ran a hand through his hair. Looked as though this wasn't the first time he'd done so today. "Yeah, it's the most excitement this office has seen in years. I drove the prisoners over to Monroe last night, but still have a lot of paperwork to file about the incident." He grinned wryly. "I'd rather be out fighting villains than doing this."

"Eddy tried to abduct Angel last night."

"Yeah, that guy's a jail sentence waiting to happen."

"He punched her face a couple of times."

Cash stared at him, eyes narrowed. "How did she get away?"

"She's a fighter, Cash."

"Yeah, I know. So she managed to fight him off?"

"Not completely. I got her out of there."

"She should press charges. Where did she go? I needed to talk to her as a witness."

"I took her home."

Cash sighed. "Timm, I get why you did it, but you shouldn't have, man. I should have interviewed her immediately, while everything was fresh."

"It seemed more important to get her out of the situation."

"I know. I'll stop by her house later and talk to her."

Timm put his hand on the doorknob, ready to leave. "I need to interview everyone and get an article written up pronto for tomorrow's paper."

"Not so fast." Cash reached for a pad of paper. "You're involved, too, so I need your statement. Tell me what happened."

MISSY SAT ALONE IN THE kitchen at lunchtime when Angel entered, yawning.

"You want some coffee?" Missy moved to rise, but Angel waved to stop her.

"I can get it." Angel poured herself a cup and sat at the table.

"What are you doing up so early?"

"I couldn't sleep." Angel pointed to the tabloid newspaper Missy was reading. "Why are you reading that trash instead of the *Ordinary Citizen?*"

Missy shrugged. The town paper was too smart for her, too focused on the issues and problems of the world. "I like to read my horoscope, but Timm doesn't put them in his paper."

"Anything interesting for today?"

Missy read her horoscope aloud. "It says I'm heading into a period of insta—instab—"

Angel leaned over and read upside down, "Instability."

"But it will be worth it for peace in the future."

She didn't need instability in her life, but peace in the future? God, Missy hoped so. Maybe after she and Phil got married.

Angel blew out a noisy breath and Missy looked at her over the rims of her reading glasses. Reading glasses. Honestly. She wasn't that old.

"Mama," Angel said, "is Phil home?"

"He went out a few minutes ago. Why?"

"I'm glad we're alone. I want to talk about him."

A cloud of fear blurred Missy's vision. "No, honey, don't." *Don't say a word.*

"I have to, Mama. He's a bum," Angel insisted. "He's no good."

Missy recoiled, pulling as far away from the table as she could.

Angel had come out swinging. She didn't know how to do things quietly, slowly. Missy had been after her throughout her childhood to do things differently. To take more care of people, to respect their feelings.

"What on earth do you see in him?"

Definitely not the sex. They had made love this morning. Sex shouldn't be a chore. In the aftermath, with her frustration riding high, she had trouble coming up with an answer for Angel.

Think, Missy.

"He worries about my financial security. That's why we clip coupons and walk a lot and don't use the car every day and things like that." That should have been a good answer, one that would force Angel to keep quiet on this topic. But when Missy said those things out loud, Phil sounded mean and cheap, not caring and protective.

"You can do all of that on your own."

"He's not as bad as you think he is." That didn't sound

right. Not strong enough on Phil's side. She tried again. "He's a better man than in your opinion."

"How?"

Oh, God, how?

"He keeps the place clean. He helps me with vacuuming and laundry. He tends the roses. Stuff like that." Stalling to find another reason why, she sipped her cold coffee.

"Is he good in bed?"

Missy choked and coughed. When she could finally speak, she said, "That's none of your business!"

There might have been too many men in and out of their trailer when Angel was little, but Missy had never discussed her sex life with her daughter—not even after Angel became an adult—and she never would.

"He wants to marry me."

"Mama, I still don't understand why that matters so much to you." She gestured around the kitchen. "You own a house. Hal left you a tidy sum. Why do you need Phil? You have security."

"I don't need him for *stuff,* Angel. I'm not that shallow." She placed a hand on her chest. "I need security for inside of me. For my emotions. I want to be with the same man for the rest of my life."

"Oh, Mama, just because he's willing to marry you doesn't mean he'll be faithful."

"Be quiet, Angel." Missy buried her face in her hands, afraid to let her daughter see how shaky she felt.

"The way he looks at me is creepy," Angel said. "He watches *me* when he should be adoring *you.*"

Missy slapped her hands over her ears. "I don't want to hear this." Because if it was true, then Missy had no hope for a happy future.

She'd waited years for a good man to come along and

sweep her off her feet, to offer her forever, to marry her and take care of her for the rest of her life.

A good man who would never leave her. That's what marriage was, right? A guarantee—or at least, a promise—to be there always? To give a person forever? A happy ending?

"The way he touches my door in the middle of the night is—"

Missy slammed a hand on the table. "Shut *up!*"

Angel leaned away from her, mouth open, chin trembling. "What?"

Missy stood so abruptly her chair fell over. The boom echoed in the quiet house.

"Get out," Missy blurted, then pressed a hand against her mouth. Oh my God, she'd said aloud what she'd been thinking since Angel had walked into her house a few days ago with her beautiful young body and perfect clear skin and…and…and eyes that didn't need glasses to read her daily horoscope, which was wrong half the time anyway.

"Not one more word, Angel." Missy might fall apart at any second, at the slightest thing. "Just leave."

Her heart tried to stampede out of her chest. What was she doing? Was this the end of her relationship with her only child?

"Mama—"

Missy slashed a hand through the air. "No. Just stop. Leave, Angel. Now."

"You can't mean it." Angel's voice sounded threadbare and raw.

Oh, but I do, darling. I'm sorry. "Yes," Missy whispered, appalled at herself that she could—that she was—choosing a man over her own daughter.

Angel stood. "I'll go pack."

"Don't come back."

Angel halted. Missy guessed she was hoping that Missy would change her mind, or would apologize and ask her to stay.

She didn't.

Angel left the room.

Missy ran down the hallway to her own room and slammed the door. She pulled down the shades and welcomed the reprieve from the bright sun that shone too harshly on her faults, on all of the parts of her life that weren't working, and lay on the bed she shared every night with Phil.

She tried so hard to be smart, but she never knew what was smart. Was she making a mistake with Phil?

No. She couldn't look at that. She needed him to take care of her. A marriage contract would mean he'd never abandon her. That's what Missy needed. A man who would never leave her.

She'd asked her baby to leave her house. Or did she mean town? She wasn't sure. All she knew for certain was that she couldn't have her daughter in the same space as Phil. Not when Angel tempted Phil by simply being young and beautiful.

From the moment Missy had given birth to her little girl, she'd sworn her daughter would always have a home with her. Had repeated that vow constantly to Angel.

And yet, a few minutes ago, she'd yanked that away.

How could a mother be that angry with her own flesh and blood? Especially when her own mother had kicked her out.

Missy lay on the bed and cringed under the weight of her own weakness. She needed Phil.

She didn't want to talk about how he stared at Angel. About how he tried to touch Angel.

Missy shivered. Things had to work out for her. She'd spent too many years fighting to stay alive, to keep herself and Angel afloat.

She'd had a good thing with Hal, but then he'd died.

Why couldn't life work out for Missy Donovan for a change? Didn't she deserve a happy ending?

ANGEL STOOD WITH HER hand on the knob. She couldn't bring herself to turn it and step out of the house. That step seemed too final.

Maybe if she talked to Mama again. Maybe they could sort this out, talk about their feelings and come up with a solution. They had always been able to talk. They were a team. The Donovan girls against the world. So surely they could work this out, too.

But, no. The expression on Mama's face had been implacable.

Angel was devastated. Mama had never yelled at her, had never told her to shut up. Mama, the sweetest, simplest woman on the face of the earth, had kicked her out of the house.

Angel fought against taking that first step outside, though, that irrevocable, probably permanent, first step.

Could she change Mama's mind? And then what? Let her marry Phil? Pretend to like the man?

She heard footsteps on the porch. Phil.

She was going to stick her hand down his throat and tear his black heart out of his chest.

She threw open the door.

Not Phil. Timm.

For a moment, she had no idea why he would be here on Missy's porch with his hand raised to knock.

"What's wrong, Angel?"

Her emotions must be written all over her face. So what? There was nothing new about that. She didn't know how to change, how to stop putting her heart out into the world to get trampled.

"I—" She seemed to be gasping for air.

"Is the moon blue? Angel Donovan is speechless." He smiled but she couldn't return that smile.

He sobered. "You want to tell me what's happening?"

Angel shook her head. She couldn't possibly talk about it right now.

"What are you doing here?" Even to her own ears, she sounded flat. Low. Lifeless.

"I came to interview you for the paper. About last night's incident at the bar." He had a pen and writing pad in his hand.

Unbelievable that in her most recent drama she'd forgotten about last night. "No." She thought she whispered, but no sound came out of her mouth. She only shaped the word with her lips.

Timm got the message anyway.

"Angel, come on, tell me what's wrong."

"Can you drive me to Matt's place?"

"Sure. No problem." He took her saddlebags out of her hands. "You going to stay there for a while?"

She nodded and followed him to his truck.

Matt and Jenny would let her stay tonight. She could catch tomorrow's bus out of town. She had enough from tips to pay for a bus ticket.

And then what?

She had to have a few hundred dollars in her pocket to survive in a strange city.

So what? She'd get a job in the first bar she found. And maybe she could ask her brother for a short-term loan…just until she got her first paycheck.

Even if Matt didn't give her the money, first thing tomorrow morning she was hopping on a bus out of Ordinary. Once again, she'd live in a place where no one knew her as Missy Donovan's daughter.

That was what she wanted most. Right?

Sure, moving to a big city and escaping Ordinary was her goal. But she'd always made those plans with the security of knowing she had her mother to fall back on, to come home to for visits, to someday bring her children to get to know their grandma. How much courage would she have without that safety net?

Angel couldn't bring herself to believe that her own mother, with whom she'd had such a warm bond her whole life, had chosen a man—a sneaky, no-good man—over her. Had booted her out of the house.

As they drove out of Ordinary, Angel's eyes and nose and throat hurt with the effort to not fall apart.

She wasn't the crying kind. And this was no excuse to become one.

WITH THE CURIOSITY THAT drove him as a reporter, Timm asked, "What's going on, Angel? Did Phil do something? Did he touch you? I wouldn't put it past the guy."

She didn't respond, and he feared the worst.

"Angel?"

She turned to look at him, her face awash with sadness. No tears, just a solemnity foreign to her. Angel lived big, with expansive emotions—blatant anger or laughter or fear—everything written on her face in capital letters. She was never subtle.

"Talk to me. Tell me what's going on."

"Mama kicked me out."

"Because of something Phil did?"

"No, because of me."

"It's hard to imagine mild-mannered Missy kicking her own daughter out of her house. What did you do?"

"Nice. Blame me. Thanks."

"That's not what I meant and you know it."

She ran her nail along the seam of her jeans and was silent for so long he thought she wouldn't answer him. "We fought."

"What about?" Rude question, but he couldn't imagine what was so bad that it would harm Angel and her mother's relationship. It was plain to anyone who saw Missy and Angel together how close they were.

"About Phil."

Of course. "Ah."

"*Ah?* What does that mean?"

"That means, enough said. Phil's a user. Missy would be better off without him."

Angel straightened so quickly she knocked her bag to the floor. "I *know*. I'm right, right? He's vile, but Mama won't listen."

Timm mulled over the problem. "What did you say to her that prompted the eviction?"

Angel folded her arms. If she'd been standing, she would have jutted a hip. Lifelong companions, attitude and Angel were never too far apart.

"That I can't let her marry him. That he's no good." She paused. "That he would be unfaithful."

A sliver of something dark wiggled under Timm's skin. "How do you know that?"

"The way he looks at me is creepy. If he's going to marry Mama, he should be looking at her. Instead, he's always checking me out. I don't like it."

That darkness grew. "Does he touch you?"

She shook her head. "But he stands outside my bedroom door in the middle of the night. Every night."

Timm saw red. No, black. No, every freaking color under the sun. A primitive, Neanderthal-like sense of possession surged. Angel was *his*.

The feeling was foreign and uncomfortable. He didn't do jealousy, or possessiveness. He lived by his head, not his baser instincts. But where Angel was concerned, nothing about him worked the way it should.

"You're better off out of there."

"But that creep is still in the house with her." Angel's stridency rattled around the enclosed cab of the truck like a bugle's blare. "How can I protect Mama if I'm not even there? How can I stop her from marrying him if she won't talk to me?"

Timm tamped down that inner troglodyte he never knew he had and forced his logical mind to the forefront. "You need to be smart about how to approach the situation. You're too emotional."

"Of *course* I'm emotional. My mother tossed me out. I'm *never* welcome back. Why *wouldn't* I be emotional?"

"Because it's *always* better to use *reason* and *intellect*. It gets better *results*. There's always a smarter, more *rational* way to do things."

"Thanks for the support." Her voice oozed sarcasm. "That's exactly what I need right now—to be told I'm not smart."

"I didn't say that."

They pulled into Matt's yard and Angel gathered her bags, threw her door open and stepped out.

"Angel, wait." He'd made her feel worse. That was pretty obvious. "Give it a few days. Maybe Missy will change her mind and ask you to come back. Okay?"

She huffed out a breath, and all of her antagonism seemed to abandon her. "Thanks."

Timm drove off the ranch, pondering the emotional roller coaster he rode thanks to Angel.

She'd practically taken his head off in the office yesterday morning because he'd put his hands where many other men's hands had been before. Yet, here he was feeling sorry for her being suddenly homeless.

He needed to get his head screwed back on properly. He wouldn't see her again until Sunday night—or would she want to cancel the self-defense lesson? That was plenty of time to realign with his priorities: become mayor, begin dating and start a family of his own.

He needed to move ahead in his schedule. In fact, he didn't have to wait until he was mayor to start dating. He could find a good woman now, a rational and sane one. Then he could get Angel out of his head.

TIMM SAT WITH HIS FAMILY in the last pew of the church on Sunday morning. His mother preferred being back here now rather than up front where the family used to sit.

He scanned the congregation, noting a few single women present. There was something vaguely sacrilegious about using Sunday services as a potential dating pool; however, this was as good a spot as any to find someone with common values. It seemed unlikely that a woman who attended the same church would turn his well-measured life upside down.

Rona from the diner sat near the front. As he watched, she shifted and fidgeted. While Reverend Wright delivered his sermon, she looked everywhere, even waved to people she saw regularly at the diner.

He knew she was tireless on the job, possessed a strong work ethic and got along with most people. Points in her favor. But, her restlessness would drive Timm crazy inside of a week. So, no.

Halfway back on the left side of the aisle, Becca Hardy sat quietly, her hands folded in her lap. A couple of years younger than he, she was a pretty girl. Sweet. Quiet. Still single.

She'd never stirred his emotions in any way, though.

Well? Isn't that a good thing?

A fleeting vision of Angel sidetracked him and he quashed it ruthlessly.

Becca was perfect. Well, other than her nickname. He didn't like it. Would she let him use Rebecca?

Half an hour later, he approached her outside the church. He greeted her mother first, then her.

"Becca, can I talk to you for a minute? Over here." He gestured to a spot slightly away from the crowd.

As they strolled, they engaged in small talk. He asked about her week, she asked about the next edition.

When they were far enough from the groups socializing, he worked up his courage. It had been a while since he'd done this.

"Do you think you would go out with me one night next week?"

She perked up. "I'd like that, Timm."

"How about if we drive over to Haven on Wednesday? I'll pick you up at seven."

"Okay." She walked away with a smile and a small wave of her fingers.

Timm decided not to dwell on why he had no sense of satisfaction. Instead, he looked around for his mother, but couldn't see her. Probably chatting with her friends. He'd wait for her in the truck. Once there, he opened the windows, pulled a book out of the glove compartment and started to read.

"Adelle, why not?"

Timm looked around for the source of the disembodied voice and noticed in his right-side mirror that his mother was on the other side of the pickup talking with Max Golden.

Max looked upset; Ma, implacable.

Timm had greeted Max before the service and he'd looked tired, his eyes bloodshot. On a Sunday morning, that was a bad sign. It usually meant too much alcohol the night before.

There had been rumors about Max's drinking floating around town for years. Some had even advised Timm to use those rumors to win the election. He refused. If he couldn't win on the issues, then he didn't deserve to win.

"Why won't you come out to dinner with me?"

Max? Interested in Ma? When had this happened?

He knew he shouldn't be eavesdropping. But to close the window now would only draw attention to the fact they had an audience.

"I don't know what to say, Max."

"Say yes." Max chuckled, but he sounded nervous.

"Max, I hear things about you that aren't good."

Timm could hear Max shuffle his feet.

"I can change. I can do better. I'm running for mayor."

"I know and I'm proud of you, but so is my son. You know how I will vote."

"Yeah, and I understand, but that doesn't mean we can't date. We had fun that one time, didn't we?"

What one time? When Papa was still alive? *No way* would Mama have cheated on him.

"Yes, we had fun, but do you remember the end of the night?"

"Yeah." Max seemed despondent. "I had too much to drink."

"That's right. I can't deal with that. I'm sorry. The answer is no."

Ma's voice was as soft and sweet as usual, but Timm heard the thread of steel that underlay it, the same one Sara had inherited from her.

How odd that his mother and his sister were currently fighting off attention from persistent but unsuitable men. Although Rem and Max had their strong points, neither of them was always reasonable. They could be wild, impetuous, using arguments that weren't well thought out. Worse, both of them battled addictions to alcohol. And no Franck woman needed another man who drank too much.

Was this some kind of curse? Were the Francks destined to experience nothing but heartache?

This was why Timm vowed to be different. He would approach his relationships with logic and reason. The woman he'd just made a date with was stable and predictable. Exactly the kind of woman he needed—as a man and as the future mayor of Ordinary.

He was moving forward in his life.

Ma opened the door and slid into the passenger seat. "Let's go," she said, spots of red high in her cheeks.

Timm drove away and put some distance between them and the church before broaching the subject of Max with his mother. "Mama, I heard Max ask you to dinner. When did you go out with him before?"

"Do you remember when you went to that publishers' convention in the spring? It was then."

"Do you like him?"

She nodded. "Max is a decent man."

He thought there was a *but* hanging after her statement. When she didn't say anything further, Timm addressed the unspoken topic. "He drinks too much, though."

"Yes, he does." She looked out the window and murmured, "I can't go through that again."

AFTER LUNCH, TIMM headed to the Legion for his book launch.

The publisher had provided him with a hundred books to autograph and sell. Personally, he thought that was optimistic. He'd be lucky if he sold a dozen.

The hall was packed when he arrived, the townspeople lined up out the door. As he squeezed by, they clapped him on the back and congratulated him.

"Great to have a published author in our town."

"We're proud of you, Timm."

"Yep. You've done the whole town proud."

Something shifted in Timm's chest, became fluid. They all wanted his book? They were all proud of him? Why?

Hank Shelter steered him toward the table with the towering stack of books at the front of the room. "Sit down, Timm. Everyone wants to buy one and they won't take them without your John Henry inside."

Timm smiled. He'd done it. He'd restored the Francks' position, had brought honor back to their name. Ma would be so pleased. A sense of satisfaction warmed him from head to toe. The Francks were a force to be reckoned with again in Ordinary.

Timm hated to assume, but he thought he might have the job of mayor in the bag. He might have already won the election.

For the next hour, Timm talked to his neighbors and signed books. His wrist started to cramp, but he never stopped smiling.

At one point, he looked up to speak with the next person and there stood Angel.

So. She'd made it home safely the past two nights—with Chester's escort, he hoped, rather than taking her chances on her own.

The bruising on her face had started to fade and assume the ugly shades of green that signified healing. She had a small scab on her lip.

Timm opened the front cover to the title page of the next copy in the dwindling pile and…stopped.

He didn't know what to write.

He'd signed eighty or so books without hesitation and, yet—

What should he say to Angel?

For a tough girl, she looked unaccountably shy.

He knew he was a good writer. He'd been published, hadn't he? But he was drawing a blank.

What to say to Angel?

Somewhere in the maelstrom of competing reactions he always felt toward her, there was a thought that he could write, but what was it?

Somehow, a dry, reasonable remark seemed inadequate. He didn't want to lay his soul bare, either, when he wouldn't have anything to do with her in the future. She was definitely not his type.

Besides, she'd rejected him.

But then, why did she watch him so tentatively? As if she, too, wondered what he would say?

He'd made a date with Becca Hardy this morning and he planned to actively pursue a relationship with her.

Mind made up, he scribbled, *All the best. Timm,* then handed her the book.

She turned the book around to read it and a split second of disappointment flashed across her face, followed by her sardonic grin, as though she knew she'd come up short in his regard, that she wasn't worth any more to him than a generic sentiment.

Despite knowing that he'd done the right thing, he felt as though he'd failed not only Angel, but also himself.

Nonsense. Get on with enjoying the spotlight.

CHAPTER EIGHT

AT SEVEN O'CLOCK, Angel rang Timm's doorbell. She was apprehensive about these self-defense lessons. She wanted to keep her distance from Timm until she had a better handle on her attraction to him. But that fight with Eddy had scared her to her bones, and she knew that Timm was right. The Roadhouse was a lightning rod for trouble. Since she insisted on working there, she had to learn how to fight effectively.

Timm answered the door. "Come upstairs."

She followed him, curious to see where he lived.

The apartment was sparsely furnished, well lit, masculine, uncluttered. Much like Timm's character. Straightforward. What you saw was what you got.

"How are you doing?" he asked. "Are things still bad with Missy?"

"I've called her so many times. She won't talk to me."

In the past few days, Angel's initial shock and self-pity had turned to anger.

"I'm mad now. There's no way I'm leaving town before they get married and I know I've failed for sure. Until then, I won't give up. Not yet."

She didn't know exactly how she would change current circumstances with Missy, but her determination was strong.

Timm smiled with a glint of admiration in his eyes.

She felt herself preen under that look. She caught herself wanting to say more, do more to earn another one. Enough of that. This attraction was going nowhere. In case she needed reminding, she was still grieving for Neil. Yet still, Timm was somehow thawing pieces of her heart one frozen bit at a time.

The second she knew that she had either succeeded and booted Phil out of Mama's life, or had failed on the day they get married, she had to run as fast and as far as she could. She needed to get out before she grew any closer to this man.

So tonight she was here to learn. That's it.

"I'm determined," she said, and wasn't sure whether she was speaking about Mama's situation or her own.

She knew Timm heard the anger in her voice because he said, "I'll show you some aikido. It's good for your soul. Trust me. It'll calm you down."

An hour later, after being thrown to an exercise mat in the middle of the living-room floor one time too many, Angel thought, *calming and good for your soul, my ass.*

She wanted to throttle someone. Anger forged a canyon through her heart and chest. She knew her mother couldn't live alone—hated it—but come on. *Phil?*

If Mama needed someone to stay with her in order to feel safe, Angel would abandon her dreams, would learn to live in Ordinary despite what people thought of her and the way they treated her. For Mama, and only for Mama, would she settle for less.

But Mama had always needed men, had never

trusted women friends to stay long enough for her to feel secure.

Timm was talking. Angel realized she'd completely missed what he'd said. A moment later, she wound up on the floor on her back. Again.

"Weren't you listening?" Timm helped her to her feet. "When I attack, use my momentum against me so I go flying instead of you. Listen, Angel."

"All right," she snapped. She felt like growling, like tearing into his flesh.

He continued to teach her and throughout, while her anger simmered and grew, he became cooler, and more and more in control, more rational.

Because she felt so irrational, his control bothered her and she resisted his lessons. She wanted him to feel as vulnerable as she felt.

After one particular throw, their lesson looked more like wrestling than anything calm and thoughtful and unemotional, as aikido was supposed to be.

"Angel, do what *I* tell you to do, not what *you* want to do. Are you here to learn or not?"

"Yes," she yelled. Timm had her pinned to the mat after she'd pulled on his arm too hard, upending both of them.

This close, his eyes—even brimming with frustration—were dark brown. A deep color she could get lost in. Tall and slim in his white *gi,* he moved with a lithe grace that belied his height. Something about aikido's discipline suited him. He looked confident and calm and sure. Masculine and in control.

When had he become so attractive to her? When had his opinion of her started to mean something? When had she started to want him to like her? And when had she begun to like him even though she barely knew him?

And why had it bothered her so much that he hadn't written anything special to her when he'd autographed his book?

Stop this. No one in town should matter to you. No one.

He sat up and so did she.

The only thing marring what was a pretty amazing specimen of masculine beauty were the scars she could glimpse in the V of his jacket.

In her self-pity, in wallowing hip-deep in her own fetid swamp of anger, she'd forgotten about Timm's scars, about what he'd lived through in his life. What the hell was she doing?

She deflated. Her anger, and her childish attempts to make him lose his temper, dissipated.

He must have noticed some physical change in her because his shoulders seemed to relax. His chest rose and fell with his steady breathing.

She looked up and found him watching her, his cheeks red. She didn't think that was from exertion. He'd been watching her stare at his scars.

The nerdy mayor hopeful and newspaper publisher was so much more than he appeared to be. She remembered him using his skill on Eddy, and how his quiet power had startled her. Still waters…

A mild-mannered reporter by day…

Angel knew she was hightailing it out of Dodge the moment it made sense. But she imagined, oh, so briefly, what it would be like to go out to dinner with Timm. To talk about what he wrote in the paper, or about normal things such as how his day had been without wondering when he was going to make a move on her. Or without knowing that dinner and conversation came with a price—the guy paid for dinner with cash and she paid for the attention with sex.

Why couldn't she look at a man like Timm and know that any sex that followed came out of respect and affection? Yes, it could be hot, should be passionate, but also tender, growing out of something real and designed to last.

She wondered how it would feel to walk home with him, hand in hand, and up the narrow stairs to this apartment knowing that he cared about her.

How would it feel to spend time with him if he'd never known her as Missy's daughter? Would he treat her with the same respect Neil had?

How would it feel to spend time with Timm as he was today? When he didn't look as though he wanted to cop a feel? When he taught her how to defend herself because he worried that she might get hurt?

Angel's eyes dropped to the V-neck of his *gi* again. The skin looked ravaged. Was his entire chest like that?

Oh, Timm. *You poor man.*

His bare feet rested close to her knee. She had never paid attention to a man's feet in the past, but his were handsome. Weird thing to think, but true.

"Does it still hurt?" she asked.

He shook his head. "No. It stopped hurting a long time ago. The skin feels stiff sometimes, though."

"Can I touch it?"

He frowned, but nodded.

She reached her index finger to the hollow at the base of his throat. The skin felt smooth, tight, warm.

"You must have suffered so much pain."

"It wasn't a picnic."

"Everything in your life changed that day, didn't it?"

"Yep. I couldn't be just a carefree kid anymore. I couldn't run around and have fun."

And she thought *her* life was bad?

In a flurry of self-disgust, she realized how truly self-indulgent she often was. She flinched and pulled her hand away.

TIMM WATCHED ANGEL flinch and wondered what went on in her head.

"It bothers you to touch the scars?" Her reaction shouldn't matter to him. He'd had years to adjust to being scarred.

Some women minded. Some didn't. He wasn't sure why Angel's opinion meant anything to him.

"It didn't bother me, no. I was just thinking how spoiled I am sometimes."

She shifted on the mat. "I know I have every right to be upset about losing Mama, but that might not be a permanent situation. Those—" she pointed to his scars "—on the other hand, are permanent."

"Yeah. I'm used to them, though. I tend to keep them covered because some people are uncomfortable seeing them."

"You don't let a lot of people see your scars?"

"Not often." Let her stew on that info for a while and she would probably figure out how few women he'd been with. Not one single woman here in Ordinary. All of his experience had been in college.

For a long time after he'd returned, he'd been so focused on the paper and on restoring the family name that relationships—hell, even sex—had been so low on his priority list to be laughable. But now that he'd accomplished so much it was past time to find a woman with whom he could have a full relationship.

He knew that quiet, sensible Becca Hardy would do well for him.

"What happened?" Angel asked, her manner soft now, her unruly anger finally absent. "I never heard the whole story."

"It was at my eleventh birthday party," he said, quietly. "Rem sprayed foam streamers on me. He thought it was hilarious to see me covered in the stuff. And I guess it probably was. But the candles on the cake were lit and...the foam ignited."

A flutter of something he thought might be regret rose in his chest. Regret that it had ever happened. Or maybe sorrow that life would never again be the same and that the easy relationship between him and his best friend would never again be as good and as healthy as it had been in childhood, that Rem would carry too much guilt for the pair of them to remain open with each other.

"Rem still feels bad about it. It put a dent in our relationship that we haven't been able to fix." Timm cleared his throat. "He still feels like he has to do penance or something for that one stupid mistake. He should get over it. I have."

"Have you?"

"Yes. I live a good life."

"Yeah. I think you'll win the mayoralty race." She smiled and he appreciated her faith in him.

He stood. "Let's do more aikido now that you're in a better mood."

Angel laughed and jumped to her feet. "Okay, what's next?"

For another hour, he showed her more moves.

By the time he drove Angel home, he felt confident that she could defend herself.

ANGEL ROLLED OVER IN bed and stretched, a little stiff and bruised in spots thanks to last night's workout. Yet she also felt good, satisfied in her ability to handle someone like Eddy.

Monday morning. She had the entire day off.

Timm's book sat on the bedside table next to the heart-shaped rock Neil had given her. She rubbed her thumb across the rock, then grabbed the book, curiosity eating at her. In so many ways, Timm was a good guy, even if he wasn't her type.

She opened the book and read the prologue. Parts of the book were from the diary he'd started after he was burned. The other parts were his observations about the town and its inhabitants.

I dream of running, of climbing out of this bed and kicking my feet high, of soaring between bounding steps, weightless and free, but no…

I am earthbound by this scarred body.

My legs remember how, but my body is weak. Another operation last week and I haven't yet recovered.

I am an invalid…so I sit at my window and watch the townspeople live active lives that I can't emulate…and I dream of doing.

Angel read for another hour before forcing herself to put the book down. She stared out the window at the calm landscape that was Matt and Jenny's ranch.

Now I know you, Timm.

She didn't want to know him this well, but his book…

It said too much about him and she understood it all. But how? Their lives had been so different.

He'd been trapped by a body that no longer worked as it should, due to a circumstance beyond his control.

She had never had a sick day in her adolescence, had been free to do whatever she wanted, whenever she felt like it.

And yet...hadn't she felt trapped in her own way? Hadn't she lived in her own kind of prison—in her reputation and the life her Mama's reputation had crowded her into, in which she'd had few choices?

Hadn't she felt free at college, to be whoever she wanted?

That's why she needed to escape Ordinary. To outrun this terrible legacy that imprisoned her, hemmed her in, limited her possibilities in this town. And the best place she knew to do that was the anonymous landscape of a city. Lots of people, lots of potential.

Because what if, at the end of her life, her biggest regret was that she hadn't lived up to her potential? That's how it would have been if she'd never left Ordinary to attend college. That's how it would be now if she stayed.

Made antsy by her thoughts, she jumped out of bed, showered, dressed and headed downstairs.

The house was quiet. Matt, Jenny and the kids were out on the ranch working. Neither farmers nor ranchers got days off.

Angel put on her most comfortable shoes and walked into town, arriving sweaty and in need of a big cold glass of liquid to soothe her parched throat. She headed for the diner to order some all-day breakfast, or maybe a burger.

Timm stepped out of his apartment as she was passing.

"How are you feeling today?" he asked.

"Stiff. A little bit bruised."

"Where are you off to?"

"The diner for lunch."

"Me, too."

"Good. Come on. I'm buying." It didn't sit right with Angel that she hadn't paid Timm for his lessons, had nothing to give him in return. She didn't like taking things from men, didn't like feeling as though she owed them something. Men who felt owed usually wanted only one thing. After reading part of Timm's book, she no longer wanted to believe he was that kind of man, but she preferred to be on an equal footing with him.

He looked surprised. "Why? You don't have to."

"I know, but I want to repay you for the lessons."

"Sure. Can't really argue with that."

TIMM STEPPED INTO the diner with Angel.

After last night's lesson, he wasn't sure how to deal with her. Although he'd always expected her to have hidden depths, it was still an adjustment for him to learn she did. It was a lot easier to stick with old habits, to continue to prejudge.

He felt on some kind of loose footing. He couldn't quite see her in the same old way, but wasn't confident enough in his assessment of who she might be. The person on the inside, the one he was catching small glimpses of, was so far removed from the woman he'd assumed her to be.

A few people turned to watch as they walked to an empty booth across from the grill. As they sat, Timm noticed George, the owner, stare at Angel while food sizzled on the grill behind him. Then he turned his gaze to Timm and took his measure.

"George is staring as usual," Angel said.

"Did you ever apply for the job he advertised?"

Angel cocked her head. "How did you know I was job-hunting?"

"I could tell by the section you studied in the paper last week."

"Why did it matter to you what I was reading?"

"I—" He wasn't sure. He ran his finger around his tight collar. "I was curious."

"Why?"

He shrugged. He really didn't know. "Well?"

"Well, what?"

"Did you apply for the job?"

Angel shook her head.

So she'd gone for the grittier job. Woman had no sense at all. "Why not? You could make good tips here without dealing with bikers."

It was Angel's turn to shrug. "George doesn't treat me very well."

"How does he treat you?"

"When I was a teenager, he used to touch me too much." She wouldn't meet his eyes. And despite the nonchalant tone, Timm got that George's attitude toward her had hurt.

She ran her nail along the edge of the table. "I didn't want to deal with that again."

"But you put up with all of those bikers pawing you at the bar."

"They aren't townspeople."

She cared what the town thought of her? In his wildest imagining, he would have never guessed, not with her no-holds-barred behavior.

When George approached the table with menus, Timm took notice. George never left the grill. Others noticed, too.

"What'll you have today?" George directed the question toward Angel and the look he gave her made Timm's stomach turn.

How did it feel to be on the receiving end of a look that dirty? He glanced at Angel. Where a moment ago she had been shy, now she glared at George with a hard jaw and mouth zipped shut.

She addressed Timm. "Do you mind if we get take-out?" That fragile honesty he'd seen in her had disappeared, replaced by the hard woman he usually saw.

"Sure," he said, because Lord knew he didn't like the attention they were attracting. "Want a burger?"

She nodded. "With mustard and dill pickles. I'll wait outside." She put a twenty-dollar bill on the table and Timm picked it up.

When Angel stood, George moved closer to her, the action subtle, but still discernible.

She shoved George and he laughed.

The exchange sickened Timm. Angel left the diner and Timm ordered their lunch.

After George returned to the grill, Timm's uncle Derick approached and asked, "May I sit for a moment?"

Timm nodded. It was hard to look at his uncle now that Timm knew something that Derick didn't. Only the eldest and the youngest boys had survived that terrible fire. Afterward, Derick had emigrated from Germany to Montana, bringing young Karl with him. Derick became more like Karl's father than his brother.

"Are you here with Aunt Edith?" Timm asked.

"Ya. I want to talk for only a moment." He paused, then said, "Why are you here with that woman?"

"Angel? We're having lunch together."

"Why?"

What difference did it make to Uncle Derick? "I taught her some self-defense moves and she's repaying me by buying lunch."

"This isn't good. You are running for mayor."

Disappointment with his uncle settled into Timm's stomach. "You honestly believe that the people of Ordinary will care whether I have lunch with Angel Donovan?"

"I think they might. You do have to consider what the voters will think."

"Think? I'm having lunch with her. I'm not sleeping with her." No matter how much he wanted to. Even if he was, whose business was it but his and Angel's?

"She has a bad reputation."

"That has nothing to do with me. She's a member of our town. A voter like everyone else."

Derick raised a hand, the one with fewer scars. "Yeah, but some voters are more important than others." He spoke with the crisp accent of his homeland and smiled grimly.

"She's a better person than you think she is."

"Maybe, but I don't think so."

"By looking no further than the surface, you're short-changing her." Timm's conscience whispered that he hadn't looked too far beneath Angel's beauty and her reputation until last night when she'd shown him sensitivity and compassion regarding his scars. He'd been certain she would be repelled, but she hadn't been.

That spoke volumes in her favor. In college, he'd

learned a lot about women by their reactions to his scars.

"Perhaps," Uncle Derick said, "but this is how most decent people in town see her. And her mother is even worse."

"Being seen with her won't make a difference to the vote."

"It will. Count on it."

"If that's true, I've judged the people of Ordinary better than I should have. I'm running on issues, not on the company I keep."

"You are ahead. Trust me. You don't want to jeopardize that."

"We'll see how tomorrow night's debate goes. Once the people understand my platform, they'll vote accordingly." Derick had reminded him of what was important, of why it was so vital that Timm keep his reputation intact, but Derick's concern seemed excessive. "I appreciate the warning, but I'm not convinced that you're right. Not by a long shot."

When Rona called that his order was ready, Timm went to pay, then left. He smiled at a few people on his way out, but the response seemed cooler than usual. Was it? Or was he imagining it? Had Uncle Derick spooked him? Was it true that Angel could hurt his standing in town, could damage a reputation he'd thought inviolable after the past two years of upstanding behavior and hard work? Would the town really overlook the fact he was a man of substance, valued for his intelligence, his opinions and his utter fairness?

Were the townspeople really that easily influenced?

Angel leaned against the wall to the left of the diner door, her expression hard.

He'd seen how upset she was by George's leering and yet how quickly that was masked by her defiance. He needed to be fair to her, but really didn't want to be put under the spotlight today.

Some kind of itchy desire to break free of the town for a few minutes burbled beneath his skin.

He made a snap decision. "Do you want to drive to Still Creek and eat *al fresco?*"

CHAPTER NINE

ANGEL PERKED UP at Timm's suggestion. "Sure. Let's go."

They walked to the alley behind the office to his truck. It seemed that Ordinary pulled Angel down, and the idea of leaving cheered her up—an attitude that Timm couldn't have related to yesterday, but possibly understood now that he'd witnessed more in Angel.

On a stretch of pretty land near the creek, they pulled into an empty spot off the side of the dirt road, worn flat by generations of teenagers coming here to swim or for make-out sessions. Along the edge of the river, they found a large flat rock and spread the food out between them.

"I ordered fries to share," Timm said.

They ate silently and he found it comfortable. In town, Derick might think Angel could damage his reputation, and Timm might worry about his family and becoming mayor, but in this place? They were just two people sharing lunch and breathtaking scenery.

"When I was a teen, Rem used to bring me here on summer evenings to swim." Late at night, so no one would see him. So Timm could pretend he wasn't a complete freak. So he could get out and have fun away from the endless rounds of physiotherapy and skin grafts. Away from Ma and Sara hovering over him. Especially

Sara, because she was young and should have been out with her friends instead of taking care of him.

"Why always at night?"

How could a woman look good eating a burger? She didn't pick at it, didn't seem to worry about calories. She dug in with a healthy appetite and, just like that, he found another quality to admire in Angel.

"Why couldn't you come whenever you wanted?" she continued.

"I liked it better at night." Yes, he did, but that wasn't the full answer. In his teenage years, his scars had never seen the light of day. If anyone but Rem had caught him shirtless, he would have died of embarrassment. At night, he could feel the air on his naked chest. He could breathe more freely. He could relax—and that was rare in those years.

"You didn't want people to see your scars."

"Would you stop doing that?"

She glanced at him. "What?"

"You have this weird habit of reading my mind sometimes."

"I'm pretty sure I would have felt the same way. Sorry you had to go through all that."

One thing he already knew about Angel was that she spoke her mind at all times. If she said it, she believed it. So, when she expressed sympathy, he knew it was sincere.

There were no baleful, pitying glances, though. She said it as a matter of fact.

She sighed, deeply. "It's gorgeous out here."

"I would never have pegged you as a fan of nature."

She swallowed the bite she'd been chewing. "There's a lot you don't know about me, Mr. Smarty-Pants-

Newspaper-Reporter." She softened the comment with a smile.

"What other secrets are you keeping from me?"

Her smile dimmed and he was sorry he asked.

"Let's talk about something else," she said. "Why do you need to close down Chester's?"

Did he want to answer her question?

He crumpled the wrapper from the burger he'd practically inhaled, buying himself time to figure out how best to approach the subject. He wanted to be honest with Angel.

"My dad drank there a lot."

"Where?"

"At Chester's bar in Monroe. Dad drove there to drink so people in Ordinary wouldn't know how bad his problem was."

"Oh." She seemed cautious, as though not sure what to say.

"One night on his way home, Dad drove off the road and into a tree. Apparently, he died instantly."

The admission made him restless, so he started gathering the wrappers and shoving them into a bag.

"I'm sorry."

"Chester shouldn't have let him drive home drunk." He couldn't meet her gaze—didn't want to.

"Do you really think that was Chester's fault? That doesn't make sense."

Timm bristled. "I'm a rational man, Angel." He didn't lead with his emotions the way she did. "Once my dad had consumed so much alcohol that he couldn't make a rational decision, Chester should have stepped in."

"And saved him from himself?"

"Yes. Exactly." He'd said that too loudly so took a breath to calm down. "Sorry." No matter how hard he tried, this was one issue about which he couldn't contain his emotions.

"I don't know what to say. I'm not sure whose fault it was. I do know Chester is a decent man."

"Maybe." Although he sincerely doubted it.

LISTENING TO TIMM'S confession was torture for Angel. His father had been drunk. He'd crashed into a tree.

An image of Neil's broken body lodged in the front of her mind.

She couldn't stand the guilt eating away at her, devouring pieces of her heart, hollowing her out.

"Tell me about Neil," Timm said. "About the accident."

"How do you know about that?" she whispered.

"I'm a reporter. I investigate things. I wanted to know why you were burning the bike."

She didn't want to talk to him about it. She hadn't talked to anyone, and he was the least likely candidate even if she was looking to confess. How could she forget the way he'd shredded her mother in print?

But he had opened up to her. And there was a reassuring air about him that suggested her secrets—her guilt—would be safe with him. "You won't print this in the paper?"

Timm shook his head. "I'm not a reporter right now. I'm just a guy who wants to know what happened to a… friend."

Were they friends? Maybe. He'd known something was wrong with her the day Mama kicked her out, and he'd been ready to help her, despite her anger toward him the day before that.

On Saturday, there had been nothing in his paper about Missy kicking her daughter out of the house. Nor had Angel been confronted with any gossip about it. He'd kept that private.

He'd just discussed a difficult topic with her.

The need to unload this burden, to put it down for a brief time overwhelmed her.

"Neil was a friend at college," she started slowly. "The best friend I've ever had. He was beautiful. Younger and more innocent than I think I've ever been."

"What happened that night?"

"It was his birthday. He worked so hard all the time. I wanted him to have fun. After I bought the motorcycle, he harassed me to teach him how to drive it. Finally, I gave in. He was doing pretty well—not an expert driver, but not bad. That night, I took him out to a bar." She stopped to swallow the emotion choking her throat. She wouldn't cry. "We had a few drinks. We danced a lot. I didn't realize the alcohol affected him so strongly. I let him drive home. He crashed the bike. I was fine. He wasn't.

"I guess the only good news is that he died instantly." She laid her head on her knees and mumbled, "I miss him so much."

Timm's hand on her back warmed her.

"I can't talk about it anymore." With the same discipline she'd been exerting since that horrible night, she shoved her memories into the mental box where they belonged. "It's too serious for such a beautiful day."

He nodded and they were quiet for a while. She focused on the sound of the creek, the occasional bird singing and let nature soothe her.

"You know, sometimes I get pulled down by all of the bad news I have to report in the paper."

A new topic. Good. "I never thought about it before,

but yeah, that would be a problem. How do you maintain your equilibrium?"

"I print as many positive stories as possible. I ask my reporters to look for plenty of good items to balance the bad." Timm looked so serious. In fact, as far as she could tell, he always did.

She could turn this day around. She knew how to have fun. How to make fun happen. She hesitated, though, because of that one big mistake with Neil. When she'd wanted him to stop being serious, to have fun for a change, she'd killed him.

Today was different, though. There was no danger here.

"We're too serious," she said. "It's a shame to waste a gorgeous day on sad stories."

She smiled. It felt strained, but what the hell. She was good at faking it. Fake It Till You Make It. That was her motto. She'd followed it for years. It had helped her to get through all kinds of dark situations.

"Come on," she said. "Let's go swimming."

"What? We don't have any bathing suits."

"We don't need them."

His face registered the most comical mix of surprise and maybe…hope? He probably thought he was going to see Angel naked.

Nope. Not a chance. No guy in Ordinary ever would again.

That didn't mean they couldn't have fun.

Angel took off her shoes then jumped into the water fully clothed.

She came up, gasping for air, the water refreshing enough to wash away the worst of her memories.

Timm sat on the rock, wearing a world-class frown.

She was too impetuous for such a stuffy, rational guy. Too bad for him. She felt great.

Maybe she'd disappointed him. What had he expected from her? She wasn't used to dealing with men on this level. With Neil, she'd been taking baby steps to become more herself.

With Timm, she was out of her depth.

She experienced a moment's regret for spilling her guts. It seemed foolish to have opened up that way. Or maybe she was a coward.

She dived under the surface of the water and let it once again clear her mind. Whatever she was, she wanted to feel good at this moment, restored to a better place.

When she came up for air, Timm still watched her with that wary frown.

She had to get him to lighten up. He spent too much time thinking and chewing on serious problems. Maybe he needed to get his reporters to work harder finding those human-interest stories.

Or she could take matters into her own hands.

She cupped her palms and splashed Timm.

"What the hell?" he shouted, swiping a hand down his face. "Are you nuts?"

She laughed and splashed him again. "Come in." She spread her arms wide. "The water's amazing."

Timm sulked like a little boy, but she detected a little envy there, too, that she was cooling off while he baked in the sun.

She sent a spray of water his way. He wiped drops from his face again. "No. I'm not coming in."

Angel rolled onto her back. "Coward."

He remained where he was, so serious, as though he carried the weight of the world on his shoulders.

Did he ever have fun, or was his life only unrelenting responsibility and duty?

She closed her eyes, floating, drenched in the sun's pure healing light, which she felt all the way to her bones.

Timm needed this, even if he didn't know it. If ever a man did, he did. If Mohammed wouldn't come to the mountain, the mountain would go to him.

She rolled over, and with a couple of strokes, she reached the rock where he sat. "Can you help me out?"

She stretched an arm toward him and he grabbed her hand to pull her out.

Jerking hard and taking him by surprise, she tugged him into the water.

Oh, you gullible man.

She laughed out loud.

WHAT HAD JUST happened?

Timm came up coughing. "What did you do that for?"

She grinned. "You looked hot."

"I was, but I wasn't going to jump in the water. Especially not with my clothes."

"I know." Her smile held a Mona Lisa secret. "Water's real nice, though, isn't it?"

Yeah. Cool. Soothing. He didn't want to tell her that, though. She looked altogether too smug. He pulled his wallet out of his pocket and tossed it onto the rock.

"How are we going to drive back into town without soaking the seats?"

"Don't be such a stick in the mud."

"I'm not." He wasn't a stick in the mud at all. He wasn't. "I know how to have fun."

"Could have fooled me."

"I'm not," he yelled, and launched a handful of water at Angel. It hit her in the face and she sputtered.

"You—" She laughed and slapped water back at him.

He returned it.

As their laughter increased, their accuracy decreased and the splashing contest deteriorated. But Timm was happy.

She sliced a perfect arc of water that was a direct hit, momentarily blinding him. Oh, yeah? Sight restored, he bore down on her, caught her in his arms, then carried her to the bank. He stumbled out of the creek and they both fell, him half on top of her.

Between giggles, Angel said, "You're stronger than you look."

I'll be strong for you. I'll be your he-man.

He wanted her uninhibited sense of fun, of joy, of carefree abandonment. He took on responsibility for everyone around him, his mother, his sister, Rem, the whole town.

"You know how to have fun," he whispered.

Teach me.

Angel smiled. Her vivid blue eyes crinkled at the corners. This woman would probably have crow's-feet when she got older, all earned through enjoying life.

What would he look like? Would he have crevices gouged into his forehead from frowning, from always taking life too seriously?

He'd succeeded, had achieved almost every goal he'd set, but had never learned to have fun. Or rather, had never relearned to have the fun he'd had as a child, before getting burned changed everything.

Timm wanted to capture her vitality to keep it close,

to carry it with him everywhere, to lighten that sense of responsibility he bore always.

He wanted to taste her smile.

When he bent close, slowly, giving her time to pull away, she didn't. He put his lips on hers. They were cool from swimming in the creek.

He took it slowly, tried not to think about how much experience this woman had with sex, how high the standards he had to meet. Last thing he wanted to feel at the moment was insecure. He only wanted to taste that amazing smile.

She kissed him back, but not with any kind of sexual prowess. They kissed innocently, like a pair of thirteen-year-olds and it felt great. Absolutely freaking great.

He pulled away from her with something like a sense of wonder.

She looked as shell-shocked as he felt.

Whoa. Too much. Feeling so much for Angel Donovan was not good. Not good at all.

He sat up slowly.

She did the same, while the brief glimpse of wonder he'd seen in her eyes turn to wariness.

"That was a mistake," he said.

"Yeah." She pushed her hair away from her face. "That was wrong."

What she said and what her face showed were two different things. She wanted to do it again. He knew it for certain, because he felt it, too.

Which made staying here a *huge* mistake. He picked up their garbage and jumped to his feet.

Exactly who was Angel Donovan? This soft-spoken, almost shy girl who confessed vulnerabilities and mistakes to him? Who kissed so sweetly? Or the flirtatious party girl, wise to the ways of men and who gave as good as she took? Or the girl who met every dare and backed down from no challenge? Or the free spirit of a minute ago, jumping into the water fully clothed?

He grabbed a sheet of canvas from the back of the truck and shook off the dirt then folded it and covered the front seats with it.

All the way to Matt's ranch, silence filled the pickup. When Angel got out, she looked pale, maybe a little shaken. Neither one of them said a word.

Timm left so quickly he sprayed gravel, crazy desperate to get to town, to his newspaper office, to normal life. Man, oh, man, how was he supposed to rid his memory of the taste of Angel?

He needed to screw his head back on and reinforce his priorities, his goals. He needed to get out on that date with Becca.

ON TUESDAY MORNING, Matt had to pick up supplies in town, so Angel hitched a ride with him so she could buy groceries. It was the least she could do considering they were letting her stay free of charge.

Yesterday's lunch with Timm had unsettled her. His kiss had been charming, without passion or heat, but so warm and tender. She didn't think she'd ever been kissed so sweetly. How did he make love? The same way?

Stop that right now.

She didn't need to think about that kind of thing.

"You're preoccupied today, sis. What's going on?"

"Nothing. I'm fine. Just a little tired." As if to prove her point, she yawned.

"Was that Timm Franck's truck I saw leaving our yard? Were you out with him?"

"We had lunch, that's all. It was no biggie."

When Matt didn't respond, she glanced at him.

He was watching her, quietly, steadily. "You could do a lot worse than Timm. He's a solid guy."

"I already told you, Matt. I'm not staying in Ordinary. There is *nothing* going on between us."

"Okay. If you say so." He pulled into a parking spot on Main. Angel saw Missy step out of Sweet Talk, she jumped out of the truck and ran across the street.

"Meet me here in an hour," she heard Matt call.

Mama saw her and stopped. Oh, her face. What was going on inside her? She looked sad and happy and angry all at the same time—much the way Angel felt.

Her smile felt so tentative, as though she didn't trust that her own mother would even acknowledge her.

Missy turned and hurried away.

"Mama, wait!"

Missy picked up speed.

Angel ran after her. "Mama, you can't ignore me."

"Yes, she can." Phil's voice came from behind Angel. "You keep away from my woman."

She turned. The malevolence on his face unnerved her—and she wasn't a woman who scared easily.

Phil showed none of the gloating or sense of victory that Angel expected to see. Rather, he seemed fearful.

She understood his animosity, but his fear? He was days away from marrying Missy and getting what he wanted. So what was the fear about?

With a final glare, he followed Missy.

Angel ran to Timm's office.

He was the last person she wanted after the way lunch had ended. But he'd taught her how to fight smart physically. Could he do the same mentally?

Her knee-jerk reaction was to come out swinging verbally and that hadn't worked; in fact, it had made the situation worse.

She entered the office and stopped cold.

Timm stood behind the counter, reading something. He looked good, calm and collected and cool even on this hot day.

His shirt was buttoned to his neck, though, and she wished she could convince him to open a couple of buttons. It wasn't going to shock the townspeople for them to see a couple of inches of his scars.

He would be more comfortable.

His comfort had nothing to do with her, though. His life, his welfare, were none of her business.

When she stepped to the counter, he looked up. His mouth fell open ever so slightly and again she remembered his lips on hers.

He shuttered his expression and she couldn't tell what he was thinking.

Here goes nothing. She didn't know whether he would agree to it, but she had no computer here and she needed help.

"Can I ask you to help me with something? You're good at research, right?"

He nodded.

"How can I find out if there is any kind of dirt on Phil? Obviously being honest with Mama wasn't enough to send Phil packing. So I need something else. How do I find out his background?"

Timm smiled, slowly and with warmth. "Now you're talking." He indicated she should join him.

He sat her at his computer and showed her how to do an advanced search, how to dig through public records. They found out where Phil had been born, how old he was. That surprised Angel. He was ten years younger than Mama, but his demeanor made him seem much older.

For the next hour, they searched the internet for any and all info about Phil but came up empty.

Finally, Timm said, "Angel, I have to quit for today. I still have work to do for tomorrow's paper."

She jumped out of his chair. "Of course. I wasn't thinking. Sorry I wasted your time."

"You didn't waste my time. I think this is a really smart way to deal with that guy. There's still more we can do, but not today."

She walked to the front door.

"They're getting married this weekend, right?" Timm asked.

"On Friday."

"Do you want me to conduct an investigation or do you want to come over tomorrow morning and I'll show you how to do it?"

"I'll come in the morning. I want to know how."

His nod looked like approval and Angel knew she shouldn't feel good about it, but she did.

ON TUESDAY EVENING, the town gathered again, this time for the candidates' debate.

Max had wanted to hold it over the lunch hour, but Timm insisted on the evening, because it made sense for all of the working people in town and on ranches.

He suspected that Max wanted to meet earlier rather than later so he could guarantee his sobriety. Even if it was unfair of him, Timm hoped Max wouldn't be as sharp in the evening as he would be at noon.

As the current mayor, Derick called the meeting to order. Timm spoke on the issues first.

"This is what I see needs to be done to make our town the best it can be, to benefit the most people.

"You know how I feel about Chester's Roadhouse,

and we had last week's meeting, so there's no point in reiterating what was said.

"The next issue that needs to be addressed is our understaffed police force. Cash and Williams are overworked. They work twelve-hour days six days a week and are on call if anything happens on Sunday. I don't know of anyone else who works so hard in or for this town. It's nearly impossible for an officer to have a normal family life with that kind of time commitment. And since Chester's opened, their workload has increased.

"My first job as mayor would be to hire two more officers. A town of 8,000 needs that many to ensure we are protected and the townspeople feel safe and secure."

Timm enumerated the smaller issues of garbage and recycling collection, and of how to deal with the rise in the raccoon population in and around town.

Then it was Max's turn to speak.

He addressed the issue of hiring police officers. "That's going to cost the taxpayers. We're not a big community. I'd like to know where my esteemed colleague thinks he'll find the money.

"If the officers are certified by the Montana Public Safety Officer Standards and Training Council, they're next to impossible to persuade to relocate to a small town. If we have to send the candidates to the Law Enforcement Academy in Helena for POST certification, we need to come up with the money to pay for it. And chances are they'll be stolen from us to work in another town that offers incentives that we can't."

Max had obviously forgotten that it was possible to have prospective recruits sign agreements guaranteeing they would either work in the town upon graduation or pay back their training fees. That was one small mistake on Max's part. Thanks to the *Ordinary Citizen,* the people of Ordinary were kept up-to-date on current issues. Many of them would know that Max was wrong on this detail.

One point in Timm's favor.

Financing two more salaries, as well as the training, could be problematic, but Timm was banking on his fellow townspeople feeling as he did—that safety and security were more important than a possible tax hike.

If he was wrong about that, well, then…he probably wouldn't be elected as mayor. He didn't want to win because his opponent didn't deserve to, but he had enough confidence in himself to know that he deserved the job and would do it well.

The question period lasted far too long and, of course, the issue of Chester's Roadhouse was raised, but nothing new was said on either side, and nothing was settled about it.

By the time the meeting ended, Timm was exhausted. He hadn't slept well last night, had dreamed of Angel. Or rather, he'd spent too many hours trying *not* to dream of her.

He'd kept his cool during her visit to his office, but not without a tremendous effort. She'd had none of her sass today, only her worry for her mother. And that vulnerability made her too human, too likeable.

Before leaving the hall, he ran a gauntlet of supporters and those who took issue with his ideas. There were some who wanted to congratulate him on his book.

Hank Shelter fell into that last group. "I finished it late last night. Loved it. You did real well."

"I lost sleep over that book, too," Gladys Graves-

Wright said. "I wasn't born here, and now I feel that I know the citizens and understand the town better."

Reverend Wright shook his hand. "Had to fight Gladys to be able to read any of it. Got a good start today and it's wonderful, son."

"Thank you, Gladys. Reverend."

It went on and on, with person after person congratulating him. Apparently, the book had been the talk of the town in the diner today because many had started reading immediately after the signing.

Speechless and a little overwhelmed by the response, Timm finally reached the back door. Angel stood outside as though waiting for him.

"I thought you'd be at work," he said.

"Chester let me come to hear the debate."

"I wouldn't have guessed you'd be interested in politics."

Angel smiled, but not as brightly as usual. He wondered if, like him, she was wary because of that kiss.

"As I said before, the great smarty-pants reporter doesn't know everything about me," she said. "You were right in there. This town does need more cops."

"I plan to fix that if I'm elected."

"Your chances are looking really good."

"Thanks. Listen, I was thinking. Wednesdays are busy for me because of getting the paper out. Why don't you come in on Thursday morning and we can investigate Phil further?"

"You deliver the papers yourself?"

"No, I couldn't keep up. I've hired a couple of people to do it."

An awkward silence ensued. They'd run out of things to say to each other. Maybe his efforts to not feel attraction toward Angel were jamming his brain. It seemed she was trying to keep a polite distance, too, and it was strange to see Angel aloof when she was the kind of person to jump right in to everything.

"See you on Thursday," Timm finally said.

"Yeah," Angel replied, and walked toward the bar.

AT SEVEN ON WEDNESDAY evening, Timm picked up Becca Hardy. She wore a plain cotton dress and carried a beige cardigan. She looked nice. Her hair was cut short and conservatively. A faint trace of mascara dotted her eyelashes.

In every way, she was unexceptional and Timm supposed that was a good thing for the future mayor of Ordinary, if he won Monday's election.

No one could ever find fault with Becca.

On the drive to Haven, he wracked his brain for things to say to her. "How do you like working at the post office?"

"I like it." Becca said nothing else.

Had they exhausted that avenue already?

"I guess it's not too busy at this time of year?"

"No."

"Bad at Christmas, though?"

"Uh-huh. The rush starts in November. People send parcels for Christmas."

"Yeah, my mom sends presents to relatives in Germany."

"I know. I weigh them and add the postage for her."

"Oh."

That was it. They'd finished with that topic, unless Timm wanted to ask her how much his mother spent on postage every year.

He glanced at Becca. She was staring out the window.

Her fingers were clasped together in her lap and he realized she was nervous.

"Do you go on dates very often?" he asked.

"No. Never. Nobody asks me out."

"I don't go out much, either. Maybe we can both relax and enjoy each other. Okay?"

She let out a sigh. "That sounds good."

"Tell me what kinds of things you like to do when you aren't weighing packages at work."

She smiled shyly and started to talk about her hobbies, one of which was knitting. He didn't think young women did that anymore, but apparently, he was wrong.

He took her to a steak house in Haven and they had a nice dinner. They talked a lot, laughed a little and learned to relax with each other.

When he dropped her off at home, he asked whether she would see him again. She agreed and they made arrangements for Saturday night.

He parked his truck behind the newspaper offices and entered his apartment. He dropped his keys onto a hall table and stared at them, lost in a vague sense of dissatisfaction.

He wandered to the front window and checked out Chester's. The usual crowd stood outside, smoking, or smoking up.

Although he tried, he couldn't help but compare tonight with the lunch with Angel by the creek. It was unfair, really, to put Becca up against Angel's vibrancy.

He'd had more fun in those couple of hours with Angel than he'd remembered having in years.

At 1:30 a.m., when he realized he was watching for

Angel to come out of the bar, he turned away from the window, disgusted with himself.

All the more reason to stop these thoughts of Angel and date Becca again.

CHAPTER TEN

ON THURSDAY MORNING at eleven, Angel walked into the newspaper offices to find Timm behind the counter.

"Did you get the stuff done that you needed to do yesterday?"

"Yep," he answered. "Let's get started."

"What do we do now?"

"Today, we'll find out where Phil's from. Then we'll check out divorce records from that state."

"You think he might have been married?"

"Maybe. If he was, we can talk to his ex to find out more about him."

"How do you know an ex would talk?"

"If they're bitter about the divorce, they fall all over themselves to tell us how rotten the guy was."

"What if she still loves him?"

"Then I'll say I'm old coworker who wants to pay off a debt. I'll chat her up then try to find out any info I can about his past life."

"You can be that sneaky?"

"When I'm investigating a story that should be told, you bet."

"Good to know."

"I've got more time today, so let's check the things we should have started with. There are all kinds of public records available to us. We'll use federal records as a conduit to national organizations and agencies that are easier and faster to deal with than the federal government."

Two hours later, with Timm using his impressive research skills, they hit gold.

"Look at that. He's Hal's half brother. It's no accident that he's here."

"Damn. He targeted Mama. I'll bet he wants Hal's money."

"Uh-huh. He's been married. I'm going to call her." He dialed the ex's number in Maine.

Angel listened while he charmed her. The man had depths and skills she would have never guessed he possessed.

She waited on tenterhooks for him to finish the call. The longer he talked, the more smug his smile looked.

When he hung up, she asked, "What did you find out?"

He didn't answer, but he emanated an energy that hadn't been there when she'd walked in this morning.

Reaching around her, he typed a name into the Google page and came up with an old newspaper article about Phil, but under an assumed name.

"That's why we didn't find anything the other day." The photo was definitely Phil, though.

"The former wife was bitter," Timm said. "He fooled around on her, bilking this other woman in another part of the state out of thousands of dollars. He served time for it."

Angel read the article. "Gotcha!"

He printed the article and handed it to her.

She turned and nearly bumped noses with him. He was studying her in his quiet, intent way. Up close, she could see the darker brown flecks in his eyes.

He had kind eyes. Intelligent eyes.

"Your cheeks turn pink when you're excited," he whispered.

Remembering his chaste kiss of the other day, and of how refreshing it had been, she stared at his lips, leaned forward and rested her own mouth on his. He tasted sweet.

With the tip of her tongue, she traced his lips and learned their curves. For a split second, his tongue came out to play.

She ended the kiss and stared at him, so closely she could almost count every eyelash, could study his broad, intelligent brow frankly, without sneaking glances at him. He smelled like the outdoors. He was clean-shaven, so he must use aftershave, but whatever it was, it didn't overpower.

The heat rolled from him in waves, melting away her resistance. The chill that Angel had felt since Mama had kicked her out thawed a little.

He touched the side of her face, ran his long fingers into her hair. He nudged her head closer, slowly, as though afraid she would bolt like a skittish horse.

No. No running today. She wanted his touch, wanted how uncomplicated he was compared to Phil.

Timm's breath caressed her face then his lips were on hers, but he didn't hesitate this time as he had before. He moved quickly, delved into her mouth with his tongue, and she welcomed it.

His hand cradled her head, held it close so she wouldn't back away, but she couldn't have if she'd tried. She wrapped her fingers around his wrists to keep him there with her.

She wanted this, had been thinking about it for days.

His tongue danced in her mouth, dueled with her own and spoke more eloquently than he did with words.

Maybe she should give in, drag him upstairs to his room and have her way with him, lean into his hard body and meld with him, become one, so her loneliness could take a hike for a few minutes.

But no. Her dreams called to her.

Get away from Ordinary. Start fresh somewhere else. You can't change what this town thinks of you. It's too late.

It's too hard.

She pulled away slowly, reluctantly, and leaned her forehead against his shoulder so he wouldn't look into her eyes and see her fear. So he wouldn't know her for the coward she was. What if she couldn't change? What if she dragged him down with her instead of him pulling her out of the gutter?

She wanted to be whole and good.

Timm desired her, yes, but did he *like* her?

"I should go," she whispered, taking the sheet of paper from his hand, where he'd crushed it in his fist.

She smoothed the creases, folded it and slipped it into her jeans pocket.

He forced her chin up to look into her eyes. She wasn't sure how much he saw. His expression was closed, wary, as though he thought *she* might not like *him.* But she did. Oh, she did.

How had that happened? She'd barely remembered him her first night here, and a week and a half later she wanted to hold on to him, to beg him to teach her how to be herself with no worries about what anyone thought of her. To be simply…Angel.

She watched him swallow. "Yeah," he said, and eased away from her. She could breathe normally again.

The outside world returned. A car gunned an engine on Main Street and Angel realized that anyone could have walked in while they were kissing and would have thought that Angel was up to her old tricks. Of course, they couldn't see inside her. They couldn't look into her heart and know that what she shared with Timm was so much better than tricks.

That had always been the problem. Who she was on the outside was so far removed from who she was on the inside.

And what exactly is in your heart, Angel, where Timm is concerned?

Affection. Wonder. Terror.

She needed to leave. She unintentionally sent the chair skidding across the floor when she rose.

"Thank you," she stammered. "I'll go tell Mama about this."

She stood suspended while he stared at her with eyes a shade cooler than they had been a minute ago. No wonder. She blew hot and cold.

Under his unwavering stare, she turned to leave but pulled up short.

Mrs. Franck stood in the doorway.

How much had she seen?

Angel nodded to her and left—ran away, really— leaving Timm to deal with whatever fallout there might be.

Timm STARED AT HIS mother.

How much had she seen?

Judging by the look of disappointment on her face, enough.

"Mama—"

She approached the counter. "Why?"

He shrugged because, honestly, he didn't have an answer. He didn't know what drove him where Angel was concerned.

"Didn't you go out with that sweet Hardy girl last night?"

"Yes."

"So why are you fooling around with that— Well, I don't need to say what she is. We both know."

"She's not what everyone thinks she is."

Ma looked at him with such pity. "So like a man to be taken in by a woman like that."

That got his back up. He didn't think he'd been *taken in* by Angel. Unless he missed his guess, she was every bit as confused as he was.

"What about becoming mayor? Have you given up on that?"

"No. Of course not."

"What will people think if you go around with her?" Ma looked over her shoulder as though to make sure that Angel was really gone, was no longer tainting the office with her presence.

Shades of Uncle Derick. "The people of Ordinary will be fine with this." Whatever *this* was. "Have you been talking to Uncle Derick?"

"He was worried about you."

"For the love of— I'm not a child the two of you should be talking about behind my back." Timm scrubbed his hands over his face. "There's nothing going on with Angel."

"Then what did I just see?"

He blew out an exasperated breath, then said quietly, "A mistake."

"Yes, you can bet on that. A mistake, all right. At your father's newspaper, where anyone could see you."

Hot all over, he flushed with shame. She was right. If he and Angel had to do anything, it shouldn't have been here. He prided himself on being a professional, yet he'd kissed her in his office. Publicly.

"Why did you come here today?" he asked.

"To take you out for lunch. You said I should get out more."

He'd meant with other people.

"I don't want to now. I don't know how many people walked by the windows and saw this."

She turned and left and he felt about ten years old and two inches tall.

He'd done a stellar job of lifting his family's reputation out of the toilet, but had almost sent it back in. Who did see him and Angel kissing? Anyone?

Logically, he knew that the opinions of a few people shouldn't matter. But he also knew what his father and mother had fought for so hard throughout their married lives. They'd fought to renew his father's faith in himself, even though it had proven too ephemeral, too easily bruised by life.

They'd fought to earn a good living, to give their children a solid life in a town that respected them. Timm had no right to jeopardize any of that.

He'd said he had faith in the townspeople's good opinion of him, but what if he was wrong?

ANGEL STEPPED INTO Mama's house—evidence in hand—and found Missy and Phil at the kitchen table.

"What are you doing here?" Phil asked. "Your mama kicked you out."

Angel didn't say a word, didn't provoke him, didn't call him names. There was no need. She knew she would win this time. The sense of power Timm had given her felt amazing. *This* was the way to do things. Know your position and don't back down.

Silently, she took the folded article out of her pocket and handed it to Missy.

Missy frowned but read it. As she finished, she looked at Phil with a question in her eyes.

He didn't see it at first because he was staring at Angel with naked hatred. When he did finally figure out that his future wife was watching him, he turned his attention to her, and his eyes widened.

"Is this true?" Missy asked, her voice laden with disappointment.

Phil grabbed the article, read it and threw it onto the table.

"I was framed."

"By a middle-aged woman? Look at her picture. She doesn't look smart enough to frame you. How much did you take from her, Phil?"

"Listen, it's all lies."

"How much?" Mama shouted.

Mama was angry with Phil and shouting at him. Hallelujah. Praise be.

"You'd rather believe this filth than take my word?" Phil was blustering and so obviously fighting a losing battle. Mama might be naive, but she believed once she saw proof.

"He's Hal's half brother, Mama," Angel said into the dense tension clouding the air in the room.

Phil surged out of his seat and roared, "You shut up."

Angel stiffened, ready to use one of Timm's self-defense moves if she had to.

"Is it true?" Missy asked.

"Yeah, it's true." Phil's mouth twisted. "Hal got the

good dad and I got the deadbeat. I was his only living relative. Why did he leave everything to you?"

"Because I nursed him until he died," Missy said. "He once told me he had a brother who hadn't spoken to him in years. Did you know he tried to find you? Gave a letter to a law firm to try to get hold of you? He wanted to tell you he was dying."

Something crafty shimmered in Phil's eyes, something he tried to hide, but wasn't fast enough.

Missy saw it and stood. "You did know. That letter reached you. That's how you found me. All of the eating? The sex three times a day?"

Angel blushed.

"What's all that about, Phil?" Missy pressed.

"There was never enough food. Enough of anything. I can't get…enough." Phil cast a bewildered look around the room, like a little boy who'd lost his mother. "Let me stay."

"Leave," she said.

"Maybe I started out wanting to take advantage of you, but I grew to love you. Honest, Missy."

Oh God, Mama, don't give in.

"It's too late. I don't believe you now, Phil." Mama didn't melt, simply pointed to the bedroom she shared with Phil and said, "Pack up."

Angel had never been more impressed by her.

Phil's expression turned hard as he stormed out of the room.

Angel hugged Missy. "I'm proud of you."

Missy rested her head on Angel's shoulder. When she backed away a minute later, there were tears shimmering in her eyes.

"Are you okay, Mama?"

"I will be. Soon." She tried to smile and Angel knew it would take her a while to get over this.

Ten minutes later, Phil stomped out of the bedroom with a suitcase in one hand and a laptop in the other.

"You'll regret this, Missy. You'll see. You're gonna miss me."

"For a little while, Phil, yes, I will," Mama said. "Goodbye."

Mama stood with quiet dignity while Phil waffled, while it appeared he searched for one last argument to salvage his position, but Missy's gaze never wavered.

Phil had lost.

"At least drive me to the bus stop."

"Walk."

He left the house. A minute later, the garage door screeched.

"Hey," Angel yelled. "He's going to steal the car."

When she started to run for the back door, Missy laid a restraining hand on her arm.

"Let him go. He can have it."

"But, Mama—"

"Angel, let him go."

Angel cocked her head and studied Missy. "Why?"

"Because he wasn't all bad. We did have some good times together."

"But—"

Missy shook her head.

"You're being too fair, Mama. Too nice." But it was her choice, wasn't it? "Okay."

Clearly Missy was barely holding herself together. Angel had done this to her, had broken her heart. Would Mama have been better off if Timm and Angel hadn't dug around in Phil's business?

No. Angel knew she'd done the right thing, but, oh, she wished she hadn't hurt her mother so much.

She stepped forward and wrapped her arms around her. "I'm so sorry," she whispered.

"It's okay, honey. You did the right thing."

On impulse, Angel blurted, "Mama, I love you," and meant it. Despite the hardship of growing up as Missy's daughter in Ordinary, Angel had to admit how much she loved this woman.

"I love you, too, Angel."

LATE THURSDAY NIGHT, Angel poured another in an endless stream of drafts. Her feet hurt. Her back ached.

At least tonight she didn't have to serve as well as pour drinks. Karen and Jessica were waiting the tables.

A shout from behind her drew her attention.

She turned in time to see a huge man pick up a smaller man and throw him onto one of the tables. Glass flew everywhere and people jumped out of chairs and scattered.

Oh, for Pete's sake.

More and more, she began to agree with Timm. This kind of thing couldn't continue.

The smaller man reared up with a flash of steel in his hand and slashed at the larger man.

Chester came out to the bar and grabbed his bat, took Angel by the arm and propelled her down the hallway.

"Chester, this is getting ridiculous."

"Yeah."

These fights were getting old. Angel wanted to be gone, like, yesterday, but Mama… She couldn't leave until she was sure Mama was okay.

"Get into my office and lock the door," Chester

said. "I'm not taking chances with you tonight. Don't let anyone in but me, y'hear?"

Angel nodded.

"Those people can kill themselves and each other, but I'm not letting them touch you. Missy would kill me."

At another shout, he shoved her into his office.

Angel slammed the door and locked it.

She listened to the fighting, muffled by the thick door. Eventually, someone knocked and she startled.

"Angel, it's me. Open up."

Chester.

She threw open the door. Gasping, she covered her mouth with her palm.

Chester half carried, half dragged Rem into the room. Rem had his hand pressed against his abdomen and blood seeped between his fingers.

"Oh, my God," Angel whispered.

"Close the door behind us," he yelled above the sounds of violence from the bar.

"What happened?"

"He got himself stabbed protecting Jessica."

Chester put Rem on the cot against the far wall and Rem fell onto his back. "See what you can do for him. Call the cops."

He ran out and Angel locked the door again.

She dove for the phone on the desk. "I need an ambulance at the Roadhouse. Rem Caldwell's been stabbed. We're in the back in Chester's office."

She placed the handset on the desk and hit the speaker button, leaving the line open in case she needed to tell the dispatcher more.

Rem moaned, mobilizing her into action. Angel might not like blood, but she could try to make Rem more comfortable.

On her knees on the floor beside Rem on the cot, she checked out his injury. It looked bad.

She rummaged through a closet and pulled out a flannel shirt. It smelled clean. She searched through Chester's desk until she found scissors and cut the shirt into strips for binding.

Angel folded the largest piece to make a thick bandage and pressed it against the wound.

Rem groaned.

"Rem, can you hear me?"

He nodded. "Hurts."

"Okay, I'm pressing a bandage against your wound. That's why it's hurting so much."

"Stop."

"Can't. Apply pressure while I bind it in place with strips."

She took his closest hand and placed it on the bandage. His hand was covered with blood and she had to avert her gaze.

"Rem, hold this tightly so I can bind it. Can you hear me?" She pressed his hand down on the wadded fabric. "Got it? That's what I need you to do. Okay?"

"'Kay."

Angel wrapped the flannel strips around Rem's torso, eliciting moans from him every time she had to pass it underneath him, and hoped like crazy that she wasn't doing him any harm.

Angel heard the dispatcher's voice say that Cash and Williams should be there.

Maybe, Angel thought, or maybe not. There was still a lot of noise.

Angel rested her hand on Rem's shoulder and he stirred.

"How do you feel?" she asked.

"Got run over…Mack truck." He tried to stand but Angel pressed on his shoulder.

"Don't move."

"What happened?" His gaze flew around the room as though there might still be danger around.

"One of the bikers stabbed you."

"That door locked?" Rem asked.

"Yep," Angel replied. "No one's getting in here unless we let them in."

Rem closed his eyes. "You think Chester has…whiskey in here?"

"Probably," Angel said, "but you're not getting any. The ambulance should be here any minute."

"Lot of pain."

Angel wiped sweat from his forehead with a scrap of flannel. "I know."

When Rem opened his eyes, Angel said, "You were trying to protect one of the waitresses. You're so brave."

Rem's mouth twisted into a wry smile. "Must have me confused with someone else."

His words were becoming more slurred.

What if he was going into shock. What should she do for shock? Rem started to shiver.

Okay. Keep him warm.

Finding a blanket on the top shelf of the closet, she covered Rem with it.

She grabbed a bedsheet and folded it in two and covered him with that, as well, but the shakes were getting bad.

A knock on the door startled her. "Who is it?"

"Timm Franck."

Angel opened the door and Timm rushed in.

"Are you okay?" he asked, clasping Angel's upper arms. His gaze roamed her body. "Did anyone hurt you?

TIMM SEARCHED HER for injury. The trail of blood in the hall had almost stopped his heart.

"Damn this place to hell and back."

Angel appeared to be all right. "You're sure you're all right?"

Angel nodded.

A moan from the other side of the room caught his attention. Rem lay on a cot, his face as white as death.

"Rem," he whispered. Nothing else would come out. He strode to the cot and leaned over. "Rem?"

Rem didn't open his eyes.

"He's been stabbed," Angel said.

"Stabbed?" Timm knelt on the floor beside Rem. "Rem, buddy…"

Rem opened his eyes, barely, and saw Timm.

"How're you doing?"

Rem closed his eyes and a crooked smile crept onto his lips. "Been better."

"I guess."

Timm's throat felt raw, his collar tight. He turned to Angel. "What happened?"

"Chester said he tried to stop someone from hurting one of the waitresses."

"He would." He squeezed Rem's shoulder. "We'll take care of you, buddy. You'll be fine."

Timm rushed out to the bar to search for Sara. She was here somewhere. When they'd heard the sirens, ever practical in a crisis, she'd grabbed a first-aid kit from the house and had run over with him. Upon arrival they had helped to sort the injured according to levels of severity.

He located her kneeling beside one of the bikers, who was sitting on the floor against the wall, nursing a gash on his forehead.

Another biker sat nearby with his arm already in a sling.

"Sara," Timm said, "we need you in the back."

"I can't go right now. I need to take care of this."

Timm bent forward until they were eye to eye, placed a firm hand on her shoulder and said quietly, "Come with me *now*."

She sent him a look of pure exasperation, folded a bandage and handed it to the biker. "Press this hard against that wound to control the bleeding."

She strode toward the rear, saying over her shoulder, "This had better be important, Timm, or I'm—"

Sara stopped abruptly inside the doorway of the office. After a moment's hesitation she moved farther into the room. She'd gone pale. His sister, the most calm person he knew, stood frozen staring at Rem.

"What happened?" she asked, her voice barely a whisper.

Timm repeated Angel's story.

He nudged Sara forward. She was training to be a nurse. She had skill. Rem needed her.

At Timm's urging, she bent over Rem and looked at his wound, checking the bandage Angel had improvised.

"I hope I did all right," Angel said.

"Yes," Sara whispered, and her voice sounded weak.

Rem heard her and opened his eyes. Timm saw a brightness behind the pain that hadn't been present for either him or Angel. Rem reached his hand toward her face and smiled. "Sara."

"Rem," Sara whispered. "Oh, you foolish man. Next time, let the sheriff take care of things."

Rem touched her cheek. Through a haze of pain, all he could think was, *She came. She came for me. If I'd known that, I would have gotten myself stabbed a long time ago.*

"Honey, you're here." All he wanted to do was hold her, but his arms were so weak.

He managed to snag one hand around her neck to pull her close. "Hey," he said. "You're the woman I'm gonna marry." He grinned, but man, oh, man, it felt sloppy.

The pain in his gut was clouding his vision and turning different colors. It had started out red, but was changing to purple.

"Trouble...seeing your face." He blinked.

Something wet hit his face. Sara was crying. For him. For no good, unreliable Rem.

"Aw, honey, don't cry."

She swiped her hands across her cheeks. She was crying for him.

"You like me," he whispered.

"No, I don't."

"You love me."

She didn't answer, but the tears fell faster. Bingo. Sara Franck loved Rem Caldwell.

His hand fell away from her neck and he closed his eyes. The pain turned black.

TIMM STEPPED CLOSE. "He's unconscious. Where the hell is the ambulance?"

Sara ran out of the room and Timm chased her into the hall.

"Sara, what's wrong?"

The skin around her lips had turned white.

"Are you all right?" he asked.

She nodded then shook her head and looked around wildly until she saw a bathroom. She headed for it and slammed the door behind her.

Timm wondered if she even realized that it was the men's washroom. Why would it matter anyway?

A commotion from the back door caught his attention. A pair of paramedics. At last.

"In here." He directed them into the office.

Timm and Angel got out of their way.

One paramedic checked the bandage and asked, "Who did this?"

Angel raised a hand away from her side. "Me."

"You did a good job. You arrested the bleeding." He worked quickly over Rem.

"Is he going to be okay?" Angel asked.

"Don't know. Hope so."

"When you get to the hospital, you make sure they take care of him before any of those bikers. Rem's worth twenty of them." Her expression was hard.

The paramedic nodded. "I hear you." He spoke into a radio, asking for a stretcher in the back room.

When it arrived, they lifted Rem onto it so carefully he made no sound of protest.

On his way out, one of the paramedics asked, "How much has he had to drink? Anyone know?"

"I pulled him four drafts and a couple of shots of whiskey," Angel answered, "but I don't know whether he had anything at home before he came in."

"He's going to be sorry he had so much. We can't give him medication with that much in his system." He frowned. "That wound's going to hurt like crazy once the alcohol wears off."

He squeezed Angel's hand. "You did good."

After they left the room, Timm asked, "How can you remember how many drinks you served Rem? Judging by the number of bodies out there, the place was packed. You must have been busy as hell serving."

"Rem's been in here every night drinking too much. I've been watching him." He took her hands in his to stop them from shaking. "I've been worried about him. If I could have gotten away with it, I would have watered down his beer. He would have noticed, though."

She looked at him with such a plea in her eyes that he felt compelled to say something. "This wasn't your fault. Rem should be in control of his own life."

It seemed ironic that Timm was defending her serving his best buddy drinks, while he held Chester responsible for every drink his dad poured down his throat.

Now was not the time to figure that out.

Angel said no more and followed the emergency personnel out.

Obviously, she cared about Rem, worried about him as much as Timm did.

He remembered what he hadn't earlier. Rem and Angel had dated in high school. Rem, the James Dean of the new century, and Angel, the baddest bad girl in town, and the prettiest, had looked stunning together.

Timm walked away before he started imagining how good they'd been together. He steered clear of asking himself why it hurt so much to remember it.

Sara emerged from the bathroom.

"Are you okay?" he asked.

She nodded.

"You don't look okay."

"I am." She sounded stronger than she had earlier, so he had to take her word for it.

He trailed her into the bar.

"Come on," he said. "I'll drive us to the hospital."

The fact that she came docilely rather than insisting on taking care of more injuries, as well as the fact that she left her precious first-aid kit behind, stood testament to her weakened state.

CHAPTER ELEVEN

ANOTHER MAN GONE.

Missy sat in her dark living room and stared at the streetlight shining through the sheers.

Despite not loving Phil, she missed him tonight, even his crappy lovemaking. Anything was better than this loneliness, this utter aloneness. She heard the faint sound of sirens on Main Street—something happening at Chester's again. As long as her baby kept safe, Missy didn't care who else got hurt.

Angel would be gone soon. Any day now.

So, Missy, what are you gonna do? Feel sorry for yourself the rest of your life?

She stood and wandered the rooms of the small house. This was all hers. She had enough cash to live on and enough stuff to keep her happy. She had every reason to be content.

And yet, no one thought of her tonight. No one missed her the way she missed others, even her rotten mama. What had ever happened to her? After she'd left, Missy had never heard from her again. She could still be alive, for all Missy knew. Or she could be dead.

Sitting on the side of her bed, she touched the spot where Phil had slept every night and most afternoons.

Let this be a lesson to you, Missy. It isn't true that any warm body is a good body.

Starting tonight, she was going to learn to live alone.

To *be* alone. It wouldn't be easy, maybe a lot like giving up a drug habit.

Although tempted, she didn't call Phil's cell phone.

She wouldn't.

It wouldn't be easy.

She hung her head.

It wasn't easy.

AT THE HOSPITAL, Timm learned that Rem had been taken into surgery. He and Sara found seats in the waiting room, uncertain how long they'd be there.

"What's going on inside that hard head of yours?" There was something behind her set jaw and hard eyes.

She glanced at him. "Nothing."

He bumped her with his arm. "Come on. This is me, your big brother. Talk to me."

"I—I don't know what to say."

"Sara Franck doesn't have an opinion about something? Is speechless? Is there a solar eclipse outside or something?"

The corner of her mouth kicked up in the barest glimmer of a smile.

"It was an accident, Sara. It happened a long time ago."

There was no need to clarify for her that he meant the birthday party. They waited for Rem, after all.

"I know."

"In your mind, maybe, but there's still a lot of emotion in you around Rem. Don't be angry with him. He's lost right now. He'll find his way."

"Yeah? How long does it take a man to grow up?"

He remembered Sara as a sweet happy girl. That had all changed after he'd been burned. In shock and overwhelmed by doctors and hospitals and his parents' grief, he'd been unable to help her.

He'd been an active kid, but all activity had stopped and that had been the beginning of his watching years.

He put his arm across Sara's shoulders. Besides his mother and Finn, Sara and Rem were the two people who mattered most to him and he wanted them happy. Unfortunately, neither were, and once again he felt helpless.

"Don't hate him," he whispered.

"I don't," she said with a tremble in her voice, and lay her head on his shoulder.

They sat in a pool of mournful silence, surrounded by others waiting for loved ones, unaware of their conversations, still struggling with an old problem that had never let them go.

Had never let Sara go, at any rate. He'd done pretty well.

Two hours later, a doctor walked through the doors leading to the working parts of the hospital.

"Anyone here for Remington Caldwell?" he asked.

Timm and Sara stood so quickly she dropped her purse.

"We are. I'm Timm Franck. This is my sister, Sara." Timm shook the doctor's hand. "How is he?"

"He's stable now. He'll be fine in time, but will need care for a while."

He blew out a gusty breath. "Thank God."

"Tell me how long he'll be here and what kind of care he'll need at home." Sara spoke with her customary take-charge tone and he was relieved to see her rally. He knew Rem would be in good hands. If anyone could help Rem to heal, it would be Sara.

Timm smiled to himself. Sara would *force* Rem to heal if she had to.

"Can we see him?" Sara asked.

"He's asleep in intensive care," the surgeon said. "Trust me. He'll be fine. Go home and get some sleep and come back tomorrow."

It was 2:00 a.m. when he dropped Sara off. Tired, but unable to sleep, Timm then drove out to Matt's ranch.

He knew he was being crazy, that this was unwise, but he wanted to see Angel. She'd been so worried. He wanted her to know that Rem would recover in time, that he wasn't going to die.

He walked around the house. A soft glow shone from an upstairs bedroom window. He'd bet that was Angel's room, that she couldn't sleep, either.

Undecided for once in his life, he debated throwing a small stone at the window to get her attention. But if she'd fallen asleep, he didn't want to wake her. Or should he knock? And awaken the whole family?

He opted for a small stone. He searched the ground until he found one and, hoping he didn't put a hole in the window, tossed it up with enough force to make noise, but gently enough to protect the glass.

When Angel appeared in the window, he let out the breath he'd been holding. He needed to see her, to make sure she was okay—she'd had a rough night—but also, not sure why, he wanted to see her for himself.

He gestured for her to come down.

A minute later, the front-porch light went on and the door opened and there she stood.

She looked like a dream.

"I woke you. Sorry."

She shook her head. "No. I was lying down but I couldn't sleep."

She wore blue satin pajama pants and a rose tank top with tiny lace straps, without a bra. She was the prettiest woman he'd seen anywhere, bar none. No swimsuit model in any magazine, or woman on any beach in the Caribbean or on the Riviera had anything on Angel Donovan. It was as if God had said *Listen up all you Adams of the world, I know you thought Eve was pretty special, but I've made some improvements.*

So what do you think?

Timm liked. He really, really liked.

The rose color of her top warmed her cheeks, so pink against her white skin. As always, she was striking in her contrasts. Sunlight skin and midnight hair. Her mane hung down her back, fell around her face in a messy tousle that begged to be touched. One strand had fallen forward over her shoulder and curled around her breast like a hand cupping a treasure.

She pushed her hair away from her face. "I couldn't sleep," she repeated, as if she was as nervous as he, but why? He had no idea why his own nerves were running laps through his body as though he were a race course.

"I don't think I will, either," he said, and meant it. What a night.

The close-fitting tank top nipped in at Angel's waist and the loose waistband of her pants sat low on her full hips.

She had incredibly tiny angel wings tattooed on either side of her belly button. In pink. He'd never seen anything so sweet or so hot.

She tugged on the hem of her tank top to cover her tattoo.

His gaze slid to her breasts, flattened ever so slightly

by the top, but not hiding that her nipples had grown hard while he'd stared.

She *liked* him looking? Her body did, at any rate.

He swallowed but unfortunately the Gobi desert had blown into his mouth. "I thought you might be worried about Rem."

Her eyes looked deep, haunted. "Is he okay?"

"Yes," he answered and, because she looked so disturbed, wrapped her in his arms. "He had surgery and the doctor said he'll be okay. He'll need time to recover, though."

Her head fit perfectly under his chin, which he rested on the silken nest of her dark hair.

"Maybe he can stop drinking now," she murmured, returning his embrace.

"Yeah."

A moment later, she stepped away, probably because of the erection he couldn't seem to control. He wanted her. Not as the Angel Donovan who mesmerized men— okay, to be honest, still about that—but also as the sensitive woman who cared about people, about a boy she'd had an affair with as a teenager.

She leaned against the wall of the house with her hands behind her back. Maybe she wasn't as unaffected as she seemed.

"Angel?"

"I won't sleep with you. Not with any man from Ordinary. I'm leaving on Monday, or as soon as I'm sure that Mama is okay on her own."

"Leaving? Town?"

She nodded. "I always planned to, as soon as I got rid of Phil."

"I didn't know."

"I thought I'd told everyone. I guess I forgot to tell you."

No reason why she should have. It wasn't really any of his business.

This was—unexpected.

He couldn't— She wasn't home for good?

"Where are you going?"

"Maybe L.A. Maybe New York."

She was choosing New York over Ordinary. Now that he knew her better, he could understand why. She liked people. She held their safety dear. Rem had been one of many boyfriends, and yet, she worried about him. Not only about the stabbing, but also about his drinking, as she would an old friend.

Angel Donovan had a depth he had only guessed at in his adolescence. Had hoped was really there.

"I've been reading your book," she said. "It's really good."

He rested one hand high on the wall and concentrated on a crack in the wood siding. "You think so?"

"Yeah."

People had been calling, telling him they'd started the book and how much they liked it so far. For some reason, her opinion meant something to him.

"Can I ask you something?"

"Sure."

She stared at the veranda floor. "Why is everyone else in Ordinary in your book, but not me?"

"You noticed that?"

"Uh-huh."

"No particular reason."

"Was it that you didn't think I was worthy of mentioning?"

"God, no! Not at all." He couldn't tell her.

She watched him. He pulled his concentration away from the crack in the wall. Her eyes looked huge and full of resignation, as though she'd accepted a long time ago that she wasn't as worthy as the other members of her town.

"Seriously," he said. He was going to have to tell her. "I didn't want the whole world to know that I had a crush on you when I was a teenager."

"You did?" A bit of her Mona Lisa, I-have-female-power smile shone through the shyness of a minute ago. "Really?"

"Yes, really." He picked at that crack some more. "For a long time."

"For how long?" She wore a full-fledged smile and he wanted to get drunk on that smile.

Okay, the situation was edging toward being dangerous yet again and he stepped off the veranda.

Suddenly serious, she moved to touch him, but stopped. "Thanks for coming to tell me about Rem."

He nodded and left quickly because all he wanted was to drag her into his arms.

No, no, no. You need someone like Becca. Someone stable.

In the morning, Matt drove Angel to Missy's house.

When she entered the house, she called, "Mama?"

Missy came out of the living room and Angel rushed into her arms.

"Are you okay?"

Missy nodded and pulled back. "I'm good." Shadows haunted her eyes like dark ghosts.

"Did you sleep at all last night?" Angel gripped Mama's hands.

"Not too much, but I'm good. Honest. I'm glad you saved me from Phil."

"Me, too," Angel whispered.

"I was alone last night, but—"

The phone rang, startling both of them.

"Can you answer it, honey? Phil's been calling and I don't want to talk to him."

Angel answered the phone, but it was Timm.

"I called at the ranch and Jenny said you'd gone home."

"I'm going to spend the weekend with Mama."

"Good. Thought you should know there's a meeting in the Legion Hall in half an hour. It's about Chester's. People are angry. You might want to be there."

"You didn't mention a meeting last night."

"I didn't know. This wasn't planned. People just started arriving. I'm phoning as many townspeople as possible to keep them in the loop."

She hung up. Not wanting to leave Mama alone, Angel said, "There's a meeting in town about closing down Chester's. Do you want to come?"

"Yes." Missy pulled a comb through her hair and put on lipstick, then they walked toward the hall.

"Where have you been staying, honey?"

"With Matt and Jenny."

Missy nodded. "I'm glad you had them to turn to."

At the hall, they took seats in the back row. The noise level hurt her ears. Angel listened to the voices around her, many of them raised, most of them emotional.

Rem's mother, Nell, sat in the front row with Sara Franck, their heads bent close together, whispering furiously. Angel had heard Nell had had a stroke last summer and maybe she wasn't able to drive herself to the hospital. That was the only reason Angel could think of why Nell would be here and not at her son's side.

Angel liked Nell. She'd never looked down on Angel.

Timm, Cash and Derick stood on the stage and yelled to get control of the crowd. Cash whistled and conversations stopped. Once everyone settled, Timm opened the discussion.

"By now, all of you know what happened at Chester's last night."

Rumblings ran through the crowd like fire through underbrush. Angel searched the room for Chester, but he was conspicuous by his absence.

"I've said it before," Timm continued, "those bikers bring a level of violence we've never seen here before. We have no room for them in this town."

Cash spoke. "Timm, you're partly right. It's a handful of the bikers causing trouble and *that's* the problem. It isn't all of them and it isn't Chester. He's doing nothing illegal. His bar is legitimate. We can't close him down."

"We need to do something," Hank Shelter called out. "Rem is lucky he wasn't killed last night."

"Yeah," Max Golden yelled. "After last night, I'm with you on this, Timm. What's it going to take to get the place closed? The death of one of our citizens?"

Rumblings again, louder now, stronger.

"If we can't force Chester to close, then how about if we put together some kind of patrols?" Max raised his voice to be heard above the rising noise. "We can get men together to watch the bar."

"Count me in."

"I'll do it, too."

"Let's show them we won't be pushed around."

"Whoa. Slow down, everyone," Timm said. "There's no room in this town for vigilantes."

"We're only talking about protecting our people and our property."

"Max, you have no idea how quickly things can get out of hand." His was the voice of reason. Angel's chest swelled with pride, even if the man wasn't hers and never would be.

"All it would take is the smallest confrontation for the situation to escalate into even more violence. We're here today to figure out how to avoid more problems, not create them. I don't care if all of those bikers kill themselves and each other. How do we keep our citizens safe?" Timm's words seemed to defuse some of the tension.

"Timm is right," Cash said. "If we have citizens on patrol, one of you will get hurt. Guaranteed. Forget that idea. Got it?"

"What can we do, then?" Max called.

"I'll talk to Chester," Cash said. "See whether he'll hire bouncers, someone to control the bikers when they get out of hand. That should help."

"Let's go on about our business," Timm said. "Cash will handle this."

The crowd dispersed, calmer and less angry than before. Seemed all they'd wanted was a sense of control, a plan to keep their town safe.

Once outside the Legion Hall, Angel said, "I'm going to stop in to see Chester. I can't work in a place that dangerous anymore. I have enough money now to head out once you feel okay."

Missy stopped and stared into the distance. "I couldn't sleep last night, but I did all right, Angel. I was alone, but I talked myself out of feeling abandoned, and about thinking that nobody loves me."

Angel wrapped her arms around Missy. "I love you, Mama, with all of my heart."

"I know, honey. I love you, too. Even when I was mad at you for trying to make me see Phil as he really was." She took Angel's face in her hands. "I'm sorry I kicked you out. I will *never* do that again."

"I know, Mama. It's okay. It all worked out in the end."

"I was unhappy with Phil," Mama said. "I stuck with him so I wouldn't be alone. That's no reason to choose a man."

"You're right, Mama."

"Give me a while, Angel. I'm going to learn how to live alone."

"Angel, wait up." She turned at the sound of Timm's voice. He caught up with her and Mama. "You're not going to work tonight, are you?"

"No. I'm on my way to tell Chester that I quit. I hate to leave him stranded, but the job is too dangerous."

"I'll go with you." Timm walked beside them.

"Mama, do you want to come, too?"

"I'll go home." She waved, then headed toward her house.

Angel knocked on the Roadhouse door. When there was no answer, Timm pounded until they heard Chester yell, "I'm coming."

The door opened to reveal Chester looking as though he hadn't slept. "Come in. How's Rem?"

"He's going to be okay."

"Thank God. I'll pay for everything. For all of his medical bills. You tell him that, got it?"

"I'll pass the message along."

"Chester," Angel said, "I can't work here anymore. Those bikers are too dangerous."

"It's not all of them, Angel. A lot of them are decent. They have their own code of honor."

"I know, but the booze and the drugs make them nuts, I guess. I don't trust them."

"I'm staying closed tonight. I've called up a couple of guys I know. Experienced bouncers from Billings. They'll be here tomorrow." He ran his hands through his hair. "I also contacted a couple of cowboys I know who'll work as bouncers for a couple of weeks. They'll be here tomorrow, too."

"Cash was hoping you'd do that," Timm said.

"Can I ask you to come in one more night?" Chester asked Angel. "Tomorrow night? Freddy will be here, too. I'll put the word out that I'll need a new bartender for next week."

"For sure those guys will be here?" She could do one more night, she guessed, if he was going to have all of that protection.

"I have firm commitments."

"Okay, but only the one more night."

"Thanks, Angel. I'll make sure nothing happens to you." He stepped out of the bar with them and locked the door. "I need to talk to Cash about getting his help tonight. I've sent the word out that the bar will be closed, but there are bound to be some who don't get the message and won't be happy about it."

Chester left them, his long stride eating up the distance to the cop shop.

"You sure about tomorrow night?" Timm asked.

"Yeah. It sounds like everything will be fine."

"I have to go write all of this for tomorrow's edition. I'm running out of time. What will you do today?"

"Spend time with Missy."

"Angel, promise me you won't come to Main Street for any reason tonight. I think Chester's right. There will be disgruntled people who want the bar open."

After she agreed, Timm hurried away.

CHAPTER TWELVE

ON SATURDAY EVENING, Angel ran a gauntlet of townspeople to reach the front door of Chester's. So Max had decided to put together a patrol, despite being warned against it.

Even though she knew these men and had never had trouble with most of them, they gave her dirty looks for consorting with the enemy.

"Why are you working here?" Max Golden asked.

"I couldn't get a job anywhere else."

"I'll give you a job," George from the diner said.

"No, thanks," she answered. "Not in a million years."

The mood of the crowd unsettled her. There was frustration and anger here in spades. Despite Timm's and Cash's reassurances and plans, these men were taking matters into their own hands.

God help them all.

She entered the bar. From across the room, Freddy waved to her. Four men she'd never seen before stood in a huddle with Chester. He introduced them. They were all big men and looked as strong as he did.

"Angel will be your first priority. I don't want one hair on her head hurt."

"You got it, boss," one of them answered.

Chester opened the doors. Just before seven, patrons started arriving.

Every time the front door opened, Angel heard the disgruntled mutterings of the patrol. Tension sizzled in the air like lightning. She counted the minutes until the night was over.

AT TEN O'CLOCK, Missy stood in front of the door to Chester's Roadhouse after being hassled by a couple of the men milling about. This didn't feel good.

She'd sat at home alone, thinking about why her life had come to this state—that she would choose a man like Phil to live with. She'd been unhappy for most of their time together.

She loved going out, seeing people, laughing with friends, socializing, but she'd stayed home for Phil.

Somehow, he'd restricted every part of her life. After a lot of soul-searching, she'd realized that Phil hadn't taken her life away from her. She'd handed it to him all dressed up on a platter.

Missy had slowly dried up in that isolation, had started to feel like a hollow husk.

She needed to get out, to sit with people, even strangers and nothing else was open tonight but the bar. When she opened the door to enter the roadhouse, her hands shook.

With all the tension she could feel on the street, she no longer wanted to socialize. She only wanted to make sure her girl was safe and stayed that way.

Inside the door, she stopped to get used to the level of noise. A couple of large men stood on either side of the door. Angel had mentioned there would be bouncers tonight. Good.

The place was packed, but Missy managed to find a stool at the far end of the bar beside a hallway that she assumed led to the washrooms. She could watch Angel from here.

The biker beside her gave her the once-over, then moved his stool to allow her room. He turned away, more interested in watching Angel behind the bar than in checking out a woman closer to his own age.

So pretty, wearing a sleeveless vest and her cowboy hat, Angel piled a tray with mugs of draft then lifted it to hand off to a waitress. Her arms were strong, her waist trim.

At that moment, Chester came in from the back and Missy's heart rate kicked up. He'd aged, but maturity had been kind, had filled him out and had added character to his face. She listed all of the things she'd been too shell-shocked to notice that day on the street.

She'd always found him handsome, but now...oh, now he was such a man.

Lucky, lucky Lisa. Did the woman understand how fortunate she was to have a strong, generous, kind man like Chester?

When he saw her, Chester stopped and stared and seemed to hold his breath.

It left him in a whoosh. He pressed both palms against the edge of the bar. "Missy."

His face turned ruddy. That streak of shyness had always appealed to her, had made her feel less self-conscious about her own shyness when he was around.

"Chester." Missy smiled, but sadly, because the timing had never been right for them.

His chest and those big biceps were even larger than they used to be. He kept in shape somehow, because none of it was flab.

When would it be her turn to have a good man stand beside her? To have a man choose her not because she liked men and sex a little too much, but because she was Missy and a good person despite her flaws?

"How have you been?" she asked, since Chester couldn't seem to find his tongue.

"Good." He cleared his throat. "Real good."

Missy checked out the room and turned back to him. "You got a nice place here, Chester. You're doing well for yourself."

"I try. I piled all my money into this place," Chester answered. "I can't see it fail."

He wiped at a spill on the highly polished wood of the bar. "Don't know if you would be interested. I'm—"

When he couldn't seem to find the right words, Missy said, "Yes, Chester?"

"Lisa and I signed divorce papers six months ago, before I opened this place."

Missy sat up straight. Really? Was he kidding? She'd stumbled onto Christmas in August. Chester and Lisa were divorced? *Santa, baby, you done good this year.*

"Really? But I saw Lisa come into the bar last week." Shoot. Now he'd think she'd been watching him and paying too much attention to his private affairs.

"We sometimes have to deal with each other about odd things. The marriage is over, Missy. We gave it a good shot, a lot of years, but couldn't make it work."

"Good." Missy said nothing else because she suspected that all of the joy she was feeling was evident on her face.

Chester smiled. "Yeah," he said in the deep voice that rose slowly out of that massive chest. "It is good."

Did he mean *good* the way that she meant it? That they were both single at the same time and should get together? Missy needed to know.

She leaned forward and placed her hand on top of one

of his. He had big hands, a little scarred and probably callused. She liked big hands.

"What are you doing later?" she asked. "After you close for the night?"

Chester's smile deepened. "Wait here for me?"

He did mean *good* the same way.

She smiled and nodded.

ANGEL WATCHED CHESTER and Mama out of the corner of her eye, saw Missy put one hand over Chester's. The look that passed between them nearly set everyone's drinks boiling.

She had to put a stop to this.

She scooted behind Chester and came around the bar. Slipping her arm through Missy's, she all but dragged her off the stool.

"Angel, what are you doing?" Missy asked, stumbling a little.

"Chester, I'm taking a break. Back in a minute." Angel propelled Missy down the hallway to the washroom.

She closed the door behind the two of them and made sure the stalls were empty.

"What are you doing, Mama?" she whispered furiously. "I thought you were going to try to come to terms with being on your own, and here you are practically undressing Chester with your eyes. What was all of that talk about not fooling with married men?"

"Chester and Lisa got a divorce. He's single."

That brought Angel up short. "He is?"

With her broad smug smile, Missy looked like the cat that had swallowed the cream. "Really. The marriage has been over for six months."

"Really?" Angel asked again, because she couldn't

quite believe that the dream she'd always wanted for her mama might come true.

Missy smiled more serenely. "Yeah, really."

Angel threw her arms around her. "You go for it, Mama. Just flat out go for it."

Missy squeezed her back. "I plan to." She opened the door and breezed out of the washroom.

Angel stood still with what she was sure was a goofy grin on her face. *Oh, Mama, have fun. You deserve it.*

Angel returned to her duties and when she left for the night, Mama was still sitting at the bar, patiently waiting for Chester as it seemed she had been doing for most of her life.

When Angel opened the door to leave, she heard raised voices outside and sighed. Did every night at this bar have to involve melodrama? But it didn't really matter to her anymore. She'd worked her last night at Chester's Roadhouse.

TIMM AND BECCA SAT in a restaurant in Haven—they were eating Italian tonight—and struggled to find conversation.

He finished his coffee and said, "Ready to go home?"

She nodded and, oddly, seemed as relieved as he felt that the night was almost over.

"This isn't going to work, is it?" he asked.

"I don't think so, Timm. I like you, but we don't have a lot to talk about, do we?"

"I like you, too," he responded, "but, no. We don't seem to have a lot in common."

They left the restaurant and he drove the highway that eventually would turn into Main Street in Ordinary.

There wasn't one single spark between them. Nada. Nothing. *Rien.*

Shared morals and ethics were one thing, as was respect, but there had to be affection to make a relationship work, didn't there?

His plan hadn't worked. Not with Becca at any rate. He needed to expand his search.

He dropped Becca off, then parked behind his building. He entered his apartment with a heavy heart, or low spirits. Or something.

He couldn't settle down. It was still too early for bed. He tried to read, but tossed the book aside. He walked the length of the apartment. He threw himself onto the sofa and turned on his little-used TV, but found nothing of interest there.

Maybe he should go to the office and get some work done—write an article, or edit a couple sent in from a freelance writer whose stuff was usually decent.

He walked down the front stairs and locked the door behind him after he stepped outside.

Noise from farther down the street caught his attention. A significant crowd had gathered. What was going on?

Timm approached and realized that it was two factions squaring off—Max and his friends on one side against bikers on the other. A recipe for disaster. Why hadn't Max left things alone?

Timm didn't recognize four muscled men standing with Max. Must be the bouncers Chester hired. Timm wasn't sure whether they would help or hinder the resolution of the standoff.

Williams stood in between the two sides and Timm didn't envy him his position. Williams was trying to reason with them, but neither side seemed to want to listen.

Worst of all, Angel stood alone, the only woman on the street.

Stay put, Angel. Don't be impulsive. Do not enter that crowd.

ANGEL TOOK STOCK of the situation on Main Street.

The bikers and the town's residents had squared off in the middle of the road. Williams stood between them to keep the peace. Cash should be here. Williams didn't have the same air of authority.

She had to cross the street to get home, but didn't want to walk around either the bikers or Ordinary's citizens. Either side would think she was making a choice and who knew whether someone would take offense?

She could walk straight down the middle, but Williams's position between the two crowds was precarious enough. She should head back to the bar.

"Go on home, now," Williams said to the men from Ordinary. "You're only making the situation worse."

"How could it be any worse? One of these idiots stabbed Rem and we don't know which one did it."

"Who are you calling an idiot?" A biker surged forward.

Williams held him back with his baton across Eddy's barrel chest. "Go home. Now," Williams ordered, but it was obvious control of the crowd slipped steadily through his fingers.

Angel felt the mood become more and more emotional. If a fight broke out, she would be caught in the middle. Even with the lessons in self-defense, she would be overwhelmed in seconds. The only woman out here, she felt keenly exposed and edged slowly toward the bar.

Timm showed up at her elbow. "Come on. Let's go inside," he said, his manner strong and sure.

He directed her into the roadhouse. "Chester, have you seen what's going on outside?"

Chester had been leaning on his elbows across the counter from Mama. He looked up with a frown.

"What's happening?"

"A bunch of townspeople are squaring off against the patrons."

Chester swore and picked up his bat, the answer to every bar problem he faced with his clientele. "You can't reason with bikers. It's their way or the highway."

"That's the problem," Timm said. "The townspeople aren't trying to reason with them. All hell's about to break loose out there."

Chester pointed the bat at both Missy and Angel. "Lock the door behind us and stay inside."

Angel didn't need to be told twice. It was odd to see Timm and Chester united on something. Neither one of them wanted this kind of trouble in their town.

After they left, she leaned her ear against the locked door, but couldn't pinpoint anything specific. It sounded like the number of voices out there had doubled, but maybe it was simply that the crowd had become more vocal.

"I'm worried about Chester," Missy said.

"I know what you mean. I'm worried about Timm."

"What's going on between you two?"

"Nothing, Mama. I like him. He's a good guy."

Missy nodded. "Yeah, so's Chester."

In response to Mama's worried frown, Angel

said, "He'll be okay, Mama. He's good at defending himself."

"He's big enough to, but how many people can he take on at one time? It sounds like there are hundreds out there."

She was right. Even though Angel knew there were probably not more than thirty people out front, it sounded like a huge crowd.

She itched to go out there to see what was happening. Never before had she cursed the absence of windows along the front of the building, but she did now. She was tempted to open the door and sneak a peek. But one look at Missy's face and the anxiety there, Angel knew she had to stay put. Regardless of how much that went against her nature.

TIMM STOOD BESIDE Chester and watched the crowd. Now that Cash had arrived, the tension seemed to be dissipating a bit. Maybe they would actually get out of this unscathed.

Timm checked out the crowd, memorizing what he saw, so he could write about it tomorrow. Something bothered him. He scanned the crowd of bikers.

He nudged Chester. "You see anything odd about the bikers?"

Chester scanned the group. "The troublemakers aren't here. These guys don't cause me a lot of problems. They don't get wound up by themselves." He craned his neck to search beyond the ensemble. "Eddy and his buddies are missing."

"Every time there's been an incident, has Eddy been involved?"

"You bet. Every time."

"So where is he now?"

The door behind them burst open.

"Chester, Timm, fire!" Angel cried.

They ran into the bar. Smoke crept in from the back.

"Call the fire department," Timm said.

"Already did the second I smelled smoke. Told them to use the alley, not Main."

Smart girl.

"Where's Missy?" Chester asked.

"In the back. She grabbed the extinguisher by the front door and ran down the hallway."

Chester pulled another extinguisher out from under the bar and tossed it to Timm. Chester started filling a bucket with water, then pulled a towel from under the counter and soaked it. He ran down the hallway with his nose and mouth covered. Missy met him halfway, her extinguisher empty.

Timm followed and sprayed orange flames consuming the back door.

Chester emerged from his office with another fire extinguisher.

The fire had obviously been started outside and they weren't putting it out, only keeping it at bay.

Angel threw a bucket of water at the door, coughing.

"Get out of here," Timm said. "Now. Take Missy with you."

"Not on your life. I'm helping."

She returned moments later with another full bucket. He tossed his empty extinguisher aside and took the bucket from her to fill in the bar sink.

"Get out," he ordered Angel and Missy. "Now."

ANGEL RAN OUT front. Cash was standing side by side with Williams and the bouncers. A lot of the crowd had dispersed. A steady stream of bikes were heading out of town.

Thank goodness Cash had shown up. She called him over.

"Back of the building's on fire. Fire crews are on their way but we have to make sure everyone's out."

She hurried to the adjacent storefront because there was an upstairs apartment. She pounded on the door. A moment later, the tenant—a young guy she didn't know—answered.

"The Roadhouse is on fire. You need to evacuate in case it spreads."

"Thanks." He followed outside. "What can I do?"

"Go to the alley and see if people have outdoor taps and hoses behind their shops. We could put some water on that fire."

"Got it." He hustled toward the alley.

Determined to do all she could to save Chester's place, she headed in the opposite direction of the tenant, taking the short way around the Roadhouse to the alley. But as she turned the corner, she came face-to-face with Eddy.

What was he doing back here?

An ugly suspicion bloomed. "You started this."

"What's it to you? You don't own the place." Before she could react, he reached out and grabbed her upper arms.

Don't panic. Keep your cool.

"I care about Chester. Why did you do it?"

"Been trying to get the place closed down."

"You've been causing the trouble all along."

"Yeah. Wasn't working fast enough so I brought out the big guns." He cocked his head toward the fire.

Angel heard sirens from the far end of town. Thank goodness.

Eddy grinned. "That's my cue to leave." He released her and ran to his bike.

She followed. She couldn't let him get away.

She punched his back to get him to turn around, then jumped away from him.

He took an angry step toward her and tried to grab her but she used one of the tricks Timm had taught her and Eddy ended up on the ground.

It worked. *Oh, my God, it worked.*

Eddy got up and put his head down to ram her. She stepped out of the way and he hit the wall.

He bounced back and shook his head, his eyes unfocused. "Where the hell are you?"

He ran for her again and she grabbed his arm and sent him flying into his bike. He landed facedown on the asphalt.

Before he had a chance to rise, she took hold of his wrist, pushed his arm up behind him and slammed her knee against it, immobilizing it.

Thank you, Timm.

Aikido really worked. She decided that no matter where she ended up, she was going to study it.

Eddy was a big man and struggling to be free. Angel couldn't hold him like this forever—she wasn't strong enough—so she opened her mouth and screamed at the top of her lungs. She kept it up until someone heard her.

Timm and Cash came running.

While Timm grabbed Eddy's other arm and did the same as Angel, Cash got out his handcuffs.

After a minor scuffle in which Eddy never stood

a chance, he was handcuffed and sitting against the wall.

Chester and Missy approached.

"Did you do this?" Chester pointed at Eddy.

"Yeah," Eddy said with a smug smile.

Missy rushed to Angel and wrapped her arms around her. "Someone said you were screaming. Was he attacking you?"

Angel wiggled out of her mother's embrace and smiled at her and Timm.

"I attacked him. I took him down, Mama. Timm taught me how."

Missy turned to Timm. "I know my opinion probably doesn't matter to a guy like you, but thanks."

"Your opinion matters, Missy," he said quietly.

"Why did you do it?" Chester had the front of Eddy's shirt in his fist.

"Remember Henry Pascale?"

"Yeah. I testified against him in that robbery trial. He tried to kill me with that shotgun of his. I had every right to press charges. He was sentenced to five years in jail. So what?"

An ugly sneer smeared Eddy's face. "He's my brother."

"All of the fights in the bar. Started by you."

"Yep."

"A lot of those bikers are decent enough, but you got them going, didn't you?"

"They're easy to rile after a few drinks."

Problem solved, Angel thought. *Now we know what was happening. It wasn't an entire evil biker population, but one man with a few crazy friends and a vendetta.*

Cash and Chester lifted Eddy to his feet and walked

him to Cash's cruiser. Before locking him in, Cash said, "Thanks for the confession, Eddy."

He turned and grinned at the group.

"Thank God that's over," Chester said. "Let's go see what the back of my bar looks like."

They kept their distance from the firefighters still putting out the fire. It seemed to be under control.

Chester wasn't going to lose the building, but would he lose the business?

There was significant damage to the wall and the door was a pile of timbers on the ground. The building was made of brick, though, as were the rest that lined Main. But for that, the row of stores that abutted each other and the Roadhouse could have gone up in smoke.

Angel shook her head. They were lucky. As bad as this was, it could have been so much worse.

CHAPTER THIRTEEN

HOURS LATER, ANGEL turned the front lock after the last firefighter left the bar.

The building reeked of smoke. Paint peeled from the walls in the back hallway. The washroom doors were destroyed. They had already determined that Chester's computer had sustained a lot of water damage.

Timm took her hand in his. "I'll walk you home."

He looked so determined that she didn't even try to protest. She was exhausted. And tonight, she wanted his company.

"Missy, do you want to walk home with us?"

Chester shot out a hand and wrapped it around Missy's elbow. "I'll take care of her."

The heat between them almost reignited the fire.

Oh, Mama, you are on your way to happiness, to your very own happy ending, with your own prince. I'm thrilled for you.

"I can't stay upstairs because of smoke damage," Chester said to Missy.

"That's okay. You'll come home with me."

Oh boy, Angel thought, *Where does that leave me?*

She knew exactly what Chester and Mama would be doing. No way did Angel want to be in the house with them. Three would definitely be a crowd.

"You can stay in my apartment," Timm whispered

in Angel's ear. He held his hands away from his sides. "That's not a proposition. I'll sleep on the couch."

"Okay." She really didn't have a choice. She wasn't about to ask him to drive her out to Matt's, and risk awakening them.

"Can I talk to you for a minute?" Missy gestured toward the end of the bar.

Angel stepped forward.

"No, honey, not you. Timm."

He joined her. They whispered and he looked angry.

Angel heard Timm say, "I promise. Don't worry."

They all said good-night, then the couples separated, with Chester and Missy walking toward the house hand in hand, while Angel and Timm crossed the street.

"What was that conversation with Mama about?"

"I'll tell you when we get to my place."

He unlocked the door, stepped inside, then relocked it. Angel followed him upstairs.

"The mood out there was ugly," he said. "I've never seen anything like it in town before."

When she moved to the living room to turn on a light, he said, "Don't. No lights."

"Okay, now you're scaring me. What's happening?"

He walked to the front window and checked Main Street.

"What are you looking for?" she asked.

"Phil."

The bottom fell out of Angel's stomach. "He left town for good. Anyway, it's okay. Mama will be safe with Chester."

"Phil isn't coming back for Missy, Angel. He's here for you." He touched her shoulder. "He left a message on

Missy's machine that this business wasn't over yet and that her 'brat' would get what was coming to her."

Weary to the bone, Angel was glad for Timm's company. "That's what Mama whispered to you?"

"Yes. She wanted me to stay with you."

He strode toward the bedroom and came back with an old quilt in his arms, which he threw onto the sofa.

He handed her a T-shirt. "You can sleep in this. You can shower first."

That was desperately needed, since they were both covered with soot.

She took the shirt and walked in the direction he indicated until she found the bathroom. She showered quickly, using a soap that smelled like a man's deodorant.

Walking into the living room, wearing only Timm's T-shirt felt weird. He checked out her legs quickly, then looked away. She liked that about him. He might look, but he never ogled.

"Go to bed," he said. "You'll be safe tonight."

"Thanks," she whispered.

When she crawled into his bed she covered herself to her ears, although the night was warm. She listened to every sound in the apartment, to Timm walking down the hallway, to his shower running and to his return to the living room.

Then silence.

Foolish girl that she was, she wanted him in bed with her, especially after last night. He'd been so sweet, driving to the ranch to let her know that Rem wasn't dying. Such a decent guy.

Even as tired as she'd been, he'd been a temptation to her.

Timm, she thought, *with you here, I'll be safe from*

Phil, but who will save me from my own follies? Who will save me from my desire for you?

WHEN CHESTER ENTERED Missy's house, she admired the view. To her, Chester had always been the best-looking man in town.

She couldn't believe this was happening, that Chester was in her house, was single and, in a few minutes, would be in her arms and in her bed.

She deserved this because she'd paid her dues in life. Oh, how she'd paid her dues.

He turned and his frank appraisal of her warmed her heart. Judging by the heat in his eyes, Chester found her more than a little attractive.

He took her hand, pulled her gently toward him and asked, "Where's the bedroom?"

No preamble. He was as anxious as she was. She liked him being so honest about it. With his hand in one of hers, she led him to her bedroom, walking backward so she could watch his eyes darken, all without a word and with his hot gaze sliding over her.

Yesterday, she'd stripped the bed of its sheets and had washed them. Now she was glad she had.

Excitement built in Missy's stomach, and in other more interesting parts of her body. She'd wanted Chester for a long, long time.

After they entered, he closed the door behind her, leaned into her until her back hit the wood. He kissed her like there was no tomorrow, as if he was trying to inhale her. She did the same to him. Their tongues danced and dueled and her blood heated and rose to meet all of the spots that Chester touched.

Were they even going to make it to the bed?

He grabbed her arms and raised them above her head,

held them there, and leaned into her. His hard chest flattened her breasts and they ached with pleasure.

His knee pressed between her legs and she rode his thigh, starting a delicious ache there.

By the time he pulled away from her, Missy was ready to jump him then and there, but it looked like Chester had other ideas.

With her hand in his, he strode across the room toward the bed. "Turn on a lamp."

She did. He dragged her close and unbuttoned her blouse, separating the two sides.

"I've been a long time wanting you." He unhooked her bra and touched one of her ample breasts. The nipple was already hard, because Chester turned her on by looking at her.

The thought of his mouth and hands on her breasts made her weak in her knees.

She leaned into his touch again, because she couldn't get close enough to him. She reached for the buttons on his shirt, but he stopped her by wrapping her arm behind her back and holding it there with one of his hands.

"But I want to see you," she whispered.

"You will. Give me a minute to look at you first, 'cause the second after you touch me, I'm going to be inside you, hard." He touched her other breast. "I want to savor you."

"You can't, Chester."

"I have to. Look at these beauties."

She threw her head back and his arm supported her while he nuzzled and licked and bit her breasts. If he didn't stop, she was going to come in her panties.

With her free hand, she grabbed his hair and forced his head away from her breasts.

"Chester," she groaned. "I can't wait."

He reached under her skirt and yanked off her thong.

In one rough movement, he had her on her back on the bed and her legs spread and around his waist, while he stood facing her.

He unzipped his pants, and Missy raised her arms above her head, stretching in pure feline pleasure.

"Give it to me, Chester," she commanded, and he entered her in one thrust and Missy cried out. He was gloriously big and powerful.

"Did I hurt you?" he asked, his voice strained because he was holding himself back.

"No," she cried. "More."

He grinned. "I knew you'd be like this."

He moved then, without hesitation, driving into her and she rose to meet him with each thrust, her thighs and muscles grasping him, wringing every drop of pleasure out of their coupling.

When Missy came, it was fast and she called out his name. Chester drank her cries from her lips and took his own forceful orgasm.

He fell on top of her and she welcomed his weight. She had always loved big men. Her body hummed while her heart rejoiced. She'd loved Chester for forever. They were finally together and she wasn't letting this man go.

She felt him burgeon inside her and she squeezed him.

"Again," she said, and his laugh was large and hearty and strong.

She cradled his face between her palms. "Chester, I'm so glad you're here."

"Me, too, love."

She moved beneath him, but he stopped her.

"First things first," he said, and carried her into the bathroom.

There, they undressed each other and Missy finally saw Chester naked in all of his stunning glory. She reached for him and he hardened in her hand.

Reaching behind her, he turned on the shower and they stepped inside. In the fog of the hot spray, he turned her around and took her standing from behind.

After another fierce release, they washed each other slowly. Now that the first crazy need was appeased, it was time to savor. Missy finally touched all of the parts of Chester's body that she'd hungered for years on end.

He was beautiful.

When they got out of the shower, he wouldn't let them dry off.

They lay on the bed and drank the water from each other's bodies, worshipped with mouths and tongues and fingers and palms spread as widely as they could to accommodate two well-endowed bodies.

For years, Missy had been too shy to talk to Chester, but now they were speaking a language they both understood and knew well and it was big and bawdy and lusty and satisfying.

They loved.

CHAPTER FOURTEEN

ON SUNDAY, TIMM stood on the veranda of the house he'd grown up in and knocked on the door.

He'd left Angel still asleep in his bed.

Sara answered. "Timm? Why did you knock?"

"I wasn't sure Ma would welcome me."

"No wonder. She told me what she caught you doing with Angel. Not smart doing it in Papa's office."

No fooling. Angel tempted him to do foolish things.

His mother walked down the hallway.

"Mama?"

She didn't look happy with him. She allowed him to accompany them to church, though, so he wasn't totally cut out of the family, but neither was she exactly friendly.

Maybe she was only keeping up appearances. He hoped it was more than that. His family mattered to him.

After church, they walked straight home. But she didn't invite him to stay for lunch, so he left.

Back on Main, most of the church crowd was gathering in front of the sheriff's office. Cash seemed to be trying to calm them down.

Fortunately, his wasn't the only moderate voice in the crowd. Hank Shelter was here again. Hank held a strong moral and ethical position in the community. There wasn't anyone in town who didn't respect him.

Today's gathering included a lot of women who were having their say, too.

"Cash, the women are afraid to walk on their own streets at night," Janey Wilson said. "Why can't we *do* something? This isn't L.A. or New York City or the slums of Chicago. Women have always been safe here." Her frustration seemed to echo that of the other women.

"I know, Janey." Cash's own voice was rife with frustration. "The situation is over, though." He explained about Eddy's arrest.

There were still grumblings.

"Look, people," Cash said, "Eddy admitted to starting every incident and to setting last night's fire. He was the one who stirred up the rest of the bikers. The situation is over. Everyone go home."

"What about the Roadhouse?" someone asked.

"I have no idea what Chester's going to do now. There will be a lot of work repairing the building, so it won't be operational for a while."

"I'm closing the Roadhouse. I'm going to fix the building with my insurance settlement, then Missy and I are going to reopen it as a restaurant," Chester spoke from where he and Missy stood across the street.

All kinds of good comments spread through the crowd.

"We haven't decided what type of food we'll serve yet, but given that this is cattle country, we're thinking we'll open a steak house."

A couple of people clapped.

Timm understood why. The diner closed at six. If you

wanted to go out for dinner, you had to travel to Haven, as Timm had done with Becca.

WIth that announcement, the crowd finally seemed satisfied and dispersed. Missy and Chester entered the diner and Cash returned to his office. Timm chatted with a few people as they strode past. Finally he returned to his apartment.

Angel stood in his kitchen, drinking a cup of coffee. "I hope you don't mind, I made a pot."

"Good. I need one."

He'd half hoped to find her wearing only his T-shirt, but she was dressed in last night's clothes.

"Thanks for letting me stay the night."

It was my pleasure, even if I couldn't sleep knowing you were so close.

"Did you see him out there today?"

"Who?"

"Phil."

He shook his head.

"What was going on with the crowd?"

He explained that Cash had updated everyone about Eddy and the bar. "Missy and Chester showed up. They obviously did a lot more than have se—" He didn't know how to extricate himself from his own bumbling.

She laughed. "I know exactly what they were doing all night."

"Well, they were also talking. Chester's going to repair the place with insurance money and…he and Missy are going to turn it into a restaurant."

"Are you serious?"

"Yeah," he answered softly, distracted by how good watching her express her happiness felt, let alone doing the other things he'd dreamed about last night.

"What are you doing today?"

"I'll have to go to Mama's at some point to get clean clothes and a toothbrush, I guess. I'll phone first."

A smile hovered on her lips. He returned it. "Yeah, definitely a good idea to warn those two you're coming, but they aren't at Missy's house right now. I saw them enter the diner."

"What about you?" she asked. "What are you up to?"

"I'm going to the hospital later to get Rem and take him home."

"How is he?"

"Apparently good enough to be released. While you're at Missy's, pack a bag. You might have to stay here for a few days until everything gets sorted out."

What there was to sort out eluded him. Missy and Chester were solid, which meant Angel could leave anytime she wanted. And that was good. Right? He didn't need her here screwing with his head and his libido.

He'd be pleased as punch when she left. He would. For sure.

MISSY AND CHESTER came home while Angel was packing her bag.

Missy hugged Angel, held her until she started to feel emotional. Chester watched with a goofy grin on his face.

Okay, so they'd had a good night of crazy monkey sex, but it felt as though her mother was crying.

Angel forced Missy away from her. Missy *was* crying.

"Mama, what's wrong?"

"Nothing, baby. Everything is all right. Every single thing."

Missy reached a hand toward Chester and he took it

and came near. "Angel, can you wait for one more week before you leave?"

"I guess. Why?"

"Chester and I are getting married next Saturday."

Angel's eyes felt like they were bugging out of her head. "What?"

"Will you stay that long? I want you there, honey."

"Of course, Mama, but are you two sure? This seems so sudden."

"It isn't," Chester said in his deep voice flavored with satisfaction and contentment. "We've loved each other for a long time."

The look they shared was hot, but also affectionate and deep. It really was true love.

Angel felt a flicker of envy, but shooed it away. Her mama needed this happy ending—she'd earned it.

Seemed she should throw a few more clothes into the bag. She wasn't going to be staying in this house again anytime soon.

REM SAT IN TIMM'S truck and tried to control his nausea. He didn't know what caused it—the meds or the lingering pain.

They pulled into Rem's yard, where his mother stood leaning on her cane. Had she been watching for him? He hoped so.

For a long time now, their relationship had been odd, strained, and he hadn't been able to get to the root of it. He didn't even know how to start to figure it out.

On his way along, he kissed her cheek.

Timm helped Rem upstairs, where he dropped onto the bed with a hiss.

"Still hurts bad?" Timm asked.

"Yeah. It's a lot better than it was, though. I'll be good in time."

"You need anything?"

Rem chewed his lip. "I don't want Ma taking care of me. She has enough trouble getting around and doing for herself without me adding to her duties. I've been doing a lot for her, but I'm not able right now. Can you come give her a hand every day?"

"I can." They both turned at the sound of a female voice behind them.

Sara stood in the doorway.

"What are you doing here?" Rem asked, unable to fathom that Sara was in his house, offering to take care of his mother. Through the haze of pain, hope flickered. Was she here for him, too?

"I've been coming over every day to help Nell."

Rem closed his eyes. "Thanks." The word sounded laden with more emotion than he wanted to admit to, but the meds were making him sloppy.

How did the world survive without people like Sara, dependable, hardworking and smart? She knew what the people around her needed before they knew it themselves.

Timm glanced between the two of them and said goodbye. He had to pass by her to leave. She hadn't budged from the doorway.

"Come here," Rem said.

"Not on your life."

"You afraid of me, Sara?" There was a time when that would have constituted a dare to the girl she was.

Now, though? She didn't crack a smile. Girl was locked up tighter than a steel drum.

Rem tried to take his boots off, but couldn't bend over. His stomach burned.

Without a word, Sara approached and pulled them off.

Rem stood shakily, holding his ribs. He attacked his belt buckle, but Sara brushed his hands aside and did it for him.

She unzipped his pants and pulled them down his legs.

When she straightened, she nearly brushed her head against his groin and it shot to attention.

She shot him what he had always called her Sara look, quelling and fierce, and pushed him to the bed.

She pulled off his pants and socks in one go. The woman was damn efficient.

He knew she was aware of his erection, but she ignored it.

"I don't do this for all the girls, you know," he said, a shaky laugh in his voice.

"Sure seems like it."

Rem sobered. "Aw, Sara, honey, don't be like that."

He stood to maneuver himself under the bedsheet, but she stopped him by unbuttoning his shirt.

After she pulled it off, she urged him under the sheet, all without a word.

"Feels good to lie down."

Before he knew what was happening, she lay down beside him and cuddled against him.

He wrapped his arms around her. "Sara, doll, welcome home."

"This doesn't mean anything." She sounded as cross as a bear with a thorn in his paw. "I'm keeping you warm."

"I'm warm, honey. I'm good." Sara was his and she didn't even know it.

TIMM MOVED INTO his mom's house for the week. No way could he sleep on the sofa in the apartment with Angel and her pretty pink tattooed wings in his bed every night.

He couldn't trust himself around her. She'd come to mean something to him. To mean too much, and wasn't that a kicker, because he couldn't come up with a name of any other woman in town he wanted to date.

Not one single name.

For the next three nights, he left her at the apartment after he made sure everything was secure.

Every morning, before he went to the newspaper office, he checked upstairs and made sure she was okay, that nothing had bothered her during the night.

When he left the apartment on Thursday night and locked the dead bolt, he stopped, certain that he smelled cigarette smoke on the air.

He couldn't see where it was coming from, but it bothered him, unnerved him. Was it Phil?

While he walked to his mother's, he pulled out his cell phone and dialed his home number.

When Angel answered, he said, "It's me."

"What's up?"

"Do you know whether Phil is a smoker?"

"I think he might have been. I never saw him smoke in Mama's house, but sometimes I smelled it on his clothes. Why?"

"Nothing. Just don't open that door for anyone other than me. Okay?"

"Go home and rest, Timm, and stop worrying about me. I'll be fine."

He sniffed once more, but smelled nothing. Had he imagined the smoke?

ANGEL ROLLED OVER. Something had awakened her. She realized Timm was sitting on the rocking chair in the corner.

"What are you doing here?" Her voice was husky with sleep. "I thought you'd gone to your mom's."

"I wanted to see you."

Phil!

Angel shot up in bed. "Bastard! Get out of here."

"No way. You're gonna give me what you hand out free to the rest of the town. Whore."

"I'm not a whore," she screamed, and ran for the door, but he caught her hair and pulled her back. Her eyes watered with the pain.

He was on her like an animal, throwing her onto the bed and straddling her.

Without warning, she thrust her hips high, hard and fast, knocking him off her. Another trick Timm had taught her. When he tumbled over the side of the bed, she ran out of the room.

He grabbed her hair again. He was too fast. He made to swing at her and Timm's voice was suddenly in her mind. *Use his momentum against him.*

Grabbing his wrist, she pulled him forward and he hit the wall beside the staircase, lost his footing then tumbled down the stairs through the doorway he hadn't closed when he'd broken in. He finally landed at the bottom.

Silent. Still.

Angel ran to the bedroom and threw on clothes, anything that came to hand quickly. She wasn't waiting around long enough for Phil to wake up and take another crack at her.

Racing for the back staircase, she unlocked the door then hurried downstairs and outside. She ran through the alley to the Francks' house, where she banged on the front door. No one answered and she banged again.

"Please, please, please," she whispered until she heard the lock and the door open.

She rushed into Timm's arms and clung to him, afraid that he might disappear and turn into Phil like he had in her bedroom.

"Angel, what's going on?"

"Phil." She couldn't get anything else past a throat that was frozen.

"What about Phil?"

"In the stairs. Not moving. Attacked me in bedroom." She was gasping for air.

"Dear God." He held her at arm's length and turned on the hallway light.

"Did he hurt you?"

"Tried to. Used aikido. Got away." Her teeth were chattering.

"What's going on?" Sara stood behind Timm, wearing a no-nonsense expression.

Rem's mother— her face as white as her housecoat— stood behind her.

"Make some tea," he said. "Angel's been attacked."

Without letting go of Angel—she wouldn't let him—he stepped into the living room and picked up the phone.

Finn came downstairs, rubbing sleep out of his eyes. "Why is there so much noise? Who's that?"

Sara soothed him and took him upstairs.

Williams arrived a few minutes later.

Timm filled him in. He instructed Angel to stay with Sara, who had already wrapped her in a comforter on the sofa and had her drinking a cup of tea she could barely hold in her shaking fingers.

They left to investigate.

"Thank you." Angel put down the cup. "I don't feel so good. Can I lie down for a minute?" She curled into the corner of the sofa.

"Do you want me to stay with you?"

She nodded. She heard Sara sit in the armchair across the room. "Mama, you can go to bed now."

Angel heard Mrs. Franck walk upstairs. The next thing she heard was Timm walking back into the house. She'd fallen asleep.

She sat up too quickly and her head spun. "Is he dead?"

"No."

She wasn't sure whether to be relieved. She never wanted to see him again, but she didn't want a man's death on her conscience.

"His leg is broken and he has a concussion. Williams took him to get a cast and then he'll be in jail."

Timm squatted in front of her. "He'll never hurt you again. Okay?"

She nodded.

He took her fingers in his. "I'm proud of you. The pretty princess was able to slay her own dragon."

She smiled sleepily. "Yeah. I did, didn't I?"

"Why don't you go up to my bed and I'll sleep down here."

"No. I'm comfortable. You go up to bed."

"You're not sleeping on the sofa. Come on."

She shook her head. "I'll go back to the apartment."

"Man, you're stubborn."

"I'm not comfortable in your mom's house," she whispered. "I know what she thinks of me."

He nodded. "Okay, I'll take you to the apartment."

They walked through the silent streets.

When Angel stepped inside and saw blood on the white wall, she recoiled.

She might have been strong enough to slay her own dragon, but that didn't mean she could handle the scene of the crime.

"Come on," he said, urging her upstairs with a firm hand on her back.

"It's Neil, isn't it?"

She nodded.

"This brings it back?"

She nodded again.

"Do you want to talk about it?"

Angel hastened to the other side of the room, putting distance between them. "No. I don't want to talk. I want to go to bed."

IF THAT REACTION didn't send a loud and clear message, Timm wasn't sure what did.

"Okay," he said, disappointed that she wouldn't accept his help. "I'll leave."

"Leave?" she asked, bewildered. "Don't you want to have sex with me?"

"What?"

"Isn't this the part in the romance novels where we have sex to make me feel better?" She sounded bitter, as though what happened at the ends of those books would never happen for her.

Those happy endings were elusive for him, too.

Maybe they didn't exist in real life. Everywhere he turned, he watched the struggle, the grasping and reaching for those mythical endings. His mother and father had been good together for a long while, but it had fallen apart after Timm's accident.

Rem and Sara performed some crazy dance with each other that only seemed to break their hearts and push them further and further apart.

He either had the most benign evenings with suitable girls or he craved the woman he shouldn't have.

There were couples who were proving that it might be, that it could be, possible to reach for a happy ending. In the past few years, Timm had seen it with Hank and Amy, and with Matt and Jenny, and with C.J. and Janey. And, apparently, now with Chester and Missy.

He had no happy ending to offer Angel, but he did want to give her comfort, if only for one night.

"Yeah, I guess this is when we should make love."

"I didn't say we should make love," she shouted. "I said we should have sex. There's a difference, you know. I'm leaving town after Mama gets married, no matter how much I like you. Too many people here still think I'm a bad girl."

"Phil?"

"Yeah, Phil. He reminded me of what I always have to fight here in Ordinary."

She'd become hard-edged and defiant, the old Angel resurrected to help her to deal with her sins and her guilt and her sorrow, or to avoid them, but Timm knew she had to live through it. She had no choice.

Life dished out what it dished out, and everyone had to deal.

"Neil is the only one who's ever seen the real me. He never called me a whore."

So Phil had called her that. No wonder she was hurting.

He knew all about sorrow and pain and regrets and *if onlys*. If only he'd never been burned, what would his life now be?

But he *had* been, and he'd dealt with it in all areas of his life. He'd healed. Now he wanted to be the one who helped Angel to heal.

"Yeah, okay," he said. "Let's have sex."

"Okay, then," she said, and started to unbutton her sleeveless blouse.

"Stop," he said. He wanted to do that.

"No. Don't stop me. Make up your mind. Are we having sex or aren't we?" She pressed her hands against her temples. "My head hurts, Timm. Help me."

"Okay." He took her hand, led her to his bedroom that now smelled like patchouli, like Angel, a retro free spirit who was currently locked up inside her sorrow, all of her goodness trapped and warped by guilt and others around her.

A lacy bra hanging from an old ladder-back chair looked like it belonged. Her pink tank top hung from the doorknob by one thin wisp of a strap. A black leather vest hung out of a drawer.

She was messing with his bedroom, his apartment, his life, his head. Angel Donovan was a messy woman.

He reached for the buttons of his shirt, then stopped. He'd shown a woman his chest so rarely. Angel had said that it didn't bothered her to see his scars, but that had been the small area that showed when he wore his *gi*. But making love with him—or having sex as she wanted—was another thing altogether.

If he had to make love to her with his clothes on to help her heal, then he would do so. Angel kidded herself. She didn't need sex. She needed love.

He turned on the bedside lamp.

"I don't want the light on."

A fat pink candle sat in a pretty dish beside the lamp.

Another Angel addition to his bedroom? He picked up the matches and lit it. "Does that work?"

She nodded. "Yeah, I like it."

He turned off the lamp. The candle scented the room. It might have been lavender, but he wasn't sure. He didn't know flowers.

He turned to her and started undoing her blouse.

She reached for him, suddenly intense, grabbing at him, trying to touch him to turn him on, like a ravenous woman who hadn't eaten in weeks.

He knew what she was doing, hoping to make him lose his control, so she could lose hers. So she could lose herself in the sex and forget her grief.

He wouldn't let her.

She needed to push through this. Sure, it would be painful, but it would work. He would be there to hold her.

"Slow down," he whispered against her hair, and held her hands still.

She tried to pull them away from his hold, but he was too strong for her.

When he let go and she reached for her buttons again, he said, "Let me."

He undressed her by the light of a flickering candle, uncovered bits of her slowly, a collarbone here, a shoulder there, as though he were a painter, a master, but rather than putting his paint to canvas to create his own work of art, he was uncovering what was already there, what had already been created with perfection, stripping away little bits of Angel to get to the woman underneath.

With each scrap of fabric he peeled away, he learned that she was a masterpiece.

His breath caught in his throat.

When he touched his mouth to her breast, he felt a featherlight touch on his hair. She might think she wanted to have sex, but her psyche craved love.

She lay down on the bed and he hovered over her. Where did a man start with such a beautiful body? Every bit deserved to be cherished first. He started at the top, with her shoulders.

If he kissed her lips, he might lose himself and end this as a fast coupling and that would be wrong on every level.

He took his time, trailed his lips along the tops of her breasts, down to the underside, which he bit gently.

She gasped a tiny breath, and her stomach hollowed out and he ran his tongue across it to her belly button.

The angel wings. He kissed first one then the other. He dipped the tip of his tongue into her belly button. Sheer perfection.

He moved lower. She tasted like a spring morning and quivered beneath his mouth. He blew on her and she shuddered and he smiled. He kissed and licked and delved until she moved restlessly, whispered words he couldn't catch, until she rose to meet him, to finally fall apart.

Her hips fell to the bed and she shivered.

He covered her with his body. When he touched her cheek, he found it wet.

She was crying.

"Are you okay?"

She turned her head into his shoulder, nodded and continued to shiver and shudder.

He cradled her and she felt his erection and reached for him, but he stopped her.

"Not yet. We need to talk."

"About what?" She sounded tired.

"I'm not sure," he said against her hair. "About Neil?"

"No," she wailed. "I don't want to. Let's have sex. Let me please you."

He nearly lost it, because that thought sent him to the edge. But he'd eased her pain a bit. Time to take care of some of his own.

"Angel," he whispered, "I'm worried about the scars. About what you'll think of them. Do you think you'll be okay?"

"Oh, Timm, yes."

She reached for his shirt. "I like you. I like *you*. They are part of you."

He grabbed her fingers before she could undress him. "They're pretty ugly."

"Shh," she said. "Let me."

She'd given herself into his care and had trusted him. He had to do the same for her.

She unbuttoned his shirt and opened it, then breathed his name. "It must have hurt so much."

"Not at first. When burns are that severe, the body goes into shock. The pain comes later with the healing."

His eyes were closed, because he didn't want to see how she was looking at him. Would he see pity? Horror? He didn't think he would see horror. Somehow, he'd grown to understand Angel in the past week. Despite her needs, she was a strong woman. Maybe one of the strongest he'd ever known.

"Look at me," she said quietly, but with command.

He did. The compassion in her eyes nearly undid him.

"I'm sorry," she said, "honestly sorry that you had to live through this."

She put her lips against his chest and remained there, breathing warmth onto him. He rested his cheek on her hair. She turned her cheek against his chest and they held each other.

He lost track of how long they stayed that way, but at some point, he wondered, who is healing whom?

When she did finally start loving him, it was slowly with kisses that she feathered over his chest.

She reached to kiss his lips and passion took over, the heat multiplied and they lost the precious control he had struggled to hold on to.

Angel knew how to kiss, treated it like an art form, and he was lost. Whatever she wanted was fine by him. Sex. Love. Animal lust. Anything. Fast. Now.

His hands took over, touching every gorgeous nook and cranny, covering all of the places he'd taken earlier with his mouth, finding all of her secrets and devouring them with hands, lips and teeth.

She gasped when he bit her stomach and pushed him onto his back. She took control now, this woman with the reckless, in-your-face, swollen, unreasonable *attitude*, and poured it over him, grabbed him with strong, sure hands and straddled him, taking him into her with greed. She was voracious and determined.

When she bent forward to kiss his chest again, her long midnight-dark hair lashed his face. He grasped her hair, pushed it from her face and brought her forward for a hungering kiss, no hesitancy now, no gentleness. His tongue explored the depths of her mouth fast and hard and she gave back as good as she got.

She moved on him, echoing the harsh need of her mouth and their fighting tongues. He drove into her hard, taking them both higher.

He sat up and held her against his chest, then turned

them, him on top of her now. Up onto his knees, he reached under her and lifted her perfect behind so he could watch himself as he drove into her, so he could watch those lovely breasts rise and fall with each thrust, so he could absorb the reality that this dream he'd had for too many years had finally come true.

This messy perfect woman was vocal, whimpered and cried and screamed in a beautiful crescendo of notes that rose and fell with their actions.

At last, they came. He collapsed onto the bed. Angel fell asleep.

He watched her while she slept. What had started as slow, sensual lovemaking had quickly morphed into all-out, no-holds-barred sex and his body still vibrated from it.

He left her slowly, kissing his way down this angel's body, sucking on those pretty pink wings.

She moved sensuously in her sleep.

He kissed her thighs and bit the back of one knee.

This was a one-time only thing. He had his reasons for not wanting an affair with her. She had her reasons for not wanting him.

In her sleep, she whimpered, but Timm finally let go of her and stood. For a full minute, he stared at the naked beauty on the bed, before finally finding his clothes and getting dressed.

He covered her with a quilt and blew out the candle before leaving the apartment in darkness.

What had happened? They'd made love *and* they'd had crazy sex. He'd eased her pain and she had eased his.

He walked home through the quiet streets and noticed that Mrs. Allen's sprinkler was still going and turned it off.

Waste of water.

He entered the family house quietly and went to bed. He'd thought he would fall asleep right away, but couldn't, not with memories of Angel simmering beneath the surface. He closed his eyes and saw images of her body in flickering candlelight, outrageously beautiful, white against his ravaged skin, soft in parts, hard in others.

She'd tempted him into sex and he'd gone without a breath of complaint, wholeheartedly, and he didn't know what to think about that. Timm Franck had lost control.

CHAPTER FIFTEEN

WHEN TIMM ENTERED the newspaper office the following morning, Derick was waiting for Timm to open the door. His grim frown didn't bode well for Timm.

"What's wrong?" Timm asked.

"You were seen."

"Seen? What do you mean?"

"Leaving your apartment early this morning after spending the night with that woman."

Timm's breath backed up in his throat. He'd been so careful.

"It's all over town," Derick continued, "that you are no better than all of the other men who have partaken of her."

Partaken of her. Old-fashioned, but yes, Timm certainly had done that and now he had to pay the piper.

"How could you do this the night before the election? At the worst possible time."

He sat at his desk and put his head in his hands. What had he done? He'd lost track of his days. He, who kept a schedule for flossing his teeth, had lost sight of the election date, a date that should have been tattooed on his soul.

He needed to be mayor. Had worked toward this for a long time. He would do it so much better than Max would. He would honor his father's memory.

"The family was depending on you," Derick said with

such disappointment that Timm cringed. He burned hot with shame. Angel's Eve had tempted and Timm's Adam had taken a bite—more than one, in fact—had eaten the whole apple.

His father would be so ashamed of him.

But what about everything that Timm had learned about Angel in the past week? She had been so much more than he'd expected, so much more than anyone in town knew. She'd given him a rare glimpse into the person inside the combative shell.

He thought that he might have seen the best of her, of who she wanted to be. Of the compassionate, caring woman she desperately wanted to show, but who the world never saw.

How could she be herself in Ordinary, though, with men like Phil attacking her and with people like George leering at her every day, dealing with men who only saw the drop-dead gorgeous shell?

And Timm was no better. He sat there and contemplated dropping her like a hot potato on the basis of the town's opinion of her.

He hadn't managed to bring her up to his level; rather, she had dragged him down to hers. In his bid to ease her pain, he had damaged himself.

He had a few bridges to mend.

Derick left the office and not long after, Angel walked in. Suddenly, it seemed dangerous that she was here. Anyone could see her.

When she approached him with a smile that reflected both her shy side and her boldness, he took her arm and dragged her to the rear out of sight line of the windows.

"Good morning," she said, moving into his arms, and he almost gave in to his insane desire to take her here on the spot. To lick that shy smile and to forge a deep kiss with the bold one, to mingle their tongues in hot, carnal bliss.

Instead, he set her at arm's length and she looked at him with a puzzled frown.

"Last night was a mistake," he said, before his rational mind gave in to the ridiculous Neanderthal loser.

She stepped out of his hold. Her face changed, lost the pretty sunshine of a minute ago. "Why?"

"Because I'm running for mayor. I have to be careful. Someone saw me leaving this morning."

"So…you're worried about *your* reputation…because of *my* reputation?"

He couldn't quite agree with her out loud—it sounded so cold—so he nodded.

"I thought you were different from the other men in town, but I was wrong." As she spoke, her words picked up speed, bitterness. "Like a worm, you slithered your way into my heart and then copped a ton of Angel Donovan feels last night. I was a fool."

Into her heart?

He remained mute, because when she put it that way, he sounded like a coward. Maybe he was.

"Don't worry," she said. "I won't bother you again."

She started for the front door, then did an about-face and strode toward the back door.

"Angel, don't be childish."

"Forget it, buddy. I've got the whole picture now." She shoved against the handle, but the door was locked.

He moved toward her, to escort her to the front, but she slammed her hands against his chest, pushing him against the wall. Tears glimmered in her eyes and he felt as low as the worm she'd called him.

He tried to reason with her. "Angel, come to the front."

She pounded one fist against his chest and, despite his scars, he felt that touch and it burned him.

Emotions flat, he flipped the lock.

She slipped through and he breathed his relief. It was over. She was gone. He locked the door, and walked slowly toward the main room. But he couldn't bring himself to actually enter where the sun and reality blazed through the windows.

Angel was gone and he wasn't sure whether he'd gained or lost. Or what he'd gained. Or what he'd lost.

ANGEL STOOD IN Timm's apartment, lost but fuming. Lost because it was time to leave. She couldn't wait for Mama's wedding. She had to leave today.

Fuming because she'd once again trusted a man and he had betrayed her. What had she missed last night? He had been sweet and attentive. Had said that he wanted to help her heal. Then he'd made love to her more slowly and more sweetly than any man she'd known.

He had treated her differently than any man except Neil. With Neil, though, Angel hadn't needed healing. She had taught inexperienced Neil how to make love and had enjoyed it. In return, he'd been shy, but inventive. He hadn't known her background and so hadn't prejudged her experience. He said he was happy that one of them knew what she was doing.

He'd been only three years younger than her in actual age, but decades younger in experience. She'd been so happy. And yet, she'd lost him.

Here she was, lost again. But also a little disappointed in herself.

Timm had offered her lovemaking and healing and

she had taken both. She'd hoped she had helped to heal some of his doubts about his scars.

Then it had all felt too intense and she'd been close to the breaking point, so she'd turned it all into hot and heavy sex, because that she knew, that she was comfortable with.

After she packed her bag, she went downstairs to the newspaper office and tossed the keys on the counter.

"Angel." Timm started to rise.

She didn't answer. With a wave of her hand, she walked out.

Somehow, her instincts had let her down. She'd misjudged Timm Franck and all she wanted to do was to roll up in a ball and cry for a week.

New York, and the desire to view Ordinary from a rearview mirror, looked more and more attractive.

She stepped onto the sidewalk and stopped. Main Street was full of people, especially in front of the post office.

A sign in the window proclaimed it election day.

Timm must be happy.

Max stood on the sidewalk. It seemed he wanted a platform. "Folks, you can thank me for getting the Roadhouse closed down. My friends and I were there the last night to protect you while you slept. You need me as your mayor."

"That's not true," Hank said. "Timm put the time and effort into rallying the crowd around this issue months ago and he persisted."

"Yeah," someone else called, "but Timm's not so great now. You hear who he's keeping company with?"

Angel felt her face heat. She wanted to disappear into the sidewalk. She'd been fighting this all of her life, so why did it hurt so badly now?

Because she saw a way out and wasn't sure she wanted to take it after all. It was the right thing to do, though, or she would be living with these kinds of remarks and innuendo for the rest of her life.

"Let's keep this race clean." Hank spoke over the mumbling of the crowd. "Leave the character bashing to the big cities. We don't need it here in Ordinary."

Angel felt her spine prickle. She turned around. Timm leaned against the large window of his storefront, watching her.

She stepped back to him. "Looks like you got what you wanted."

He nodded. "At what cost?"

"Rem's stabbing."

His jaw worked. "Yeah."

"It wasn't your fault. You tried to avoid violence."

He tried to touch her arm, but she stepped away. "Why are you defending me?"

"I'm not sure. Is the town right about me, Timm?"

He shook his head, one hard brisk jerk. "You're worth all of them put together."

"So, would you see me again?"

"No."

"I thought so. Good luck in the election. Goodbye."

Her smile felt infinitely sad as she walked toward her mom's house.

As soon as Missy saw her, she wrapped her arms around Angel.

"Do you want to talk about it?" Missy asked.

"No." Angel leaned her head on her mama's shoulder. "I'm so tired, Mama."

"I'll make comfort food. What do you want? Chocolate cake? Ice cream? Potato chips? Custard?"

"Yes."

She felt Missy's shoulder shake with laughter.

"Which do you want?"

"All of it."

Chester joined them in the living room. "Chester, honey," Mama said, "can you run to the grocery store and get me some eggs and a box of baking chocolate? We also need ice cream."

"Mint chocolate chip."

Chester gave Angel a one-armed hug on his way out the door. Her mother was definitely in good hands. So Angel could do this.

"Mama, I'm taking the six-o'clock bus out tonight."

Missy didn't answer, simply embraced her again.

Angel felt better already. Sort of. To her surprise and disgust, what she really wanted was to crawl into bed with Timm and have him love her tenderly, the whole night, the way he'd originally wanted to do. No sex, but a lot of loving. She needed it now, but the coward wasn't available to her.

She'd been cherished and the feelings invoked by his tenderness were so intense and perfect and glorious that she had retreated from them.

Maybe she'd only thought she wanted to change. Maybe, even though she was convinced she wanted gold instead of dross, maybe going for gold terrified her. Maybe she thought she really didn't deserve it.

She shouldn't accuse him of cowardice, when she herself had avoided the honesty of her emotions and of what he had been offering.

What a pair of craven fools.

TIMM SAT WITH HIS family and friends in the diner.

Hank leaned close and whispered, "You still have this election in the bag."

Timm smiled grimly. Maybe, but why did he feel so bad. Why was there no sense of victory?

"You might be right, Hank."

"I am. The town appreciates you. They know you were the one who lobbied to get Chester's closed for months. Not Max."

"Yeah."

"There's nothing wrong with Max, but the town likes you more. They want you to win."

"Thanks, Hank. I appreciate that."

The truth was that he wanted today over with.

Both the lovemaking and the sex with Angel had been stunning. He couldn't get the taste of her out of his mouth, or the feel of her from his hands. He wanted her in his bed, but he'd given her up.

He'd made the right choice. He would keep the family's legacy alive. Ordinary needed him. He needed Ordinary.

If only he could get the look on Angel's face out of his head. Her shock and disappointment in him shamed him.

Derick came in with a big smile on his face. "You are in the lead, Timm."

That was good, so why didn't he feel better?

They all went outside, to where a lot of the townspeople had gathered to await the election results.

Hank stepped into the post office, then returned and said, "You're leading by a wide margin. You're our new mayor. There aren't enough citizens left to vote to upset you now even if they all voted for Max."

When the crowd heard that, they let out a huge roar.

Timm found the victory bittersweet.

A little farther down Main, the six-o'clock bus honked

to come through. The crowd dispersed and that's when Timm saw her.

Angel.

Standing at the bus stop, with the saddlebags she'd brought from college hanging from one hand. That was the only luggage she carried.

He remembered that first night, stopping her from burning the bike. She'd been a mass of adolescent memories and dreams. Since then, he'd come to know so much more about her.

She was just flat-out amazing.

Where was she going? New York, as she'd said?

He couldn't stand the thought of her there.

New York would chew up Angel and her world of contrasts, her sunshine skin and midnight hair, her bright shiny star of vulnerability and chutzpah.

His heart ached, felt physically broken, watching her get on that bus. When would she come back? Once a year at Christmas? To see her mother, but not him?

The bus pulled out slowly, careful not to hit the celebrating crowd.

He felt it then, the great crack that started in his hard head and ended sharply in his scarred chest, in his heart. He didn't realize it had started with the accident.

He'd been a bright, vibrant young boy suddenly reduced to watching, to separating reality from dreaming. To believing that he could never have a normal life. He would close off his heart to emotion for more than twenty years. He ruled his life with his head, and his intellect, to keep everything under control, so he could never feel the desolation he'd felt after the accident. He'd closed off his heart.

In doing so, he blocked off all joy.

Angel had changed that. She had brought color, and

crazy, nonsensical contrasts, and irrational dips in the creek, and big, bold sex.

That crack shifted now, leaving a gaping wound in his heart.

If he didn't keep her, he would never be whole again.

Angel Donovan was on a bus leaving town and Timm Franck's heart was breaking in two.

He ran from the crowd and their accolades. It was wrong, so wrong, to put their needs ahead of love, to deny love between himself and a woman because he was afraid of what people would think.

Talk about watching instead of doing. Watching the woman he loved drive out of town was dead wrong.

Max would make a fine mayor—not as good as Timm—but just fine.

Ordinary would survive. The town had plenty of people living in it and on the land surrounding it, really good people, who loved the place so much that it would never go wrong for long.

Those same people had fought for it in the past months and had won.

Right now, Angel needed him more than the town did. Right now, this very minute, he needed to fight for her and the future they should have together.

His heart raced with each long stride he took.

When he reached the alley, he jumped into his truck and started the engine.

The guy who didn't believe in speeding tore out of the alley as though banshees were on his tail.

The bus had a good head start, but Timm had a V-8 engine, determination and love on his side. Angel was going nowhere without him.

He caught up to the bus and honked. Nothing. No reaction.

He pulled out to pass, but a tractor approached in the oncoming lane with a load of hay. He honked for the bus to stop. Still no reaction.

It lumbered on ahead of him, while he sat on the vehicle's bumper.

He checked the tractor's progress. Slow. Lord, was it moving backward? His heart rate kicked up. He had to get Angel off that bus. If the bus wouldn't stop and he couldn't get her off, he was following it to the end of the line.

He glanced at his fuel gauge and swore. He didn't have enough gas to follow the bus that far.

He had to get her off. Now.

"C'mon. C'mon," he muttered to the tractor. "Pass already."

Finally, *finally,* the bus inched past the tractor and the tractor tore past his truck with the speed of a snail.

He swore and pulled into the passing lane. All clear. Thank God. The road ahead was empty as far as he could see. He moderated his speed to match the bus's and honked to get the driver's attention, gesturing to him to stop on the shoulder.

The guy shook his head.

Again, Timm gestured that he needed the driver to stop.

Again, he shook his head.

Timm noticed a car come out of a driveway ahead and enter the oncoming lane. Timm pulled in front of the bus and carefully applied the brakes, slowing the truck easily so the bus wouldn't slam into him. The driver had to stop with Timm because he couldn't pass him. The car was still approaching from the other direction.

The bus pulled onto the shoulder behind Timm.

He jumped out of the truck and ran to the bus as the driver stepped out.

"Buddy, are you nuts? What do you want?"

"I want a woman." Timm tried to step around him.

"We all want a woman."

"No, I mean, a woman who's on your bus. I don't want her to leave town."

"Timm?"

They both turned at the sound of Angel's voice. She stood beside the driver's seat.

"What are you doing?"

He stepped around the driver, climbed the steps and threw his arms around Angel. "Don't leave. Stay with me."

"Oh, *that* woman," the driver said behind him. "I don't blame you, buddy."

She felt like treasure in Timm's arms, rare and precious and real and his.

"Don't leave," he whispered again.

She didn't say anything, simply held him while he picked her up.

It sounded like she sniffled. "No, I don't cry. Ever."

He held her and grinned. She was trying hard not to cry. "I don't care about the election. I don't have to be mayor. I only want you."

He breathed her in. "Please. Marry me."

She hiccupped and he knew she was crying. "But the town—"

"I don't care about the town. I don't care what people say." He set her on her feet and eased back so he could see her.

"We've both been given the short end of the stick in life and we've dealt with it, but I've been lonely."

Her lower lip trembled. "Me, too."

"We deserve happiness. We deserve each other."

"Say yes," a woman shouted from farther down the bus.

Someone in one of the seats whistled. "Way to go!"

A female voice said, "He's cute. I'd go for him."

Angel had her chin tucked against her chest. Timm bent his knees to put his eyes level with hers. "I love you, Angel."

"Oh, my God, this is so romantic," another female voice said. "If you don't say yes, honey, I will."

The passengers broke into laughter.

"Yes." Angel launched herself into his arms.

Applause and catcalls rang through the bus. Behind them, the driver said, "Great. Now can we get this show back on the road?"

Timm laughed and said, "Yes," taking Angel by the hand to leave.

She squealed and said, "Wait. I have to get my stuff."

She grabbed her bags, then left the bus with him. After he helped her into his truck he closed the passenger door and waved to the driver.

The bus pulled back onto the highway and drove off. Timm got into the driver's seat and dragged Angel across his lap and into his arms. He kissed her with a fervor he'd never felt before.

He had learned a lesson today. Self-control was overrated. This was not.

This woman felt right in his arms, felt perfect, as though she'd been custom made for him. He couldn't have crafted a more perfect woman for himself, not only her body and pretty face, but also the soul tucked inside her. He even liked her warrior woman, the battle-ready girl who'd grown up scrapping.

He kissed her until they were breathless.

"I used to watch you all the time."

"I remember," she said, brushing his hair from his forehead.

"You must have thought I was such a loser."

She frowned. "Never. I always felt bad for you, that you couldn't do all the stuff that my friends and I were doing."

"I wanted to. I've changed my life since then. I don't sit at home watching anymore. Now I'm actively involved in town and life."

While he talked, he touched her, everywhere and anywhere. She feathered her fingers through his hair again and again. She unbuttoned his shirt to kiss his throat. He swallowed and she kissed the motion.

"Don't button up your shirt so high," she said. "Be comfortable. Be yourself."

"I'll make a deal with you. I'll show the world who I am, if you'll do the same yourself."

She started to pull away and he growled, "You're not going anywhere, lady. You're staying in my arms, where you belong."

When he had her settled as close to his chest as science permitted, he said, "You've got this beautiful soft side that I want everyone to know about. You don't have to fight anymore. I'll kill any man in Ordinary who makes a pass at you. I'll defend you."

"You don't have to. My friend taught me these great self-defense moves…"

Her voice trailed off because Timm had unbuttoned her blouse and was kissing her neck and the tops of her breasts. He slipped one breast out of the cup of her bra and kissed the nipple. She gasped and shivered.

"Oh, Timm, you have a good mouth."

"Yeah?" He grinned. "I came out of my shell everywhere but with women. I want to come out of my shell with you. Only you. Last night was amazing."

He watched the nipple harden on her plumped breast and smiled.

Then he started kissing her again, because it was too hard not to. He held her while he ran his hand to the juncture of her thighs and pressed.

A minute later, they were breathing hard and Timm knew he had to get her home fast.

"Are you broken down, Timm?" Cash walked along the side of the truck toward the open driver's window.

Angel squealed and tried to tuck her breast back into her bra, but Timm was holding her too tightly. He saw Cash in his side mirror and knew how close Cash was, knew there wasn't enough time for her to get decent, so he pressed her snugly against him and wrapped his arms higher around her back, smashing her face against his neck.

Cash wouldn't see a thing.

His face appeared in the window and registered shock when he saw Angel. Then he grinned. "You caught the bus."

"Yeah," Timm drawled. "I caught the bus." He kissed the top of Angel's head. "And the girl."

"Any news you two want to share?"

"She's going to marry me, Cash."

"Is that true, Angel?"

She nodded her head against Timm's neck and giggled.

Cash's eyebrows did a suggestive Groucho Marx

thing. "Hot damn." He started walking to his patrol car. "You two get home safely," he called over his shoulder.

After he moved on, Angel sat up and tried to repair herself, but Timm kept trying to lift her breast back out.

They wrestled and giggled until her hip hit his erection and he winced.

"Let's go home and take care of that."

He stared at her in wonder, because both lovemaking and sex were all rolled into one and were so damned beautiful with this woman.

"How am I supposed to get us home safely without touching you?" he asked with a thread of pain in his voice.

She moved to her side of the truck and buckled herself in. He did the same.

"You'd better not pull any more stunts like stopping buses on the highway," she said. "I want to have a bunch of kids and I'm going to need you for that."

He smiled at her, so glad that she'd mentioned children. He wanted a lot of them, too.

CHAPTER SIXTEEN

EVERYWHERE TIMM TURNED, someone clapped him on the back, offered congratulations or smiled and laughed.

In his victory in winning over the girl he loved, he'd forgotten that he'd won the election.

He kept a firm grip on Angel's hand. As he wandered through the crowd, she tried a couple of times to jerk her hand out of his grip, but he wouldn't let her. She was part of him now. This town would accept that or he would opt out of it.

Forging a path through the crowd, he headed toward the sidewalk in front of the police station, still forcing Angel along with him.

He whistled a couple of times and the crowd turned toward the sound.

"Listen up." He raised his voice to make sure everyone would hear what he had to say. This was important. Pivotal.

"I want to thank everyone for your support and your votes. And thank you to those of you who helped out on my campaign."

The crowd hooted and whooped.

He gestured for quiet.

"But I have to decline to be your mayor."

For a moment, a shocked silence reigned, then all hell broke loose. Angel's hand jerked in his.

This time he had to whistle four times for order.

"As some of you may know, I have been seeing Angel Donovan." He glanced down at her and gave an encouraging smile.

"I don't doubt for a moment that I lost votes to Max because of this. For those of you who didn't know about this, perhaps you would have changed your vote, too."

To his surprise, he suddenly became emotional. "For that I would call each of you a coward, as I have been, for not publicly announcing my love for this wonderful woman. I'm announcing it now, with pride."

He looked at her again and held her gaze. Her deep blue eyes sparkled in the sun.

"Angel has been given a bum rap by this town. Not one of you knows her the way I do. I've asked this amazing woman to marry me and plan to do so as soon as possible."

Then, in front of the town, the world and whatever entity ruled this universe, he kissed her long and hard, pouring his heart into it.

When he finally lifted his head, the clapping started slowly with one person.

He searched the crowd until he found the source. Hank Shelter.

Another pair of hands joined from the rear of the crowd. Cash Kavenagh.

Slowly, more people followed suit. His friends. His family.

A few people wandered away sporting dark looks, but they didn't matter to him. In the future, only those who would treat his wife with respect would earn his in return.

If he were never voted in as mayor in the future, he would be happy anyway.

This time when he pulled Angel along behind him, it was to take her to his apartment to love the daylights out of her.

ANGEL'S HEAD WHIRLED. She followed Timm, not quite sure what had happened. Her life had changed irrevocably.

He had actually come after her. She'd never been so happy in her life than to hear him make a commitment to her. But to have him repeat it in front of all of Ordinary and to abdicate his position as mayor flooded her with more joy than she'd thought possible for one woman to hold.

Timm Franck had taught her about courage—true courage. Not her old fists-raised, damn-the-world, take-on-all-comers attitude, but the courage to put your heart into someone else's hands and *trust* them.

After everything he had given up for her, she trusted him completely.

She switched positions and led him into the bedroom, where the setting sun turned everything to gold. She undressed him slowly to watch the sun turn him to gold.

Remembering when she'd realized that she no longer wanted dross in her life, that she deserved gold, Angel smiled. She'd found her gold in Timm.

She kissed his scars, still awed that he not only survived the fire and his enforced separation from the world, but that he had excelled and had overcome his fears, had actually forced himself out into the world to become an active member of his community.

Oh, such beautiful strength.

She ran her hands over his square shoulders. They bore too much responsibility. He needed to learn to have fun and she would be the woman to teach him how.

She'd come home to Ordinary devastated by Neil's death, and now here she was, ready to start a new life. Neil had taught her to value her own worth. Timm had totally cemented that in her heart.

Gently, she pushed him onto the bed. He'd finished stripping her as she'd been worshipping his body.

"Look at you," he breathed. "So beautiful. The sun is making you all golden." As she straddled him, he touched her breasts and her angel wings and her dark curls.

He might have done well in his community, but where women were concerned, he hadn't valued himself, either. She would teach him that lesson as he had for her.

When she reached down and took him in hand, he closed his eyes and sighed. She laughed.

"Your laugh is sexy," he said, shifting to take her mouth with his. "I want to swallow that laugh."

"Oh, Timm," Angel said with her own happy sigh. "I have so much to teach you."

She started with the gorgeous flesh she held in her hand, bending to love him with her lips and tongue.

She knew when he was close to fulfillment because he grabbed her and brought her up for his kiss.

"Come here," he growled, and lifted her onto him.

He filled her beautifully, perfectly, and she started moving on him. He cupped her breasts and his eyes followed where his hands led, his gaze so hot it might as well have been another pair of hands.

His fingers played over her, driving her to release. A moment later, he followed her over the edge and she collapsed onto him.

TIMM TRIED TO catch the breath that Angel had stolen from him. If this was what he had to look forward to for the rest of his life, he was ready to surrender body and soul.

He felt the scars on his chest loosen and expand with the love he felt for this woman.

She still straddled him, her head on his chest. He combed his fingers through her long hair, over and over again, paying homage to her beauty.

"I'd like to ask Hank if we can have the wedding on the Sheltering Arms ranch. Do you want an outdoor wedding?"

She nodded against him. "I would love that."

He felt a subtle withdrawal in her and asked, "What just happened? What's going on inside that head of yours?"

"How many people do you think will come?"

"Angel, I know you'll find this hard to believe, but more people love you than you think. Everyone who attends will be a friend."

"I guess I can't wear a big white gown, can I?"

"Because of your reputation? Honey, you wear whatever you want. I would marry you in a gorilla suit."

She relaxed against him, then sat up. Before she moved off him to lie beside him, the blazing red sunset set her skin on fire. As she'd done with his heart.

CHAPTER SEVENTEEN

SOMETIME IN THE middle of the night, Timm heard the front door of the Franck house open. Out of respect for his family—especially his mom—he had come here to spend the night rather than stay wrapped in Angel's arms.

He sat up. He listened for noise, footsteps, but whoever was there moved stealthily. Pulling his pants on without a sound, he moved into the hallway and toward the top of the stairs.

A shadow moved up those stairs and he flattened himself against the wall. A split second before he lunged at the intruder, he recognized his sister.

"Sara," he whispered furiously.

She jumped and emitted a scream, truncated by his hand across her mouth.

"Don't wake Finn or Ma."

"Timm," she whispered as furiously after he'd removed his hand. "You nearly gave me a heart attack. What are you doing up?"

"Wondering who was breaking in. Where have you been all this time?"

"Taking care of Rem. He wasn't feeling well, so I stayed late."

"Uh-huh. What did you have to do for him?"

"He developed a slight fever." A tremor ran through her voice.

"Sara, you couldn't lie to save your soul. What's going on between you and Rem?"

"Nothing."

"Lie. I can read you like a book. What's going on?"

"Nothing after tonight." She sounded too sad. "Finn and I will be catching a bus out today."

No. Don't take the boy. "Why? I thought you had until next week."

"Rem is healing well. He doesn't need me anymore."

"But—"

"Good night, Timm." She entered her room and he knew he'd get nothing more out of her.

"Sara, I'm marrying Angel. Are you okay with that?"

She nodded but there was no joy in it. "Let me know when the wedding is." Then she shut the door between them.

THE FOLLOWING MORNING, Timm drove to the Caldwell ranch.

Nell let him in. She walked with a slight limp. One corner of her mouth drooped, slightly. Otherwise, she was the same woman he and Sara had adored when they'd come here as children, running in and out of Nell's home as though it was their own.

She let him go up to Rem's room.

Rem sat in front of his bedroom window, his arm cradled protectively against the healing wound in his stomach, an ironic reversal of roles. During their teenage years, it was Timm at the window and Rem out doing and bringing the news to Timm.

"Rem, did you know that Sara is leaving today?"

Rem laughed soundlessly. "She mentioned it."

"She won't tell me what's going on."

Rem nodded.

"*You* tell me what's happening here."

"Can't," Rem said, close-lipped and determined.

Timm wanted to pull someone's hair out. What was wrong with the pair of them? They were old enough to have settled their differences by now.

Sara needed to learn to forgive Rem. Actually, he needed to forgive, too—forgive himself.

THE WEDDING TOOK place on a stunning sunny September morning on Hank Shelter's front lawn.

Timm looked out over the family and friends who had come to share in this blessing.

Sara looked happy but a little overwhelmed, wondering how on earth her hopelessly scarred brother had attracted the most beautiful woman to ever walk the streets of Ordinary. Ma hadn't attended, refused to accept Angel as her daughter-in-law. It hurt. He hoped she came around in time.

Timm heard a disturbance near the back of the crowd and glanced down the length of the grassy aisle they'd left open for Angel.

A second later, she appeared, her hair midnight black in the sun and her blue eyes blazing with love for him.

One slim leaf drifted down from the weeping willow and landed on her hair, gold-green against the black.

Her long dress swirled around her ankles as she walked toward him.

Timm smiled.

The bride wore white.

HOURS LATER, ALONE at a bed-and-breakfast in Haven, surrounded by chintz and lace, Angel and Timm stood across from each other, sporting the goofiest grins, drunk with happiness.

"Close your eyes," she said.

Still grinning, he took another sip of champagne and shook his head. "No. I want to see you. You're beautiful in white. In the future, wear it often."

"Sure." But her smile was one of her Mona Lisa mysteries.

Oh, what did the woman have in mind?

He closed his eyes and heard the rustling of her lacy gown as it hit the floor.

"Open your eyes," she whispered, and he did.

His wife stood before him, wearing a tiny black leather waspie, those magnificent alabaster breasts gorgeous above it. The curls below those pretty pink angel wings were bare. She hadn't worn any panties.

His heart nearly stopped beating. She hadn't been wearing panties at their wedding. If he'd known, he would have never survived. He would have dropped of a heart attack. He would have taken her into a bedroom in Hank's house and loved the daylights out her while the guests partied outside.

"What do you think?" she whispered.

His neighborhood bully reared his possessive head and devoured the playground of her body with greedy eyes. *Mine.*

Timm rushed toward her at the same time she did

and they met in the middle. He lifted her into his arms and she wrapped her legs around him.

He laughed and she giggled.

Oh, his wife knew how to have fun. He looked forward to a lifetime of her lessons. Long into the night and the wee hours of the morning, fun they did have.

* * * * *

COMING NEXT MONTH

Available August 9, 2011

#1722 STAND-IN WIFE
Twins
Karina Bliss

#1723 THE TEXAN'S SECRET
The Hardin Boys
Linda Warren

#1724 ONE GOOD REASON
Going Back
Sarah Mayberry

#1725 HER SURE THING
An Island to Remember
Helen Brenna

#1726 FULL CONTACT
Shelter Valley Stories
Tara Taylor Quinn

#1727 FEELS LIKE HOME
Together Again
Beth Andrews

You can find more information on upcoming
Harlequin® titles, free excerpts and more at
www.HarlequinInsideRomance.com.

REQUEST YOUR FREE BOOKS!
2 FREE NOVELS PLUS 2 FREE GIFTS!

Harlequin®

Super Romance®

Exciting, emotional, unexpected!

YES! Please send me 2 FREE Harlequin® Superromance® novels and my 2 FREE gifts (gifts are worth about $10). After receiving them, if I don't wish to receive any more books, I can return the shipping statement marked "cancel." If I don't cancel, I will receive 6 brand-new novels every month and be billed just $4.69 per book in the U.S. or $5.24 per book in Canada. That's a saving of at least 15% off the cover price! It's quite a bargain! Shipping and handling is just 50¢ per book in the U.S. and 75¢ per book in Canada.* I understand that accepting the 2 free books and gifts places me under no obligation to buy anything. I can always return a shipment and cancel at any time. Even if I never buy another book, the two free books and gifts are mine to keep forever.

135/336 HDN FC6T

Name	(PLEASE PRINT)	

Address		Apt. #

City	State/Prov.	Zip/Postal Code

Signature (if under 18, a parent or guardian must sign)

Mail to the **Reader Service:**
IN U.S.A.: P.O. Box 1867, Buffalo, NY 14240-1867
IN CANADA: P.O. Box 609, Fort Erie, Ontario L2A 5X3

Not valid for current subscribers to Harlequin Superromance books.
**Are you a current subscriber to Harlequin Superromance books and want to receive the larger-print edition?
Call 1-800-873-8635 or visit www.ReaderService.com.**

* Terms and prices subject to change without notice. Prices do not include applicable taxes. Sales tax applicable in N.Y. Canadian residents will be charged applicable taxes. Offer not valid in Quebec. This offer is limited to one order per household. All orders subject to credit approval. Credit or debit balances in a customer's account(s) may be offset by any other outstanding balance owed by or to the customer. Please allow 4 to 6 weeks for delivery. Offer available while quantities last.

Your Privacy—The Reader Service is committed to protecting your privacy. Our Privacy Policy is available online at www.ReaderService.com or upon request from the Reader Service.

We make a portion of our mailing list available to reputable third parties that offer products we believe may interest you. If you prefer that we not exchange your name with third parties, or if you wish to clarify or modify your communication preferences, please visit us at www.ReaderService.com/consumerschoice or write to us at Reader Service Preference Service, P.O. Box 9062, Buffalo, NY 14269. Include your complete name and address.

HSR11

*Once bitten, twice shy. That's Gabby Wade's motto—
especially when it comes to Adamson men.
And the moment she meets Jon Adamson her theory
is confirmed. But with each encounter a little something
sparks between them, making her wonder if she's been
too hasty to dismiss this one!*

*Enjoy this sneak peek from ONE GOOD REASON
by Sarah Mayberry, available August 2011
from Harlequin® Superromance®.*

Gabby Wade's heartbeat thumped in her ears as she marched to her office. She wanted to pretend it was because of her brisk pace returning from the file room, but she wasn't that good a liar.

Her heart was beating like a tom-tom because Jon Adamson had touched her. In a very male, very possessive way. She could still feel the heat of his big hand burning through the seat of her khakis as he'd steadied her on the ladder.

It had taken every ounce of self-control to tell him to unhand her. What she'd really wanted was to grab him by his shirt and, well, explore all those urges his touch had instantly brought to life.

While she might not like him, she was wise enough to understand that it wasn't always about liking the other person. Sometimes it was about pure animal attraction.

Refusing to think about it, she turned to work. When she'd typed in the wrong figures three times, Gabby admitted she was too tired and too distracted. Time to call it a day.

As she was leaving, she spied Jon at his workbench in the shop. His head was propped on his hand as he studied blueprints. It wasn't until she got closer that she saw his eyes were shut.

He looked oddly boyish. There was something innocent and unguarded in his expression. She felt a weakening in her resistance to him.

"Jon." She put her hand on his shoulder, intending to shake him awake. Instead, it rested there like a caress.

His eyes snapped open.

"You were asleep."

"No, I was, uh, visualizing something on this design." He gestured to the blueprint in front of him then rubbed his eyes.

That gesture dealt a bigger blow to her resistance. She realized it wasn't only animal attraction pulling them together. She took a step backward as if to get away from the knowledge.

She cleared her throat. "I'm heading off now."

He gave her a smile, and she could see his exhaustion.

"Yeah, I should, too." He stood and stretched. The hem of his T-shirt rose as he arched his back and she caught a flash of hard male belly. She looked away, but it was too late. Her mind had committed the image to permanent memory.

And suddenly she knew, for good or bad, she'd never look at Jon the same way again.

Find out what happens next in ONE GOOD REASON, available August 2011 from Harlequin® Superromance®!

HSREXP0811

Celebrating
Blaze 10 years of
red-hot reads

Featuring a special August author lineup of
six fan-favorite authors who have written
for Blaze™ from the beginning!

The Original Sexy Six:

Vicki Lewis Thompson
Tori Carrington
Kimberly Raye
Debbi Rawlins
Julie Leto
Jo Leigh

Pick up all six Blaze™
Special Collectors' Edition titles!

August 2011

www.Harlequin.com

HBCELEBRATE0811

SPECIAL EDITION

Life, Love, Family and Top Authors!

IN AUGUST, HARLEQUIN SPECIAL EDITION FEATURES
USA TODAY BESTSELLING AUTHORS
MARIE FERRARELLA AND *ALLISON LEIGH.*

THE BABY WORE A BADGE
BY *MARIE FERRARELLA*

The second title in the **Montana Mavericks:
The Texans Are Coming!** miniseries....

Suddenly single father Jake Castro has his hands full with
the baby he never expected—and with a beautiful young
woman too wise for her years.

COURTNEY'S BABY PLAN
BY *ALLISON LEIGH*

The third title in the **Return to the Double C** miniseries....

Tired of waiting for Mr. Right, nurse Courtney Clay takes
matters into her own hands to create the family she's
always wanted— but her surly patient may just be
the Mr. Right she's been searching for all along.

**Look for these titles and others in August 2011
from Harlequin Special Edition wherever books are sold.**

BIG SKY BRIDE, BE MINE! *(Northridge Nuptials)* by *VICTORIA PADE*
THE MOMMY MIRACLE by *LILIAN DARCY*
THE MOGUL'S MAYBE MARRIAGE by *MINDY KLASKY*
LIAM'S PERFECT WOMAN by *BETH KERY*

---

www.Harlequin.com

SEUSA0811